# A Lifetime Long Ago

# By Mary Hughes

# A Lifetime Long Ago

## By Mary Hughes

This book was first published in Great Britain in paperback during May 2018.

**ISBN-13: 978-1986865142**

# Introduction

Elizabeth Reid is a lady who has it all. She came from a very troubled and violent background but now lives a fairly quiet, self-sufficient life, running a very successful fashion business.

She has two beautiful daughters and had a late husband who loved her dearly. She is well liked and admired by all that know her. She is a strong lady, quite unaware of her own courage.

Her extraordinary life was all going to plan until she met Poppy Rainsford!

Poppy by contrast once lived a rather privileged life in a middle class family until a tragic accident suddenly hit home, resulting in her life taking an unexpected and disastrous turn. Life suddenly became very complicated very quickly.

A chance encounter however, would then change both of their lives forever. It would take both women on an unexpected journey beyond their comfort zone. It would challenge them in so many different ways.

We all have history and we all pass judgement on other people's lives, but do we ever really know what is really going on in another person's life? What roads have they walked down?

"Don't judge me until you have walked a mile in my shoes," has never rang so true as it does in this story. It is a worthy tale about two proud women whose strength and courage and above all else, their independence helps them to overcome all the curve balls that life has thrown at them. It is an engaging story of determination and grit, which will probably tug at your heart strings.

# About the Author

Mary Hughes has lived in Co. Kildare, Ireland, for the past sixteen years with her husband Paul and their children Amy and Owen. Mary was born and raised in the West of Ireland, moving to London when she was seventeen. Mary is the eldest of four children. This is her first book, which was not only a surprise to her but a shock, as by her own admission she is no story teller.

I guess you could say she would call herself an accidental author. So when the idea first came to her to write this book around Christmas of 2016, the words flew onto the pages and the main text was on paper within a few days. Never did she imagine she would ever complete this book.

# Acknowledgements

I would like to acknowledge the support my husband Paul over the course of writing this novel. A big thank you to my two sisters Ann and Kathleen for the long phone calls sometimes from across the Atlantic Ocean and for their excitement and encouragement and most of all to the famous words "Hurry the Hell up, don't keep us waiting tell me more, no, no, don't spoil it."

## Dedications

I dedicate this book to Amy and Owen, who have inspired me since the day they were born. They are both intelligent and beautiful inside and out.  May you always dream big and follow your heart.

Thanks also to Don Hale for editing the mumble jumble of words on the pages and to Dr Steve Green for his production and design work including the beautiful front cover.

# Chapter 1

# Elizabeth Reid

It had been lashing down with rain all day and it was now bouncing back off the ground. In Ireland, we would say it was 'hammering it down!' There were loads of umbrellas dumped all over the place as each offered little protection from the wind and heavy downpour.

Everyone was sick of it and given the opportunity, all of us would have probably jumped on the first flight out to sunny Spain.

It had been like this for most of the past two weeks and there seemed little sign of it stopping. The Met Office confirmed it had been the wettest November on record, dating back to more than a century before. They also announced serious flood alerts all over the country.

Somerset, Devon, and Kent seemed the worst hit areas, with many towns remaining under siege due to the rising water levels. The loss of homes and businesses was also on the rise, and with no sign of the rain stopping anytime soon, it was hard to imagine what the overall damage would be.

In some areas, the entire infrastructure seemed completely wrecked, with whole villages under water. The River Thames was on the verge of spilling over into the streets. All along the river banks many hundreds of sandbags suddenly appeared. Every shop front and home appeared surrounded by these same horrible protective measures.

It baffled me that with all our knowledge and technology why we didn't have a more efficient way of dealing with this problem? We have some of the best minds in the world and yet, somehow, we always lacked the will to make any purposeful changes.

Why people are always so afraid of change, I will never know. In some ways, we are still in the dark ages. We are a first-world country with a third-world attitude. It's time we started to take global warming seriously and stopped pushing the can down the road.

It would be great, however if we could keep some of the millions of pounds worth of investment that is constantly sent abroad and use it to help our own people and to stop this sort of damage happening in the first place.

The official line is that they are committed to dredging the rivers as part of their work to protect people, property, and the land. Hello there, Mr Brains! I think we might need to do a bit more than river repairs.

All I know is that I would have been much better off that particular day wearing a pair of Wellingtons rather than risking my own lovely boots. Stylish they may be, but waterproof they were not!

I considered prioritising the design of shoes and boots that are both stylish, comfortable and most importantly waterproof, fully equipped to cope with our uncertain British weather.

As I walked down the main street I looked up to the Heavens and at last, I could see the hotel sign. It was such a welcome sight. The Ashbrook Hotel had been my favourite place since first arriving in London. From the very moment I stepped inside, I found it relaxing and calm, and over the years it has been my very own piece of Heaven.

My dearest friend Isabelle Hastings and I first came here to celebrate my plan to open a fashion shop. We were both filled with enthusiasm and dreams, but we were so young then, and so full of life.

In the early years when my confidence began to slip away, she became my rock, and for every obstacle that I found, she somehow knew how to remove them. She is incredible and has always been able to lift my spirits, to make me feel as if on the top of the world again.

From the very beginning, we were instant friends. She arrived in my life at just the right time. We were like twins. We liked the same food, movies, and music. She was an Oxford graduate, with 1st Class Honours in Finance and Business.

She had expert knowledge in how to deal with banks and the right approach to get the best rates that I could afford. She had a great way of getting people to do exactly what she wanted, and it was her own unique way of sweet-talking that finally persuaded the banks to take a risk and support my venture.

Originally, they thought I was too much of a gamble and that the business wouldn't work. Isabelle though had other ideas and diligently filled out all the paperwork, helping me put together a revised business plan. She later applied for start-up grants.

She was amazing, and oh, how she worked the room. In the beginning, she didn't want to join my business at all, as she was still working her way up the corporate ladder.

She would laugh and claim she knew nothing about fashion, but after the company she had been working for suddenly went bust, she readily joined me at 'Wear with Confidence.'

Since then we have never looked back. She's now responsible for sales and marketing, and I look after the staff and designs. Together we have taken the company beyond our wildest expectations. When we started we would have never considered or believed we might open a new store in America.

A visit to the Ashbrook was our special place to take time out for celebration, or whenever we needed a valuable pick-me-up. On that particular day we were planning to have afternoon tea, and to go over some paperwork before I flew back out to the States to see if we could get the contracts signed, and finally open our new store.

It was great to get away from the office, as it was always so busy. It was so hard to find a brief moment to think or plan. We really needed to take on more staff to be able to keep up with the demand and get the new season launched.

As I ran up the steps to the hotel, I was already feeling excited that special atmosphere and the anticipation of enjoying a relaxing afternoon.

The doorman was always well dressed in his single-breasted black jacket with red epaulettes and white gloves. The uniform had changed little over the years since the hotel first opened back in 1889, and Jack greeted me with his friendly and familiar tone.

He was a little on edge that day, however, and said he was concerned about the rising water coming down the street. He was also contemplating whether it was time to put out the newly delivered sandbags but believed they looked unsightly, and not fitting for a hotel of its stature.

The hotel was a mix of the contemporary and the traditional. It had olde-worlde charm. It was lavish without being ultra-posh. It somehow felt as if the place had been frozen in time, and the staff were always extremely professional and attentive, yet low key, sensitive and unobtrusive.

It amazed me they were always able to remember the names of all the regulars, together with noting all their likes and dislikes. Their attention to detail was outstanding.

The lobby was extremely busy that day. I thought there must have been a large group of people checking in as new luggage was scattered everywhere. The staff too appeared unusually anxious and were rushed off their feet trying to get everyone checked into their rooms

I loved all the hustle and bustle of this place but quickly made my way towards the drawing room. It was always much quieter in there, so I headed towards a luxurious plush sofa, which I just sank into. It was conveniently located just in front of a huge ornate fireplace with an enticing log fire.

I was still fairly early so whilst I waited for Isabelle I ordered a glass of champagne. It may have been unusual to order alcohol at that particular time of the afternoon, but I thought,"Sod it!" I deserve a glass, as I had finished all my work for the day.

It had been a very hard twelve months. The planning for our flag-ship store in the States had been a complete nightmare - between finding the right location, getting all the essential work done on the store, together with all the branding Stateside and the hiring of new staff.

We should have opened within four months, but there was still an issue or two to resolve with the wording of the contracts. The

Unions were unhappy, and there was some new legislation that the lawyers claimed we had yet to comply with.

I believed that when I arrived over there I would soon be able to get it all sorted out. At that stage, I didn't know what the objections were, or if it was just the American lawyers pushing to make a few extra dollars.

As I drank the cold glass of champagne, I gradually started to relax. The rest of the day was set for chill-out time. I had already packed and the US paperwork was prepared.

I could now feel the heat of the blazing fire starting to warm my cold body and calm my troubled mind. This time tomorrow I would be in Washington DC, but I was beginning to feel slightly guilty sitting there on my own and drinking champagne in that cosy little room.

I always loved people-watching so I settled myself down, leaned across the arm of my chair and studied nearly everyone battling against the elements on that cold, wet, and half-deserted street.

The horrible weather conditions had obviously affected the number of people out shopping on that day, as normally there would be hundreds upon hundreds of people passing by, but I reckoned that the most sensible of people had opted to remain inside, safe and dry. The traffic too seemed equally quiet.

I soon drank my first glass of champagne so ordered another. I was beginning to feel drowsy again and hoped Isabelle would hurry up, but just then my mobile phone rang. Annoyingly, it was Isabelle to say she would be at least another half an hour, or so.

# Chapter 2

The alcohol had certainly dulled my emotions but I was feeling very thankful for the way my life had turned out. I never imaged my fashion designs would be so successful. I still felt humbled by the whole experience. It was so surreal. I hadn't planned for this particular lifestyle at all, and I always intended on going to college to study, then perhaps to become a nurse.

I thought it funny how my career had developed but wished my late husband Edward had been with me to share in my success, as it would have meant so much more to me having him by my side as well as my best friend Isabelle.

He was the only one person that I had ever truly loved. He had been my soul mate. I was lucky to have met him.

I was just about to start day-dreaming again when suddenly there was a lot of commotion outside. First, there was a rather loud and annoying car horn blaring away, and then I heard the horrific screech of brakes.

A cold shiver ran down my spine. I was hoping no one had been injured. I took a closer look out the window and tried to wipe some condensation from the glass but I couldn't quite see what was happening and was just about to turn away when I heard another disturbing high-pitched scream. It didn't even sound human. It was more like that of an animal caught in a trap.

To my amazement, I could now see a young lady with two small children. She looked panic-stricken and was sat crouched in the middle of the wet road. They all appeared to be soaking wet and what looked like the contents of her shopping now lay scattered about the street.

I was sure she was the very same girl that I had seen passing by my window some fifteen minutes or so earlier. At that time she was pushing a buggy and had been accompanied by a small boy, who was jumping up and down in the puddles, laughing his head off.

I wondered what was happening, so I moved a little closer to the window and could now see that this young lad with curly blonde hair had started to kick out and strike at his mother whilst screaming uncontrollably.

To my shock and horror, however, everyone seemed to be totally oblivious to her predicament, and they just kept on walking past as if the mother and children were invisible.

Just then a car drove straight through a very large roadside puddle and sent a huge wave of water cascading everywhere and drenching the already bedraggled young woman and her children. The car didn't even stop to acknowledge its deliberate action.

The distressed lady was now on her knees whilst trying to hold onto the young boy, who she had wrapped in her arms as he continued to lash out at her.

One passing man angrily shouted at her to take her kids home immediately and to teach them some manners, saying she was "Unfit to be a mother". He added that if they'd been his kids, he would teach them a lesson they would never forget in a hurry.

The young woman remained still, however, and continued rocking the little boy gently in her arms. I could see that she kept wiping the tears and driving rain from her eyes and face, and could then hear her softly singing as she tried to soothe the child's fears in the hope he might calm down.

Before I knew it, I found myself by her side in the rain. I helped her get to her feet and moved them off the wet road. I also asked if I could help, but she shouted out, "Go away, you rich bitch. We don't need your help! You think that you're so much better than the rest of us. You rich people sit in your ivory towers judging people like it is a pastime."

Out of the corner of my eye, I could see a black cab approaching so I quickly stepped back into the road again and flagged it down.

As soon as it stopped I popped the buggy and the child inside and helped the screaming Mother and child into the cab. Next, and for some completely unknown reason, I jumped into the taxi with them.

"Where to?" asked the Cabbie.

She gave the driver her address through tears and sniffles and just sat there rocking the young boy who was still screaming, but his pitch had dropped and thankfully, he had now stopped hitting and kicking out at his Mother and gradually seemed to be calming down.

The cabbie said he couldn't take us to that particular address as it was not a "safe area," and said that no one in their right mind would ever go near that place. He claimed it was a well-known 'no-go area.'

I, of course, was not aware of this and had no idea what he was talking about, or why he wouldn't take us there.

I told him I would make it worth his while if he just drove, but he still refused, so I somewhat out of character told him that we were not getting out of his cab, and would happily sit there all day if need be, and if we did this he wouldn't earn a penny.

We sat in silence for a few minutes and I began wondering what I would do if he made us get out. To my relief, he eventually pulled-out and drove off in the right direction whilst mouthing something rather unpleasant about me under his breath.

The young lady continued to sob as she cradled the boy, but she seemed to be in some weird world of her own where no one else existed.

At last the driver stopped in front of a very scruffy old block of flats. It looks semi-derelict. I thought, "Surely nobody could live there?" Most of the windows were broken. It was filthy dirty and rubbish was strewn everywhere.

I asked the driver if he had the right address. He nodded and said, "Yes," adding, "If you want my advice don't go anywhere near that place, or you will become a target with your expensive clothes and bag.

"You'll stick out like a sore thumb. You're asking for trouble Missus. It's not a safe place for anyone, never mind a rich lady like yourself."

I must admit, I felt extremely intimidated by what I saw. I was not the weeping violet type by any standards, but this stretched me to my limits.

Just then the young girl spoke for the first time in ages. It was barely a whisper, adding, "He's right, lady. You should not stay here. You're on the wrong side of town and you should go back to your own type."

I paid the taxi driver and gave him a generous tip and thanked him for his advice and assistance. I then helped the young lady out of the cab with the boys and lifted the buggy out. The lad was now clinging to his Mum for dear life.

I turned to her and said I was made of stronger stuff and it would be OK. I must have said this with some conviction, but actually, I was bricking it.

I was also doing my best to ignore all the warnings and the horrific surroundings, and told her "I was only trying to help."

As we walked in silence towards the flats there was an extremely loud bang. It was like nothing I had ever heard in my whole life. It was more like a mini-explosion, then two young lads wearing black hoodies suddenly appeared directly in front of us. They had black scarves covering half of their faces and came at us so fast they practically knocked us for six.

They looked us straight in the eyes and shouted that if we were ever asked if we had seen or heard anything we should deny everything.

They told us in no uncertain terms that if we opened our mouths at all, they would be back and knew where we lived.

One of the guys lifted up his dirt-stained shirt up to show us a gun, and then they ran off as fast as they could and laughing like two mad March hares.

I was lost for words and for the first time in my life my knees began shaking and knocked together. I was now urgently asking myself, 'what the hell was I doing there!'

I was beginning to regret getting out of that very safe, warm and dry taxi. I thought, "Surely I could have ended my 'Good Samaritan' act in the street, and just gone about my own business," but no, for some reason, I had been inexplicably drawn to this particular girl but still had no idea why.

# Chapter 3

When she opened the front door to the hallway inside the block of flats the smell was overpowering. I found myself spluttering like crazy. It was all I could do not to vomit, but as I stepped inside the building, nothing could have ever prepared me for several other disgusting sights and smells before me.

The whole place stunk of urine and stale alcohol. There was a drunk lying on the floor in a pool of his own vomit. There were bags of rubbish everywhere. There were dirty needles and used condoms all over the place, and yet four young innocent children still continued to play amongst all these terrible objects as if they were not there.

I thought, "Why aren't these children in school?" and wondered if they ever went to school. Then the stench of choking black smoke from a smouldering burnt-out metal object in the foyer and the further smell of sick became overwhelming again.

Several young teenagers walked about half-naked, and as we headed towards the stairway, there was a sharp increase in the noise level as people slammed doors, banged things against the walls, and shouted obscenities.

I worried about the dirt and risk of disease at that horrid place and wondered why anyone would ever want to live there. I also asked myself how could society allow people to live in these conditions. If we saw animals living like that we would be outraged, yet we have constantly closed eyes to people who live this way every day.

The level of poverty was unbelievable. These people were the forgotten people of society. I wondered how many more estates existed nationally with similar conditions.

I asked myself does anyone know, or even care that people are being forced to live like this? The lift was out of order so we had no choice but to tackle the concrete stairs where I had to carry her buggy up the stairs.

I shook my head and thought "What in the name of God was I ever thinking?" I was now becoming concerned that the taxi driver had been right and I quickly started to worry that I might not make it out of that place alive.

I could just see the headlines now…. "Elizabeth Reid's body found in a run-down block of flats…. The police are at a loss to explain how or why she went there.  What possible motive could she have had to go there in the first place? Had she been kidnapped? To date, there have been no ransom demands. If anyone has any information please contact the police immediately…"

I thought what will my girls think? Why had I done this to them? I felt so sorry for everyone.

I appealed to the 'Angel in Heaven' above to help me. I asked, "Archangel Michael, please protect me and  let me survive this, and I promise I will never be so stupid again."

The young lady said she lived on the third floor. I began shaking again and muttered, 'Mother of God,' I didn't think I had the strength to carry the buggy all that way, yet somehow I made it to the top.

I realised now that if I survived this ordeal I would go to the gym and get myself fit as I felt completely exhausted by this hike. When she opened the door to her flat though, I was totally flabbergasted!

I was not expecting much but to my surprise, it was extremely clean, tidy, and very orderly. It was also remarkably peaceful and tranquil. It felt like a bizarre oasis in the middle of a war-zone. The furniture was old and well used but had been well cared for.

Now I was really intrigued by this girl, and about her life.

She put the young clingy child down and pulled the other one from the buggy. She went to the bathroom and I could then hear her fill the bath. She returned a few minutes later with clean towels and suddenly started to see me as if she had forgotten about me completely.

She stared at me as if I was an alien, she asked, "What are you doing here?" She had a startled and bemused look on her face.

I was just trying to help. "Let me introduce myself. I am Elizabeth Reid."

"Thank you for your help, but you can go now," she replied.

The little boy with the blonde hair shouted, "No Mummy. I want her to stay. She is nice."

I smiled in acknowledgement and quickly suggested that I should put the kettle on while she changed their wet clothes.

The kitchen was tiny, possibly one of the smallest I had ever seen. The fridge sat in the corner of the room making a loud noise it sounded as if it was preparing for take-off at any moment.

I filled the kettle and switched it on. From the other room, I could hear her and the children laughing as they splashed around in the bath. It was so surreal to hear such a normal sound amongst this otherwise chaotic environment.

It was like the meltdown had never happened. You could almost forget where you were. I thought that I must send Isabelle a text, as she might have had a search-party out looking for me after all of this time.

I sent, 'Sorry Izzie something came up. I will call you as soon as I get a chance, Love Liz.'

Sitting at the table and waiting for the kettle to boil I found myself looking out of the window at the sheer madness that surrounded that awful place. The flat was a complete contradiction to the crazy world just outside her door.

I started to pour the hot water into the cups to make the tea, but when I went to get the milk from the noisy fridge, I found there wasn't any, and also noticed there was very little food.

I considered that we would just have to have our tea black.

When the young woman returned she had mellowed, and said, "I am sorry for being so rude to you earlier when you were been very kind to help. My name is Poppy, Poppy Rainsford, and these are my boys Blake and Ollie."

She flopped into the chair by the window, and when she looked up I realised her face was very red and swollen. She had obviously been crying.

She asked, "Tell me, why would someone like you be so kind to someone like me?"

I replied, "Truthfully, I am not even sure myself as this is so out of character for me. I have never done anything like this in my life before.

"I guess I got really mad at that horrible man in the street. The way he kept shouting at you and I was so shocked that no one even bothered to acknowledge you. They could see that you and your children needed help. They acted as if you were invisible."

Poppy gave a little laugh, and said, "That happens a lot, so much so that I don't even notice it anymore."

With a smile on her face for the first time she added: "I can relate to that, when you are poor like me you ARE invisible! I guess most rich people think we choose to be like this? That we deserve this life and maybe they are afraid, that they too could end up like this.

"It's not a choice I have made. I never chose this life. Do you know this is the poorest estate in London? You can't get any lower on the life-scale. This is the last place on earth you would want to be.

"Even the police won't come in here... it's like this place doesn't exist. On the rare occasion, they have been here, they arrive in full riot gear and are armed to the teeth. They never really make any difference as life just goes on as normal as soon as they leave.

"This place is plagued with drug addicts, dealers, pushers, and gangs. There are also a few young girls on the first floor that run a 'lady of the night' business.

"So you never know what's going to happen and you certainly don't open your doors or windows day or night. There is always someone fighting and shouting. Many husbands beat their wives and kids and people are mugged on a regular basis, especially on Giro Day.

"You learn very quickly not to make eye contact or have a conversation with anyone. One word to sum this place up is a 'ghetto,' it's so grim and slimy.

"Somehow you worry more when the place is quiet, as it normally means something major has happened or is about to happen.

"I'm terrified most of the time, and I am also very scared that my son Blake might open the door and get out by himself, especially when he's in the middle of one of his meltdowns.

"Not everyone here is bad though. Some people are kind and watch out for you. I am one of the lucky ones as the neighbours' on this floor are fine and if they don't see you for a day or two, they will call to make sure you're OK. I'm shocked that I've ended up here. It was not in my life plan."

I asked her: "Tell me, Poppy, how did this come about? Judging from your accent, you don't seem to be from around here."

"I'm not stupid. I just made a mistake, and this is the price I'm having to pay for it."

I was totally taken with this girl. For some reason, she lived in this rat-infested ram-shackled building surrounded by thugs, drugs, and people that were completely off their heads.

There were prostitutes all over the place, and the building was falling down around her, yet she had made her apartment a safe and pleasant haven for herself and her children. She had somehow carved out some sort of normality amongst all this chaos. The place was spotless with everything in pristine condition.

The children played on the floor of the sitting room and their laughter was refreshing.

Blake, who had been the subject of the meltdown, now seemed settled and happy as if he had never had a problem at all. He remained well behaved and even helped his younger brother to make a jigsaw.

Poppy prepared some beans on toast for the boys. She said it was all she had as her shopping had spilt all over the road. With all that commotion, I had never even thought to pick any of it up.

When the boys had eaten, she made them comfortable for a nap, then returned to the kitchen and told me I should go now as my family were likely to be concerned. I told her not to worry about them, as they would be OK.

# Chapter 4

I sat back down and pleaded with her to continue and to explain her current situation, I insisted, "Please Poppy, tell me all about yourself."

She replied, "Surely you have better things to do without listening to me?"

I said, "No, not at all. I am very interested. You've done a great job on making this flat homely, comfortable and safe. Anyone can see you are a great Mum. I would love to know how, and why you ended up here."

Poppy replied, "Well, it is not what you are thinking. I come from a fairly wealthy family in Liverpool. My father is a local businessman and also does work for the local council.

"He's also the part-time Pastor of our local Church, but he's a strong man with very strict rules and opinions. I had a great childhood and many would say that I had a privileged upbringing.

"My father is a tough man with high standards and he expected his two daughters to fall into the role he had set out for us. We were never allowed to have any friends, sleepovers, or to go on any sleepovers. There were no parties and definitely no boys."

"As strict as my Dad is, my Mother is an angel. She is gentle, kind and funny and loved us beyond belief. We were her life. Strange as this may sound, Mum and Dad loved each other and they both loved us equally, or so I thought.

"They gave us the best of everything. We laughed a lot and we had a strong unit. My sister and I didn't think we had strict parents and it never entered our heads to rebel. We were just happy.

"We were also lucky too as we went abroad every summer for three weeks. We were enrolled in swimming classes, music, and dance lessons. I also played the piano and my sister the guitar. We even went horse riding every Saturday.

"At school, some people would have said I had it all. I was getting good grades and loved sport, and I was very popular with my peers. I enjoyed school and found school life very easy and comfortable.

"The teachers all loved me and they were surprised by my constant thirst for knowledge. I always wanted to know more and always had more questions.

"Can you believe it? I was even head girl for two years and was voted the girl most likely to succeed. I had the perfect childhood. I could not have asked for more. Do you know I got four A Levels and was off to University? I was the girl they all wanted to be. I loved my life. I know how that makes me sound.

"If only they could see me now they would have a great laugh and say look at how the mighty has fallen."

I tried to discreetly wipe a tear from my eye, and asked, "What were you going to study in University?"

She said, "I had my place confirmed to study to be a vet"

"Why a vet?"

"I just love animals they make me feel like a better person. I have always felt comfortable around them. It was my dream job, I couldn't think of anything else that would make me happier.

"They don't judge or criticise. They show you total and complete love. They are not worried about your income, or if you are rich or poor, fat or thin. They are always happy to see you. All they want from you is a hug and a rub.

"At the beginning, Dad was not happy with my decision. He felt it was not a job for a young girl. He had wanted me to do a business degree and afterwards to join the family business. I had my mind set and there was no way he could stop me, so I had Mum's blessing, and she eventually talked him around.

"He later gave me his blessing too and even offered to pay the College fees and for my student accommodation. I was over the moon. Life was amazing, it could not have been better."

"Did you start University then?"

"No, sadly not."

"Why, what happened?"

Just then my mobile phone rang and the shrill sound made us both jump. I said, "Please excuse me. I had better answer this."

To my shock, there were 15 missed calls from Isabelle, and I thought, she is going to be really mad at me.

"Hello, Isabelle?"

She replied, "Jesus , where the hell are you? You have me freaking out! I have been trying to call you for hours, why weren't you answering the phone?"

"I am sorry Izzy, I didn't realise the time. Did you get my text?"

"Yes I did, and let me tell you that it did nothing to ease my fears. I have even called the girls and they don't know where you are.

"I also called Mick, my friend who is a policeman in Battersea, and he said I can't report you missing until you've been gone for at least twenty four hours. I thought he was joking!"

"Thank goodness for that," I replied. "Izzy, I am totally OK. I am sorry I had you so worried. I will explain everything, but just not now... You have to trust me on this one."

When Izzy was satisfied, she hung up on the proviso I would call her later that evening.

When I walked back into the kitchen, Poppy was making toast. She turned to me and asked if I would like some. Until then I had not realised just how hungry I was.

"Yes, please," I said.

She was apologetic and explained: "I am sorry, but I don't have anything else to eat."

We just sat there like old friends eating our buttery toast with a strong cup of tea. Poppy then asked, "Are your friends annoyed with you?"

"Don't be thinking about them, they will be OK," I replied.

She said, "I'm sorry if I have caused you any trouble."

"Nonsense, where were we? Oh yes, did you go to University?"

"Sadly not."

"Why was that? What happened?"

As the tears started to roll down her face, she took a deep breath. She closed her eyes, began to speak slowly, and chose her words very carefully. I could tell the effort it was taking for her to re-visit this traumatic time in her life.

At times, she spoke so softly that it was hard for me to tell what she was saying. She started to talk about her last holiday and how happy everyone had been then, and that if only she had known it would be their last holiday together, she would have cherished it a bit more.

She began, "I was due to start College in September. I had so much to do so Mum and my sister Daisy said they would help out and that we should go shopping together to get some bits for College before I left.

"It was a lovely warm day and we set off into the City centre. We got the last of the items on my shopping list in record time so we stopped and had lunch at our favourite Italian restaurant.

"Afterwards we went together to get our nails done. We were all in good form laughing and joking and were travelling home on the A41 to Ellesmere Port.

"As we left the City traffic and headed home, I was driving. I had passed my test earlier in the year and Mum insisted I drove as much as possible to get all the experience I could before going off to University.

"The traffic was much lighter than normal. There seemed nothing out of the ordinary then suddenly – bang – and we were rear-ended by a huge truck. It just ploughed into the back of us forcing our car into an uncontrollable 360-degree spin before we eventually crashed into an embankment.

"I don't remember a great deal but the police told me afterwards that by the time they and the Fire Brigade arrived the car was on fire. The three of us were unconscious and they had to work at record speed to get us out.

"By the time the ambulance got us to the hospital, Daisy had died. I was in intensive care for a week. I had a broken leg, fractured ribs, and a head injury.

"Thankfully it was not so serious for me but for Mum, however, she went into a coma and suffered a stroke as a result of the accident.

"She stayed in this catatonic state for about three months. She just lay there in hospital completely unaware that Daisy had gone for good. Dad was emotionally broken. He sat beside Mum day after day talking to her and praying, begging God for her to wake up and be OK.

"He made deals with God on an hourly basis just for her to live. He stopped eating and sleep was no longer part of his day.

"He barely spoke to me. He blamed me for the accident, after all I had been driving. The following week he arranged for Daisy's funeral. It was just me and Dad, as Mum was still in a coma.

"It was horrendous. We just stood side by side and he never spoke a word to me. He never held out his hand or looked me in the eyes. I don't know which was worse: losing Daisy, or standing there beside a total stranger.

"She was not just my sister, she was also my best friend. The one and only person who both knew and understood me. We had so many plans for the future. She was the other half of me. We were so alike we could have been twins.

"The morning Mum woke up from the coma I was so relieved she was going to make it. Then we had to tell her about Daisy and she just crumbled again.

"We thought the day couldn't get any worse, but then the consultant called myself and Dad aside and gave us the devastating news that Mum had not made as full a recovery as they had first hoped. They were still uncertain as to whether she would ever walk again.

"A month later though, she was ready to leave the hospital. But still, Dad rarely spoke to me. Most of the time he didn't even notice if I was there or not. Before Mum came home we had some work done on the house. Dad converted the drawing room into a bedroom with a bathroom.

"It would be easier than trying to get her up and down the stairs. He had the doors widened and a ramp put outside the front door. Anything he could do to help, he did.

"The afternoon Mum came home she was a mixture of happy and sad as she was still coming to terms with Daisy's tragic death. The first thing we did after leaving the hospital was to go to the Cemetery to visit her grave.

"Dad was so gentle and understanding with her it warmed my heart that he might be softening a bit. He told her that he didn't choose the headstone as he wanted her to be there because she had missed the funeral and felt it would help her with closure.

"It was as if I was transported back to the day of the funeral and all the pain and heartache came racing back to the surface. My tears made Dad so angry. I had never seen him that angry before.

"Mum put her hand on his shoulder and asked him to stop as none of this was my fault. I was never so filled with love for my Mum as I was at that moment.

"It was such a relief that SHE did not blame me too. Over the next year, I became my Mum's chief carer taking her to her physio appointments, hospital check-ups, and counselling sessions. I was even helping her with her physio exercises at home.

"Her progress was slow and steady, but she began smiling a little bit more. She was determined to get her independence back. She pushed herself day in, day out. There were times during that year when I questioned her as to why Daisy had died and I had lived. "

"I would have happily changed places with her if she could have been saved. A year after the accident we were informed that the court case against the other driver was to be heard at Liverpool Crown Court."

"There was enough evidence against the male driver so we were not called to speak at court, which was a God-send, as I didn't remember much in the first place."

"On 26th August the three of us headed into the courthouse to see what was going to happen. The case though was much harder to take than I ever expected, and nothing could have prepared me for that awful event."

"The driver Dan Hunt, a 45-year old man, had previous convictions against him for drunk-driving and on the day in question he had already been banned from driving and shouldn't even have been on the road."

"The Judge said Hunt had shown a huge disregard for the law and the Court and had not displayed any signs of regret for the loss of life or the injuries inflicted on his victims. He was sentenced to five years in jail and given a lifetime ban from driving.

"In November that year, Mum and Dad suggested it was time for me to move out and get on with my life and perhaps go back to College, as that is what Daisy would have wanted for me.

"Shortly afterwards I found a small apartment in a nice modern block in the City centre. I started working for a local estate agent. It was my first job and I loved it.

"I really enjoyed showing off the new houses and apartments. But my real love was for second-hand homes. I had re-applied to College and was accepted so for the second time in my life I was given a date to start Uni.

"Life was good. Slowly I was starting to rebuild my life but without my soul partner Daisy. There is still not a day that goes by that I do not think about her or the day that changed all of our lives.

"This was my first Job, first apartment, and my first time to go out clubbing. Life became a series of firsts. I had the freedom I yearned for as a teenager.

"Then the handsome Luke Ryan entered our office. He was looking for a flat to rent. He was Tina's client and she should have been the one to take him to the appointments, but my luck was in, as she had called in sick that day and I was taking care of her diary.

"Luke was a charmer, tall, dark and handsome. His accent and his 'come to bed' eyes soon had me melting. I was putty in his hands when he spoke. I showed him the apartments Tina had lined up for him. He was happy to take a one- bedroomed place on Duke Street.

"He was a stockbroker and often worked late and wanted somewhere where he could just crash out after a hard day at the office.

"He came back and signed the contracts straight away. He asked if he could buy me a drink to celebrate the new pad. At first, I said no, but once he turned on the charm, I couldn't resist. So we went to the nearest pub and he ordered champagne. I had never tasted champagne before. I drank it as I didn't want to be rude, but I didn't like it at all. A drink turned into dinner and then a club.

"Over the next few months, we saw each most days. He was always charming, and polite. Our day never seemed complete unless we saw each other. He became my drug. I was in love, hook, line and sinker!

"I could not get enough of him. I had never imagined that love would feel like that. How could I be so lucky, to find true love so soon?

"Luke loved life, he loved to party and didn't take anything too seriously. He never planned anything, and everything was a spur of the moment decision. He was the complete opposite of me. He would make fun of me for having a life-plan.

"He kept staying over more and more and it was rare that he went home. I spoke to his landlord to see if he could get out of his contract. He said he would agree to let him break the contract if he would pay the rent until a new tenant was found.

"I agreed to this as I had at least ten other clients looking for an apartment. It was hard to find a nice apartment in the City, so Luke moved in with me.

"On occasions, however, he would stay out with friends, or he could be working away in London or Manchester, or at the Paris office.

"Six months later I missed a period and then found out I was pregnant. I was not sure quite how I felt. My emotions were mixed. I was happy and excited, but then sad and scared, as I didn't know how Luke would react. We had never even spoken about this possibility or discussed any long-term plans.

"With Luke's work commitments, we didn't really live together. He had not met my parents and I had not met his. We were so tied up with each other we never thought about the wider family.

"That night I told Luke the good news. He was like a young child at Christmas. He was jumping up and down, punching the air and talking to my belly, even at that stage he was calling the bump a boy, his son.

"Over the next few weeks, we were so happy. He came to the hospital for all the appointments, and at around thirteen weeks, I said we should tell our parents.

"He said his parents were living overseas, as his Dad worked for the United Nations and travelled a lot, and said that when he next rang them he would tell them. He said they would be delighted as this would be their only grandchild.

"I had to confess I was terrified at the thought of telling my parents. I had to ask Luke to come with me, as Dad might not be so mad if he was there, but Luke didn't think it was such a good idea.

"I never saw him doubt himself before. He said he was afraid that my Dad would not like him, and would try to split us up. I reassured him that I loved him, and that would be enough for my Mum and Dad.

"It took a lot of persuading and bribery for Luke to come with me to meet my parents. And he was right ,they didn't like him! Dad thought he was too arrogant and cocky.

"They took an instant dislike to him, and I had not even told them about the baby. I was shaking like a leaf as I gave them the news of their grandchild.

"The shock and look of disgust on Dad's face had me in tears. It was like I was a five-year-old again. His eyes were cold and hard as he asked me to leave and not come back again.

"Mum was in such shock too that she never spoke a word. She had tears in her eyes. I could not make out if this was because she was happy or sad.

"I hoped the baby would bring us closer just like the old days. I thought if only Daisy had been there, she would have known what to say to make them accept me and the baby as a blessing.

"Dad said I was upsetting my Mother and should leave, so with a heavy heart, I walked out the door of my family home, unsure as to what to do next.

"Luke put his arms around me and told me he loved me but sarcastically said, "I think that went very well." He then added, "I told you so."

He said, "From now on I think it would be best if you visited your family without me." A few days later, I called Mum and although she was chatty and asked about the baby and how I was doing, there was something in her tone that I didn't understand at the time.

"At the beginning, Mum kept in touch and seemed happy about becoming a Grandmother.

"The night Blake was born was amazing. The pain was forgotten as soon as I held him in my arms. I had never felt this happy before. I knew straight away that I loved this little bundle with all of my heart. It was unconditional love.

"Luke was by my side the whole time. He was wonderful, kind, caring and in awe. Blake had his Dad's eyes and my mouth. I called Mum and Dad to let them know they had a grandson. Mum was overjoyed and said they would be in to visit us in the morning.

"True to her word, they arrived just after breakfast. Dad was beaming as he looked at Blake. When he took him in his arms, his whole body softened. It was like the barrier he had put up after the accident had come down. There was a warmth in his smile as he said he was the most beautiful baby he had ever seen.

"Over the next few months, life was good. My relationship with Mum and Dad improved, and they would just drop by to see us. Strangely, they never asked about Luke, and Luke was never in when they called.

"Luke was working away a lot in those days. When he returned he was always in good form. Life was amazing. Every day was a day of firsts. Luke was a loving, kind and doting father. We settled into our new roles with great ease and excitement.

"Blake though was only four months old when I missed another period. I was not overly worried at the time as I thought it was just my hormones being all over the place. Can you image my surprise when I found out I was pregnant again?

"This time I was happy, as I was sure Luke would be over the moon.

"It would mean I would have to take some extra time off work but I knew the office would not have a problem with me taking another leave of absence.

"I had just got used to looking after Blake, and had so much love for him, but questioned myself whether I could love another baby just as much? How would I be able to manage two babies under two?

"It was going to be a lot of hard work. I admitted to being exhausted for much of the time, and wondered what it was going to be like after baby number two arrived?

"I also wondered if other women felt the same? I told myself that it would all work out as I could still go to University part-time, or maybe even do an online degree.

"I was over the moon with excitement. It was all going to work out. I just knew it would. Luke was earning more than enough to start paying some bills. Up until then, he hadn't paid for anything. His idea of any contribution towards the bills was to pay for a takeaway, or to bring home a bottle of wine."

# Chapter 5

I could tell that this next stage was going to be particularly difficult for Poppy to explain, so I touched her arm gently and gave her some comfort before she continued.

She confirmed, "To my horror, Luke was not happy. He said I had trapped him and he didn't want another baby. He even booked me into a clinic to have an abortion.

"When I refused to go, he changed, saying he would be away more than normal, working longer hours etc. When he spoke to me, his tone was not the same. He stopped paying attention to me, and would just request his dinner, or ask if his laundry was ready.

"I suppose he treated me like a maid. Slowly, he stopped playing with Blake and started talking to him the same way he did to me. He started acting strangely and began drinking more and more.

"Sometimes he would be gone for days at a time and I never knew where he was. When I asked him, he said I was becoming too clingy and needy and he didn't appreciate it. He became nastier and less supportive.

"At times he would be verbally abusive, bang on the wall, or would knock the furniture over. More and more, he came home smelling of drink and cigarettes.

"He also began taunting me with how he could have any woman he wanted, and how lucky I was that he was here - especially as I was becoming so fat and ugly and all I did was whine and was so boring because I would not go out clubbing any evening.

"He thought it would be OK to go out and leave Blake alone. I could not believe it. Who in their right mind would ever leave a sleeping baby alone to go out clubbing?

"All I wanted to do was sleep and I needed to wash my hair more frequently, as I constantly smelled of baby sick, and the flat became a tip. He asked why I didn't clean the place as all I did all day was to sit on my fat arse watching daytime television.

"He was fed up with baby stuff all over the flat. He would scream 'you can't swing a cat in this place.' He demanded to know how we could ever fit another baby into it? He asked when I was going back to work so that we could get a bigger place?

"The months passed quickly and before I knew it the familiar labour pain re-started. I left a message for Luke to tell him to meet me at the hospital. Maria, a Spanish friend of mine from work offered to take Blake for me for a while until Luke came back from the hospital.

"She was my rock in the earlier days. She had four children but her husband left her after the fourth child was born. That was fifteen years ago, and she had never heard from him since.

Luke finally arrived at the Hospital just before Ollie popped out to say hello to the world.

"The nurse joked that this baby was in a hurry and was not going to wait for anyone. Luke stank of alcohol. I couldn't believe it. He arrived very drunk, very rude, and was very obnoxious to all the nurses.

"He even started to ask some of the nurses what time their shifts ended. Asked if he could take them for a drink to celebrate. He never once looked at Ollie or me. When I spoke to him he just started to shout and poke his fingers into me and said, "Well you're not going to be any fun tonight.

"His voice boomed out and all around the room. The senior nurse asked him to keep it down and even offered to make him a strong coffee to help him sober up. He began causing such a disturbance that they had to call security to have him physically removed from the ward. I didn't have the words to express just how bad I felt.

"For the next three days, I just sat there by myself watching the other mothers' with their doting partners by their sides. It took all my strength to hold myself together. I never understood how someone could be so lonely in a room full of people before.

"After the visitors left all I had was the other mothers' pity. I think that was the worst. I did call my Mum and Dad to give them the news but they said that they were taking a mini break before Dad had to take on a new client.

"Once he had secured the contract it would be all systems go and consequently there would be no time for a break for at least twelve months, so there was no chance that they would be able to visit.

"I did have a call from Maria to say that Luke had collected Blake the day before, so I guessed that was good news at least. Against the advice of the doctors, I discharged myself on day three. I just couldn't do another day watching all the happy families.

"Outside I breathed fresh air into my lungs and wrapped my arms around Ollie and whispered Mummy loves you now and forever, and explained, 'Let's go home and meet your brother Blake.

"I had missed Blake so much over the last three days, I had never left his side until now. I jumped into the first taxi that came and for the first time in three days, I had a big grin on my face. I thought I can do this! I was filled with pride and optimism."

# Chapter 6

Poppy took a sip of water and then resumed telling her story rather nervously, she explained, "When I arrived back at the flat I was expecting Luke to be there full of apologies, and for him to say he had been too embarrassed to come back to the hospital after his previous behaviour. I had not heard from him since the birth and all my calls had gone unanswered.

"I thought that hopefully, now I was back home he would be OK. The flat though sounded very quiet as I approached the door but I was not overly worried as Blake would normally be down for his nap at that time.

"When I opened the door my heart crashed. I nearly dropped poor Ollie out of my hands. Jesus, you should have seen the state of the place and the smell was awful. It made me want to vomit. The place was nearly destroyed and there were empty beer cans everywhere, some still half-full and stale, and there were some half-eaten takeaway cartons and rubbish was strewn all over the floor, together with numerous cigarette butts.

"It looked as if Luke had had a party and never cleaned up. The place looked like a squat. Panic set in when I went in search of both Blake and Luke, but neither of them were there. I tried contacting Luke again. No answer, and then I wondered what on earth was I going to do?

"I put Ollie into Blake's bed as I had not had the time to set up the crib before he was born. I opened the window to let in some fresh air in the hope I could reduce the smell, then suddenly, there was a loud hammering on the door.

"I thought this must be them, but when I opened the door, it was our neighbour from across the hall, holding Blake in her arms. She had the face of thunder on her.

"I couldn't understand why she had Blake. She explained that Luke had asked her to mind him whilst he went to the Hospital to see me as there was some sort of emergency. That was a lie on two counts, as there had been no emergency and he never came to see me.

"She said that was two days ago and she had not seen or heard from him since. He had given her no food, no clothes as he had been anxious to leave. She said she had tried to call him several times since, but to no avail.

"She kindly suggested we don't ask her to look after him again. To say she was angry was an understatement. I thanked her for her help and apologised a hundred times. I tried to explain that I didn't know she had Blake as I too had not seen Luke for days.

"She handed a smiling Blake into my arms and I spent the rest of the day cleaning and tidying the flat, then I ordered a home delivery from Tesco as there was no food in.

"Over the next few weeks, I settled into a routine with the boys. I had come to terms with the fact that Luke was gone for good this time, and after a lot of tears, I was beginning to accept it was probably for the best. It was at night that I missed him the most.

"About a month later, however, Luke came back full of regret and with his arms full of gifts for me and the boys. He was on his knees asking for forgiveness, wanting to try again. He said he had changed and wanted to be a father to his children.

"He put down all of his actions over the past few months to the pressure he had been under at work. We sat and talked for hours. Blake loved having his Dad back and there were tears in his eyes when he held Ollie for the first time.

"Afterwards he ran me a lovely bubble bath and cooked dinner for me. We sat for hours planning our future and it felt like the old days again. He was easy and relaxed. Regrettably, I fell for his charm once more, hook, line and sinker again.

"He would be home by 5.30pm each evening to help feed and bath the boys and to put them to bed. It was bliss! About six months later, however, the warning signs appeared again and all was not well.

"Once again he started coming home later and later, and some nights he didn't even come back at all. He would never explain where he was or what he was doing. It was always my fault if he didn't come home, as he said he couldn't stand the sight of my ugly fat face.

"In one breath he told me that no one would ever look at me as I was so disgusting, and in the next, that I was sleeping with every man in town, which was a joke, as I never had a minute to myself, never mind have time to see anyone else.

"My days were spent cleaning and looking after the boys. My only highlight was going to the park. Then one night he started hitting me. At the beginning, he was careful not to leave any bruises and would never hit anywhere that marks could be seen. Needless to say, the violence escalated and over time it didn't seem to make any difference where he would leave his mark.

"It was again, always my fault, and he would always promise never to do it again if only I didn't keep getting on his nerves. After a while, he couldn't control himself any longer and didn't care where he hit, or what marks were left behind.

"I ended up with a broken arm, fractured ribs, and burn marks on my hands and legs. If I cried or asked him to stop it would just send him into a real frenzy. He said I was an 'adult and should just take it.'

"The final straw was the evening Blake came into the room and said, 'Daddy don't hurt Mummy.' I was lying on the floor with blood running down my face praying that he would stop and for it to be over. Luke walked over and picked him up by the back of the neck and started to shake him.

"When Blake began to scream he threw him across the room as if he were a rag doll. Luke left both of us on the floor and walked out. I slowly crawled over to Blake where he was lying and at first, I thought he was dead.

"When I touched his beautiful hair he turned around and suddenly wrapped his body around me with relief and shouted out, 'Daddy is bad, I love Mummy.' After I tidied up that night I knew I had to do something before Luke came back, so, I called my parents.

"I told them everything and asked if me and the boys could come and stay for a while until I sorted something out. They were crystal clear in their response, NO WAY! I had made my bed so I should now lie in it.

"They said they had tried to tell me he was 'bad news' and told me that I, of course, wouldn't listen.

This was my life for the next four years, he would beat the crap out of me and then disappear to allow time for the bruises to heal.

"I was on tenterhooks waiting for Luke to return, and as usual he came back a few days later as if nothing had happened.

"But, Blake wouldn't go near him. He would cling to my legs every time he came home. He started bed-wetting and would also wet himself several times a day.

"I knew I had to get out when the school called to say Blake was acting out in school. The Headteacher was always on the phone saying he was concerned about Blake, asking if I knew of any reason for his sudden change in behaviour. He was also getting into fights with other children.

"He even stopped eating and wouldn't sleep for more than an hour a night. He would sit and scream non-stop for several hours at a time.

"I spent my days praying to God to make it stop. Luke physically hurt me, but my parent's coldness hurt me much more. I called several times but they wouldn't change their minds. I was now out on my own. I had got myself into that mess, so now had to get myself out.

"I couldn't let Luke hurt the boys. I knew it was only a matter of time before he seriously hurt one of them, or me.

"Later that day I started to plan my escape. I contacted the landlord and gave notice on the flat. I researched Women's Refuges. There was one fairly close to me. They gave me loads of information and made me realise that I was not alone and didn't have to do this by myself.

"I spoke to a lady called Barbara. She told me that thirty years ago she had been in the exact same position.

"When Luke went to work one morning, I packed our bags and left. I told the landlord he should change the locks straight away. I went to the Shelter, and over the next month or so, they gave me the strength and confidence as my bones and heart started to heal.

"They made me believe that I was an attractive young lady, and deserved to be treated like a princess.

"With counselling, I also started to believe in myself again and was looking forward to rebuilding a better life for me and the boys. Before they could re-house me, however, the Centre was forced to close down when their funding was suddenly withdrawn due to Government cutbacks.

"They were given just fourteen days to close the place down. I was panic-stricken, as I had nowhere else to go. I could not go back. Barbara sorted out all the forms that needed to be filled in so that I could claim welfare benefits and she also gave me the details of this place.

"Barbara even paid the first three months rent and for the train fare down here, and I also received some other funds to help get me started.

"She arranged for someone to meet me at King's Cross Station in London, to bring me down here, but I don't think she really knew what this place was like. If she had, she would never have sent me here.

"She believed it was a starter home, and to some degree she was right, but I don't want to stay here, as no one ever receives any help.

"I know I am one of the lucky ones, and although I have not heard from Barbara since I left, each night I always keep her in my prayers, for without her, I don't know where I would be today.

"I have tried to make the place as homely as I can. I know it doesn't look like much but you should have seen it when I first moved in. And I know that once I close that door we're safe. There is no other feeling that comes close to that."

I took a deep breath, and asked Poppy: "Do you ever worry that Luke may still be looking for you, or that he could still find you?"

"At times, yes, but honestly this would be the last place he would look for me."

I queried, "Did you ever get back in contact with your parents to let them know you are OK? They must be very worried about you and the boys."

"I did on a few occasions, but they were not interested. As far as Dad is concerned, both of his daughters are now dead. He said Luke had been round to the house to threaten them and to cause trouble if they refused to tell him where I was.

"He told them he was going to call the police and have me arrested for kidnapping his kids. I sometimes call Mum when Dad is at work just to let her know we are OK. She talks, but she can't help as she cannot go against my Father's wishes.

"She said Dad has disowned me. She did tell me she saw Luke in town a few times with another woman and with three children that were all older than Blake. She said she heard them calling him Daddy.

"When she and the children went into a shop he came over to warn her not to make trouble as they were not really his wife and children. Mum said she had asked around and was told they had been happily married for the past fifteen years and were once childhood sweethearts.

"She was told he was an amazing husband and father and very involved with his kids' school and was even a coach to their football team.

"I was totally shocked! He was married! Where did his wife think he was when he was with me? How could she not know what was going on?

"I often wondered if he used to hit her as well and if his other children were also afraid of him.

"Well, that's my story Elizabeth. I am really sorry for ruining your day. I bet when you got up this morning this was not part of your plan."

Poppy then asked me with a look of determination, "Tell me, what's your story? Why did you really help me and why are you still here?"

I smiled back at her and told her she was right, and half-heartedly admitted, "It had not been part of any plan, but plans are made to be broken."

She could tell that I now seemed a bit uncomfortable and had caught me glancing at my watch, and asked, "Elizabeth, can I call you a taxi? There is only one firm that will come out here especially after dark. It is like the Wild West here. It is not safe to be out at night."

Poppy called the taxi firm and whilst we waited we sat in a comfortable silence, smiling back at each other. As I left, Poppy gave me a massive hug and thanked me so much for an 'interesting day.'

I then asked her, "Would you mind If I called on you again in a few days?"

She looked surprised, and said, "Why would you want to? We are obviously from two very different worlds. You are not going to call Social Services are you?"

I replied, "No, not at all! Why would I do that? You are doing such a great job, anyone can see that."

"I don't know anything about you Elizabeth."

"I'm not sure why you would want to."

"You have done more than you will ever know."

Poppy said, "I'm sorry if I bored you with my life story, but for some reason, you are the only person I have ever told, apart from Barbara. I'm not sure what came over me."

I put my hand on Poppy's shoulder and said it had been a pleasure. Just then the taxi buzzed to say he was waiting nervously outside.

Poppy said she would walk me down to the ground floor, as people didn't always react well to strangers, especially if they were dressed like me.

We said our goodbyes and Poppy watched as my taxi drove away, no doubt still wondering what it had all been about.

# Chapter 7

Poppy thought she was must be living in some sort of parallel universe and kept wondering what had come over her as she had normally been such a very private and guarded person.

She had never spoken about her life in such detail before to anyone and kept thinking about how stupid she had been.

As she walked back up to the flat she asked herself if Luke had somehow sent Elizabeth there, and was she now going to come back with him, or the police?

For a moment she became panic-stricken again then thankfully logic kicked in, believing that there was no way he would be looking for her as it would definitely impact upon his own alternative life with his other family.

Poppy thought she would probably never see this woman again, and this made her evening seem a lot easier and worry-free. Back inside the safety of her flat she had to deal with the practical matter of having no food and very little money to replace all the shopping she lost earlier.

Poppy believed she had just enough food for breakfast and possibly lunch the next day, but after that, she didn't know what the hell she would do.

She kept asking herself why she hadn't picked up the shopping in the street, but realised she had been very worried about Blake. His tantrums seemed to be getting worse and were happening more frequently and lasting longer.

Most of the time Blake barely spoke and just sat there in his own little world, rocking and screaming. He was becoming more and more isolated from his peers at pre-school, yet his reading and writing remained very advanced.

Poppy knew his pre-school teachers were concerned and she knew she would have to arrange a meeting with them to try to work out what was happening and why. She also wanted to check to see if Ollie had been given a place at the Nursery.

She was grateful to Elizabeth for her help. She thought she was a very quiet and kind lady, but remained both puzzled and amazed that someone like her would want to help a total stranger for no apparent reason.

She considered that Elizabeth had hardly said anything about herself and wondered what she was really like, where she lived, and what kind of life she had. She cursed the fact that she should have asked more about her instead of just rabbiting on about her own crazy problems.

She thought, however, that there was something 'special' about her visitor that had somehow stirred a fire in her belly and put some hope back in her life.

Standing in the kitchen as she washed up Poppy started to daydream about the life she had always wanted with the boys smiling, happy and playing in their own back garden, and then hearing the screams of laughter as they played on the swings shouting, "Please Mum, just a little bit higher."

Then they would be racing down the slide again and running back into the kitchen with rosy cheeks and completely out of breath. They could even make fairy buns together.

She also began to think about whether she should go back to University to study.

There seemed no obstacles in her way, yet in reality, she didn't really know if going back to study to be a vet would actually work, as it would mean being away from her children too much. Then she thought, maybe she should do something else?

Sometimes Poppy wished her Mum and Dad would come to visit and spend some time with Blake and Ollie and take them to the park like normal Grandparents.

She loved her children so much, that she could never imagine not having them in her life. She could never close the door on them, no matter what they did. Poppy said she would never stop telling them she loved them and said she would always be there to love and support them.

She went to bed that night feeling more optimistic and happier than she had felt for a long time. Tomorrow was going to be a brand new day and a new start for the three of them. It was to be positive thinking from now on.

Poppy slept like a baby. It was the best night's sleep she had had for a long while. She eventually woke refreshed and full of energy, as she stretched across the bed, she whispered, "Today is going to be a good day."

She could feel something unusual in her bones, then suddenly she was startled by the absolute silence. She checked the clock and couldn't believe it was now 10.30am and the boys were still asleep. They were usually up and about by 6.30am, jumping up and down and looking for their breakfast.

As Poppy raced into their room to check on them, to her surprise they were still well away in the 'Land of Nod.' They looked so peaceful. Blake's blonde curly hair was spread out on the pillow and Ollie was snoring gently, so she crept out, closed the bedroom door and went to make a cup of coffee.

As the kettle was boiling she replayed events from the previous day over and over again in her head. She thought, what a weird day it had been!

And then with a steaming cup of coffee in front of her, she took out a piece of paper and a pen and started to write down a list of things she needed to do to help kickstart her life back in the right direction.

She thought that if the previous day had taught her anything it was that she couldn't stay in THAT awful place forever. She considered that anything was possible if only you believe and take the first step...

**Poppy's to Do List**

1) To go down to the local council office to see about alternative accommodation

2) To go talk to Blake's teacher.

3) To go to the health nurse to see about Blake's behaviour.

4) To look for a nursery place for Ollie.

5) To go to the Job Centre and look for a part-time job.

6) Look at the local College and check out what courses and options are available.

As she wrote down her list, she also said silent prayers for all that she was thankful for. She was so grateful for the boys and that she had been lucky enough to have escaped from Luke.

Meeting Elizabeth had given her some new confidence and in a funny way, it reminded her of who she had been before the accident, and before Luke.

Poppy readily admitted she had made mistakes with Luke but knew she shouldn't have to spend the rest of her life paying for them, after all, she had done nothing wrong, just fallen in love with the wrong guy.

She had no doubt, that to make the changes needed, it would not be easy, and so she told herself just to take it steady, taking one step at a time.

Poppy was surprised at the way Elizabeth had just sat there and listened to her and never once judged her. She never interrupted or rushed her, so again she began to ask why. And to wonder who she really was, or if she would ever see her again.

Either way, she believed she was an angel, sent to steer her in the right direction.

When the doorbell rang it startled her and she spilt her coffee over both herself and the table. She muttered, "Nobody's ever rung the doorbell before", so with trepidation, she slowly opened it, not quite sure what to expect.

To her amazement, there was a courier standing there with a large box. He nervously checked to see if she was Poppy and when she confirmed, he pushed a piece of paper at her and asked for her signature. The man seemed agitated by these unusual surroundings.

Poppy was unsure whether to sign it or not. She too was a little apprehensive and when she signed, the man quickly took the paper then ran off as fast as his legs would carry him.

She carried the box inside unsure what she was going to find and opened the attached envelope...


**Dear Poppy,**

*It was a pleasure meeting you and the boys yesterday. They are a credit to you. I hope you don't mind but I put some groceries together for you as I never thought to pick up the shopping from the ground yesterday. I hope you will not think I am interfering in your business, I am just trying to help. I have set up a meeting with my colleague Isabelle Hastings, 10.30 am Tuesday at 'Wear with Confidence,' 331 the High Street, Kensington, London W8. We have something we would like to run by you. I am sorry that I will not be able to make the meeting as I am away in the States on business. I hope you will be able to make the meeting.*

*Best wishes*, **Elizabeth Reid**

Poppy couldn't believe it. She thought Elizabeth was such a strange but generous woman and wondered what else could she be up to. She asked herself, why did she want her to meet Isabelle? And she had never heard of 'Wear With Confidence' before, and was puzzled as to what to do, and what they did.

She was so excited to see what was in the large box that she ripped it open rather roughly like a young child would at Christmas. It was full of food, and to make it better, it was from M&S*. Previously Poppy had only bought cheap stuff.

*\*Marks and Spencers.*

This was a real treat. There was bread, milk, eggs, fresh croissants, cakes, pasta, sauces, fruit and vegetables, meat, juice and fizzy drinks and a lovely bottle of red and white wine.

Poppy had not had a glass of wine for such a long time that she no longer remembered what it tasted like. There was enough food for nearly two weeks. She knew this must have cost a fortune. So, not for the first time, this strange woman had left her totally lost for words.

She decided to make French toast for breakfast. What a treat this was going to be for her and the boys. She started mixing the eggs with milk and cinnamon in a bowl. She put some butter into a pan and watched as it sizzled and melted.

She placed the bread into the egg mix and then put the bread into the pan, and while the aroma spread around the kitchen, she chopped up some blueberries, strawberries, and bananas.

Her mouth was watering and just as the French toast was cooking the boys arrived in the kitchen asking what the funny smell was. They started to lick their lips and asked if they could have some.

Poppy said, "Yes, of course, take a seat," she placed the toast in front of them topped with fresh fruit. They were also drizzled with maple syrup.

She couldn't recall whether the boys had ever had French toast before but noticed they both cleared their plates in record time and amazingly both had remained silent whilst they gobbled down their food.  That was new, as normally they would be chatting ten-to-the-dozen.

Poppy felt so much happier than she had been for a long time. The world suddenly seemed to be a better place that morning.

Afterwards, when dressed, she took Blake and Ollie to the park, and then they went on to the Job Centre.

The assistant was helpful and took time helping her to fill out her application details. She seemed impressed by Poppy's school grades, and her previous work experience, and even typed up her CV for her.

The lady told Poppy about a few jobs: one was for the hairdressers, another a receptionist at a local hotel, but her favourite was in a school as a part-time secretary. They both agreed that the school job would be perfect as she could work when the boys were at school and she wouldn't need to worry about childminding.

It would be a win-win for her. She couldn't have planned it any better. The lady said she would send her CV off to all three places but would call the school to personally recommend her. Poppy thanked her again for all her help and promised to let her know how things went.

Before she left, however, she was told not to get her hopes up too much as sometimes things didn't always work out the way she would like them to.

Her words failed to deter Poppy, who believed it would all work out, and that she probably would get that job at the school.

Her spirits remained high and she felt like celebrating, so Poppy took the boys back to the playground for a second time that day. They even had ice cream afterwards.

Poppy thought, what a productive day, and asked herself why she hadn't done it before. She then told the boys they would have to go to another office and told they had to be 'good boys' – to which they agreed.

They took the Tube to the Council offices and went in search of the housing department. The man on the desk was unfriendly and not very helpful, but she persevered and he eventually gave her a smile and then handed her some forms and an information booklet.

He explained they would not be able to get her an appointment for at least three months as there was such a backlog.

He said there were so many applications and not enough people to process them. Poppy calmly explained the conditions they were living in and that she was afraid for the boys' safety. He seemed genuinely shocked, but at the beginning, she didn't think he believed her.

The man then stood up and walked away after she had given him her address and Poppy was unsure if he was going to come back or not. She was just about to go when he returned with a female manager.

She approached Poppy as if she were an alien. She had a really sour face and spoke with a harshness in her voice that took her by surprise. She began to lose faith as to whether any of this would work out.

She asked her to repeat her address and demanded to know what the real problem was. Poppy began shaking as she told her about her living conditions. She was close to losing her nerve but then found the courage to continue with a new confidence she had not felt before. The manager responded in a very sharp and disapproving tone, saying it was a disgrace and not a suitable place to bring up children.

The woman even had the cheek to say SOME people belonged in

places like that and didn't deserve anything better, implying that somehow it was all their own fault.

She tapped some keys on her computer and then let out a sigh and told Poppy to come back on Tuesday morning at 10.30 sharp, where she would interview her, and fully assess her case.

The manager warned her that she would need all the paperwork filled out – and not to be late – as she was very busy.

She explained that even if her circumstances fitted their criteria it could still take years to find an alternative or suitable accommodation. She also added, not to build up her hopes. The manager also confirmed that a letter from Blake's teacher would help her case.

Poppy thanked her, yet didn't know why, and hoped it would be months rather than years before things could be sorted out.

The boys were tired and fed-up with all the waiting around, so she decided it best to leave Blake's teacher and the health issue until the next day.

She was pleased with how the day had gone and wanted to end it on a high note. They headed back home to watch a movie and for dinner, she told them she would cook a carbonara with bacon and prawns. She also wanted to treat them afterwards with chocolate brownies and ice cream.

This had been a good day and a chance to celebrate the first of many, she hoped, believing life was gradually improving and could only get better.

Back at the flat, the children played with their toys whilst dinner cooked and both lads seemed much more relaxed for a change.

After Poppy had put the boys to bed, she opened a bottle of wine. It was a treat for her to a have some quiet time and a rare bonus to have a glass of wine.

Once again, she thanked Elizabeth in spirit, wherever she was.

It was only 8.30pm, but it felt like so much had happened in that one day. She opened her old laptop up to look up some colleges online to see what courses were on offer.

Poppy needed to prepare for an early start the next day as she wanted to continue to build more positive steps towards her new life, yet somehow awoke later with a start to find she had fallen asleep on the couch.

It was now 3.30am. She had a stiff neck and was freezing cold.

She sleepily crawled into bed, clothes and all, and continued her dream almost at the same place where she had woken up.

The following morning she again woke early, refreshed and full of energy. She went into the kitchen but was disappointed to note she had not done the washing up from the previous evening.

She just finished as the boys came in search of their breakfasts. They each began chatting as they ate their food, and asked if they could go to the park again.

"Maybe later," Poppy explained, as it had just started raining outside, and told them she needed them both to be 'good again,' as she had to talk to a few more people.

Blake pulled a face and said that was boring. His mother promised him another ice cream if he could be good again, and Blake replied that he would try.

Eventually, they went off to school to talk to Blake's teacher. The boy was not impressed as he didn't like school and was already under suspension for hitting another child, and had even bitten a teacher.

This was the meeting Poppy had been dreading the most as it made her feel like a total failure as a mother. She was terrified they would call Social Services as they had threatened to before on more than one occasion.

His teacher Mr Gilfoyle was a patient man, but Poppy feared he was now at breaking point, as nothing seemed to be working. He said he was nearly out of options and said it was looking as if Blake might have to go to another school for children with 'challenging behaviour.'

This was the main reason why he had not gone down that road sooner, he was afraid it would only have a negative effect on Blake.

Sitting In front of Mr Guilfoyle, she felt like a small child again as he explained that he was unsure as to whether Blake should be allowed to return to school.

He believed Blake would need to see a psychologist, as he was showing signs of autism. She had never heard of autism before, so she was close to tears. He filled out the forms for the assessment and the more boxes he ticked the more it looked like he was a really troubled child, and she was a bad mother.

When he finished, Poppy thanked him for his help, but it was with a heavy heart that she headed towards the doctor's surgery to talk to them, and to see if she could get any help whilst they waited for an appointment with the psychologist.

She told herself, thank goodness she hadn't started this process yesterday, or she might not have had the courage to continue.

The doctor was very kind and helpful and told her that an occupational therapist would call her back within the next few days to see if there was anything they could do to help and to try to get him back to school.

Poppy thought that at least the doctor had done his best to keep her spirits high. By the time they left they were hungry, and the boys had reached the stage where they were almost pulling the heads off each other.

She was close to tears and quite unsure as to what to do next. They headed out towards the park and the boys quickly ran over to the swings. They had not been put off by the constant drizzle of rain and their screams of delight boosted Poppy's mood as they shouted, "Higher, Mum, higher!"

It soon put a smile back on her face for the first time that day. Their laughter also lifted a great weight from her heart and she couldn't stay sad for long.

They reminded her that she would have to charge ahead whatever happened next. She could no longer afford to stay still and allow life to happen around her. She had to remain in charge of her own destiny.

She knew there would be a few hard days ahead but she was now a stronger woman and needed to take back control of her life. She was determined to be a victim no longer.

She also told herself, that she wouldn't feel any guilt for being alive or for having made a mistake with Luke.

Without Luke, she wouldn't have had two fabulous boys and although neither had been planned, they were certainly not a mistake. She believed they were, in fact, a gift from God. So she decided she would no longer live in the shadow of the past and decided NOT to allow her parents or anyone else to dominate her life.

She was sorry if they thought she had been a disappointment to them, but knew she had NOT been responsible for Daisy's death.

Poppy said she owed it to herself to be strong for her children and wanted to provide them with the same opportunities she had with Daisy whilst growing up. They were now her life and she needed to do everything in her power to show them that if you work hard, life will provide for you.

# Chapter 8

Poppy had two interviews set up for the following week. She was beside herself with excitement as the school interview was one of them. Before she knew it, it was Tuesday morning and she found herself back in front of the housing officer.

The manager seemed a lot softer this morning and went through her paperwork and then took her to another office to meet Mr Lockwood, who would review her case.

He was a jolly man in his mid-sixties. He seemed friendly enough as he studied all the documents and explained he would have to inspect the building before making any final decision.

He said he believed it would just be a formality as he had been to the flats a few years before and had recommended the place to be knocked down.

He said Poppy's case would be a 'High Priority,' but even so, added it could take up to twelve months for her to be re-housed as there had been a serious lack of investment in housing stock over the past ten years.

The man said it was a disgrace that people were still being forced to live in those conditions, and agreed it was no place to bring up children. He said it was not a safe place for a young girl to be on her own with two young children.

He was outraged that the powers that be would not intervene. Over the years he had campaigned for some further investment and had tried on several occasions to gain support from local politicians.

The officer had wanted them to personally visit the place and felt that if they spent just one night sleeping in any one of the flats they would have soon found extra funds to invest.

His motto was "What is good for the cat is good for the kitten", and said that if they would not let their kids live there, then no one else's kids should be allowed to live there either.

One major concern was a distinct shortage of alternative accommodation and he asked her if she would be willing to move to another area, to which she readily agreed.

He then asked if he could call around later that day as he wanted to get the ball rolling quickly, and informed her that she was his last case, as he would not be taking on any more clients due to his pending retirement in six months. Mr Lockwood wanted to try to ensure that all his clients obtained suitable alternative housing before he left.

She was now very grateful she had met this man and knew he would do everything he could to try and help her. Two hours later, Poppy and the boys eventually left the Council's housing offices to rush home, feed the boys and give the place a quick clean.

By the time Mr Lockwood arrived at 4.30pm, she felt ready for bed and thought she must have lost a few pounds due to all the running around. She was completely exhausted.

The housing officer was really surprised at how she had decorated the place and said that her boys and the flat were a credit to her.

He confirmed that he could justify her as being an 'At Risk' family on the housing list, which would mean she could be offered a new place within six months.

When he left Poppy danced around the room and was overjoyed and thought things could not have gone better. She told herself how bonkers it was that life could change so quickly, saying you never know from one moment to the next what is around the corner.

On Friday morning Poppy received a letter from Isabelle at 'Wear with Confidence,' it simply said she was disappointed she hadn't been able to attend their meeting on Tuesday but would like to offer her another appointment for the following Monday afternoon. She said that if that did not suit, to please call and arrange another time.

Poppy had totally forgotten about the meeting Elizabeth had set up. It never entered her head and seemed like a distant memory. She admitted that if she was honest, she had not really planned to go to it in the first place as it was all a bit strange.

She was at a loss as to what it was all about. Who was Elizabeth Reid? What was 'Wear with Confidence?' And why did they still want to see her?

Poppy was sure that once Elizabeth had left her flat, she would never see or hear from her again. She was considering whether she should go just to see what they wanted, believing it wouldn't do any harm.  Finally, she made her mind up, she would go and see what the meeting was all about.

The weekend quickly came and went and by Monday morning, Poppy was a nervous wreck, still questioning her own intentions. By twelve o'clock though, her curiosity got the better of her as she prepared herself and the boys to head over to Kensington High Street to meet Isabelle.

Blake though was off in one of his 'dark moods' and Poppy thought that unless she was very careful he might suddenly go into one of his meltdowns. He had been very difficult already that morning and to make matters worse, Ollie was running a temperature.

It took much longer than normal to get the boys ready, and in part, she was taking this as a sign that maybe it had not been a very good idea to go in the first place.

Just as they were leaving the flat, Blake had one almighty meltdown. There was nothing to be done other than to hold him tight and rock him until he calmed down.

She used her soothing voice and rocked him back and forth. Poppy promised them both that they could go to the swings as soon as he stopped, then some twenty minutes or so later, Blake finally dried his tears, picked up his coat and demanded, "Come on Mummy."

They headed towards the Tube station with Poppy thankful the boys loved trains. She had never been to Kensington High Street before and was taken aback by all the shops. Everything was there, from expensive clothes to antiques, vintage specials, and children's toys.

Suddenly she became overwhelmed because everyone else seemed so well dressed, and again she questioned her motives as to what she was doing there.

When she finally arrived at 331, The High Street, she was surprised to see how different this particular building was. It was not as 'flash' as the others.

She thought, maybe this will be OK after all and taking a deep breath she pushed open the doors and the boys dashed in and jumped up onto a big white couch.

Poppy was breathless. The décor was simple, yet very stylish. The young girl behind the reception desk smiled at the boys and asked if they each wanted a lollipop.

The receptionist then turned to Poppy and asked if she could help her. Poppy explained she had an appointment with Isabelle Hastings.

She asked, "Ms Poppy Rainsford I presume?"

"Yes, it is," she replied."

"Great, Isabelle is expecting you, please follow me and I will take you up to her office now."

She chatted away as they walked up a beautifully carved staircase. Poppy could smell the polish from the wood and the walls were full of large paintings of beautiful women and men in gorgeous clothes, and just like the building, they were exquisite by their simplicity.

The boys were so quiet that she even forgot they were there. When they reached the top of the staircase, Poppy was led into a large room which again seemed elegant and was most impressive.

A few minutes later Isabelle entered. She was stunning from her shoes to her hair and looked picture perfect. She asked the boys if they would like to play with a box of toys on the table whilst the ladies sat down and talked at the other end of the room.

Finally, Poppy found her voice. She wanted to know what it was all about.

"Why am I here?" she asked.

Isabelle smiled and told her Elizabeth was sorry she couldn't be there but said she was still away in the States on a business trip, so she had asked her If she could meet up with Poppy instead.

"I hope that is OK with you?"

Poppy replied, "Sure, I guess."

"Let me start by saying that Elizabeth was very impressed with you, let's just say you made a great impression on her, and believe me when I say that, it doesn't happen very often. Now, let's get down to the reason why you are here as I bet you have a lot of questions.

"Elizabeth has seen something special in you and before you ask, she has not told me what it is, and I do not question her judgement as she is never wrong."

Poppy intervened, "Once again, I ask, what is it that I have missed, why am I here?"

Just then, there was a knock on the door and a lady entered the room carrying a tray full of biscuits and some fruit juice for her children, she turned and asked Poppy if she would like a tea or coffee.

She thought she might as well play along with all this as Isabelle didn't seem to be in any great hurry to let her know what was really going on.

"A coffee, please. Milk and two sugars."

Isabelle poured the coffee, "Tell me, Poppy, what are the boy's names?"

"Blake and Ollie."

"They are beautiful. I love the blond curls."

Poppy just laughed and said, "I hear that a lot." sitting in these chairs you could easily forget all about your worries, she felt so comfortable

Isabelle chatted away to her for what felt like ages about the weather and other general conversation. Finally, she asked Poppy what she knew about 'Wear with Confidence.'

With a very red face Poppy admitted, "Nothing at all, and to be honest, I don't really know Elizabeth either, so I am still at a loss as to why I am here.

"Elizabeth was very kind to me when we last met and I am very grateful to her for the parcel she sent, but to be honest, I never expected to hear or see her again, and she never spoke about herself."

Isabelle gave a very loud hearty laugh, and said, "This is going to be very interesting!"

She spent the next hour and a half telling Poppy about 'Wear with Confidence.' Poppy then replied, "But I still don't understand. I am none the wiser. What is this all about? How does all this affect me?"

"It's simple, Poppy. We would like to offer you a job."

"What?" she queried, "Why? Is this for real? Doing what?"

Isabelle just laughed again and replied, "I can see you're overwhelmed by all of this. But one step at a time. Let me tell you about the position. It would be 9am to 5pm, Monday to Friday. The starting salary is £20k with 25 days holiday plus Bank Holidays.

"In addition, you will get an extra day of leave for each year up to a maximum of 35 days. Your salary will be reviewed annually. As you have no experience, Elizabeth has suggested that you start in the warehouse and work in each department for the first six months and afterwards you can choose which department you would like to stay in.

"I know that might sound a bit strange, but everyone here has to work in each department before they start the role they have been employed to do, as it is only then that you can appreciate that we all have to work together as one. We can't function without each other, that is what makes us so successful.

"You will also find that our staff turnover is very low as most people tend to stay. We are like a family here. If you work hard we like to think that we will look after you."

Poppy was amazed, and said, "But I can't work full time. I was only looking for a part-time position, to work around the boys, who are at school."

"That's not a problem; we have child care facilities that cater for babies to teens. We currently have twenty children. Also, Elizabeth said you were looking for a new place to live.

"She has arranged for you to stay in the flat that we sometimes use if we have visitors from overseas. Occasionally the staff use it if they are working late on a project.

"If you have time we can go and see it now. I hope you like it, and that it will suit your needs. But, finish your coffee first, and don't look at me like that! I can see you are in shock and looking for the catch, but there really isn't one.

"Before you try to say no, I must remind you that Elizabeth has left strict instructions that no is not an option, and when you get to know her a bit better, you will find out she is not someone that takes no as an answer.

"If you were to say no, it would also mean I have not done my job properly.

"Will you excuse me for a moment whilst I make a quick call and get my coat? We can go over there now and have a look, it is only a ten-minute walk, so it will not take up too much of your time."

Before Poppy had a chance to respond, Isabelle had left the room. It all seemed so surreal, and she had to pinch herself so she could quickly wake up.

Ten minutes later Isabelle returned with her coat on and keys in her hand.

Next, they all trotted off, with Poppy more like a puppy, and still a little unsure about what was going on. Isabelle pointed out different places and things of interest on the way but Poppy remained bemused and lost for words.

They soon arrived in front of an elegant terraced property.

As Isabelle opened the door she apologised that the place was so small and hadn't been used in a while, claiming it needed a good clean.

She said she would get the cleaners back before they moved in, and explained, "The flat was redecorated when we bought it a few years ago."

Poppy thought this was madness, saying to herself, this place was NOT small!

It comprised of an entrance hall, an open plan living area and kitchen/dining room with polished oak floors. The kitchen had stylish high-gloss cabinets with granite worktops. There was also a large American fridge-freezer, a double oven, dishwasher, washing machine, and even a coffee machine!

It had all the mod cons you could ever imagine. It also had two double bedrooms with one ensuite and a full bathroom suite tiled from floor to ceiling.

There were French doors at the back of the kitchen that led out and into a small garden, to which the boys made a quick beeline. Isabelle walked over and opened the door and told the boys to have a good look.

The walls were painted in soft grey and cream. There was so much light streaming through the windows that it flowed into every corner of the room. Poppy was stunned. It was still so surreal! Since arriving at the flat the boys had remained in the garden.

Poppy thought these type of things never really happened in real life. She was speechless. Isabelle finally broke the silence asking, "Why don't you have a look upstairs at the bedrooms and let me know what you think of the place."

The upstairs did not disappoint either. Not only was the main bedroom also ensuite but in addition, it had a balcony that looked out onto the garden. It was so peaceful and serene.

Poppy knew she could be happy there and became lost in her own world until Isabelle and the boys came back inside. Both children said they loved it there but quickly ran back down the stairs and out into the garden again.

Isabelle asked, "What do you think?"

"I think the place is amazing, but there is no way I can afford anything like this even with your generous salary."

Isabelle let out another hearty laugh, and explained, "You don't understand. This is all part of your package; there is no rent to be paid."

She handed Poppy the keys and said, "Welcome to your new home. I hope you will be very happy here. No buts, all you have to do is show up for work next Monday at 9.00am, and then everything will fall into place."

"Are you sure, as I have no idea of what I am doing, or why Elizabeth is offering all this to me."

"Let's just say Elizabeth is a very wise lady and she always has a plan. Elizabeth saw something very special in you, and she has not been wrong yet. She believes everyone should be given an opportunity to try something new.

"It will all work out in the end, just wait and see. When would you like to move in? If you want to you could start to move in later today. If you need any help just let me know and I can organise a van to collect your things."

Poppy held out her arm towards Isabelle and insisted again, "Tell me, why would Elizabeth be doing all this, as she does not know me at all?"

Isabelle smiled and replied, "Elizabeth works in mysterious ways at times. She is a strong woman who has built this business from the ground up single-handed. The best advice I can give you is to work hard and hold on to your hat as things move very quickly here. I can promise that you will never be bored.

"I have to go back to the office now. Here are the keys. Stay for as long as you like. I will send Frank over to your flat in the morning to help you move."

As she made her way towards the door Isabelle shouted, "Elizabeth has left a letter for you on the side in the kitchen. I hope you will be very happy here." Then she was gone.

Poppy walked back into the kitchen, she was watching the boys through the window, rolling around in the grass. Blake went over to Ollie and gave him a kiss on the head, telling him that he loved him and that he would always look after him and keep him safe.

Blake fell to the ground laughing. He was now the 'man of the house.' It brought tears to Poppy's eyes, and she just wished more people could see him as a kind, loving and happy boy, and not the boy who would have frequent meltdowns and tantrums.

She was hoping to get an appointment for his assessment fairly quickly, as there had to be a genuine reason for his behaviour and she wanted some guidance on how to help him.

When she went out to the boys, they came running into her arms and said, "Mummy, we like it here, please can we stay?"

She explained, "We will come back, but first we have to go to the old flat to pack up all our stuff, then tomorrow we can move in here."

# Chapter 9

When she returned to her own flat, she soon realised how desperate and drab it all looked and just how unsafe it was for everyone. She was relieved to know that that night would probably be her last night at that address.

When the boys went to bed that evening Poppy started packing away all their clothes. She began thinking about what to do with all the furniture and kitchen equipment when it suddenly hit her that she didn't need to worry anymore, as her new place had absolutely everything, and anything transported from this old place would look really shabby.

"Sod it," she whispered. "I will leave everything," thinking that maybe the person who comes in after me will need them more than I do, so by 9.00pm she had finished and sat down with a lovely glass of wine.

Not for the first time that week she said a silent prayer to whoever was listening. Poppy was eagerly looking forward to a fresh start but had no real idea as to what it all entailed. Her new motto was 'In for a penny, in for a pound,' and she muttered to herself, "Roll on tomorrow, I can hardly wait!"

At 10.00am the next day there was a loud knock on her door. It was Frank and Gerry from "Wear with Confidence", with a van to help them move. Their faces looked pale with the shock of the place. They took one look at each other and without saying a word made her feel somewhat ashamed.

Poppy had lived there for over two years and kept asking herself how and why she hadn't moved before. The men said they were unsure as to whether it was the right address.

Poppy apologised for them having to come all the way out here and for the state of the area. They both laughed, and said, "No bother at all. We'll soon have you out of here no time at all!"

Frank had obviously noted the look of shame and desperation on Poppy's face as her tears welled up, so he quickly nudged her, gave her a smile, and said, "Not to worry Love. You're in safe hands now."

Within the hour they had all of their belongings safely packed in the van, and the men gave the distinct impression they were in a hurry to get out of that place as quickly as possible.

Poppy was highly relieved to be leaving this place. As they left the building, some of her neighbours came out to say goodbye and all seemed genuinely pleased that she was moving on.

One of them even joked, "You never belonged here in the first place, you were much too good for this horrible place. Best of luck for the future." It felt a bit strange as she had never really spoken to many of them before.

Frank talked non-stop during the entire journey without ever once waiting to hear a response. Gerry, on the other hand, remained quiet, and the driver confirmed the young man was on work experience with him for a month.

They arrived about an hour later outside her new 'Little piece of Heaven.'

Frank and Gerry kept running in and out with all the bags and boxes. They were in a hurry as they still had some deliveries to complete by 4.00pm. Frank said, "You will be very happy here and you will love working with 'Wear with Confidence.' It's a great place to work."

Before Poppy had a chance to thank them for all their help they had gone.

She began to unpack and soon put the clothes and other personal items away, but before she knew it the boys came racing in from the garden to say they were hungry.

Poppy went into the kitchen to get her bag so that they could all go to the shops and get some food, but when Blake opened the fridge, he shouted, 'WOW, look at all this food!"

Elizabeth had really thought of everything, as the fridge was crammed full.

Whilst making some sandwiches she noticed the letter that Isabelle had been talking about the previous day. After lunch, she sat by the patio doors drinking a hot steamy cup of coffee and looking out as the rain began to fall.

She carefully opened the letter and £500.00 in cash fell out and onto her lap. She was jumping for joy and couldn't believe her luck.

Blake and Ollie came running to find out what had happened and joined in with all the excitement, asking, "Mummy, are you happy?"

She replied excitedly, "Yes, boys, I really am. Let's have some ice-cream to celebrate."

**Dear Poppy,**

*Welcome to the team, please use the money to get anything you might need.*

*I put together a list of schools for the boys in the area, you might want to go and have a look at them before you make a decision. I highly recommended Kingsgate. If you call the Headmaster, Mr Keith Burnsall, tell him that I have sent you and he will see you straight away.*

*Many of our staff are using the school and have children who are very happy there. It is a lovely school and I'm sure the boys will enjoy their stay there. You will hopefully find it's a lot different from their current school.*

*If you need anything else please do not hesitate to contact me. I will be in the States for longer than planned, but I look forward to catching up with you and the boys when I return. I hope you will enjoy working with us.*

*Regards,* **Elizabeth**


That night Poppy went to bed thankful for her good fortune, praying it was not just some weird dream. She told herself that if it was a dream then please don't let her wake up until the next morning!

She awoke the following day at 8.00am sharp to the unusual sounds of the traffic outside. Slowly she climbed out of bed still half-afraid it was all a dream.

When the boys came into her room at 8.30am they all went downstairs to make breakfast and while they were eating she had a look at the list of schools. She decided she would start with Kingsgate, as it was the closest to their new home.

The school had asked her to come in later that morning. As she was unsure as to exactly where it was, she decided to take the Tube, but in the end, they found they could easily have walked it, as it was very close.

They were greeted by the Headmaster, Mr Burnsall, as soon as they arrived at the school. He immediately put Poppy at ease. He was tall, dark, and handsome with a very soothing voice.

He completed all the necessary paperwork and was really good with the boys, asking them if they would like to see their new classrooms and to meet their new teachers. At first, they were reluctant.

Blake was already showing signs of a possible tantrum. Mr Burnsall was very quick to notice and reacted speedily to avoid any possible meltdown. The boys were later then taken to be introduced to their new teachers.

After they had left, Mr Burnsall said his school had an excellent track record in supporting all students, and explained, "We strive to inspire, motivate and excite all of our students to become lifelong learners. Everyone is treated equally regardless of his or her background or grades.

"It's our job to develop their confidence and to foster self-belief. We really encourage them to try new things and to step out of their comfort zone. We want them to experience success and embrace the future challenges that life will provide."

Poppy was falling in love with this school and considered there was no way she could ever think of her children going anywhere else.

The Headmaster asked many questions about the boys and how they were getting on at their current school.  She was afraid to tell him about Blake's behaviour thinking perhaps it could change his mind, but with a silent prayer, she decided that full disclosure was essential in order to progress.

When she had finished speaking, he just smiled back at her, and said, "That didn't sound too bad." Poppy was in shock, at Blake's current school he had been labelled the 'Demon Child,' and her a 'Bad Mother.'

Mr Burnsall was sympathetic, and replied, "I think you will find we are fully staffed to deal with any 'challenging behaviour,' and over the years we have seen it all. The programme we use has a great success rate.

"I think the boys will be fine here. Would you like to confirm their places today? Or would you like time to think about it?"

"No, I mean yes, I would love the boys to come here. When could they start? "

The Headmaster checked his records, and asked, "How does next week sound?"

Poppy looked slightly bewildered and replied with a smile, "That sounds great!"

"Alright then, I will need their birth certificates and a report from their current school. If it is OK with you I can call them this afternoon, and sort out the transfer and reports.

"If you have any further questions you can always call the office. Goodbye Ms Rainsford, it was lovely to meet you."

"Yes, Goodbye Mr Burnsall, and thank you."

Right on cue the boys suddenly appeared, their faces flushed with excitement. Poppy could tell they had enjoyed it almost as much as she had.

On their way home, they were full of chat about their new school, claiming one child did this, and another said that... "Mum you should see all the paints they have," demanded Blake, whilst Ollie loved the Lego table. Blake also talked about all the books that were there and said they all looked like new.

"Mum they were not torn and they had nothing written on them. Mummy, can we please come back again, please, please? We love it there Mum!"

"OK, yes boys!"

They quickly jumped up and down, "Thank you, Mum." Yippee, they chorused.

Poppy and her children walked home on cloud nine. Later that night she again revised her 'to do' list, she had never believed it would have been nearly completed so quickly.

The next few days passed quickly and gave her little time to even think about starting work the following Monday. It was Sunday evening before reality finally hit home.

The next morning Poppy was a typical nervous wreck once more. Not only were the boys starting a new school, but she was also starting her new job and had no real idea of what she was going to be doing.

She prayed it would all work out but remained terrified of failure and worried about the absolute torture of having to return to her old life and flat.

# Chapter 10

Poppy stood and waited for a moment outside the offices of 'Wear with Confidence' before being greeted by Isabelle, who took her to meet the warehouse manager Mr Lavin.

By the time she arrived there, she felt weak at the knees with nerves and her head was spinning with apprehension and excitement. Mr Lavin appeared to be a very serious man in his late sixties with a very strong East-End type, London accent.

He made Poppy slightly nervous at first and asked if she had had any similar previous work experience. She was ashamed to reply that she did not, adding that she was still unsure as to why she was there. He just rolled his eyes and shook his head.

"Well then," he said, "Let's just start from the beginning. We will start by showing you the archives of previous sketches. The shop was opened in 1970 by Elizabeth, she started off by making and selling items at the local markets and over a short time, she gained a reputation for creative, stylish, and elegant pieces.

"She began making hats, scarves, and children's clothes. Later, she made communion dresses, christening gowns, bridesmaid's dresses and suits then she moved into the wedding dress market.

"In the beginning, everything was sewn by hand. Today she is still known for her unique designs for all budgets. As you will see we also make everything on site. Recently, we branched out into jewellery and headpieces.

"Her work is amazing, especially all the early stuff made by hand. I would advise that you look at all the early sketches when you get time. It will really give you a sense of the woman.

"For the next few weeks, you will be helping out in the jewellery section as there is a backlog of orders. And, as I am sure you are aware, anyone who joins the company has to work in each department. You will find it's a great place to work. We are like a family here. Most people stay all their working lives.

"You will be expected to work hard, and in return, you will be well looked after. Elizabeth is a very fair boss, but be under no illusions she is no pushover and is a tough business lady.

"Rule number one: - work hard and be honest, and don't be afraid to ask, or to make suggestions or suggest ideas. If you don't know about something, just ask!"

Later Mr Lavin introduced her to Mrs Jackson, who was a jolly woman in her mid to late fifties. She was the 'go-to' person. If anyone needed to know anything, she was definitely the person to see. Poppy was told to pay strict attention to her and informed that you can never buy knowledge.

By the end of the day, her head felt like it would explode, and she was worried about how she would ever remember everything she was told on that first day.

There seemed to be so many different types of metals, including gold, silver, platinum, different diamonds and their cuts, gemstones, and crystals.

It seemed to be a huge task. On the plus side, she reminded herself that everyone she met appeared helpful and very willing to share their knowledge.

They all seemed happy and loved their work. She thought it

seemed a testament to its founder.

She considered that life was strange and there was no way you could ever have predicted what was likely to happen. For some unknown reason, however, Poppy had never given up on her dreams, despite being told she was wasting her time and hoped that one day everything would eventually turn out for the best.

She still found it hard to believe that one extraordinary meeting had somehow changed her life. Poppy believed her late sister Daisy was probably up there somewhere moving Heaven and Earth to help turn her life around.

She muttered, "I promise you, Daisy, I will make the most of this opportunity. I will not let you down. I will work harder than I have ever worked before. I may feel out of my depth but one thing I am sure of is that I will come out on top, as opportunities like this don't come around every day."

The weeks soon passed and each day she learned more and more. Poppy even looked forward to work. She was happy and believed the mood of the place was infectious and said that even her children now seemed more content.

The school was working out better than she could ever have imagined, and Mr Burnsall remained true to his word. The school carried out a full assessment on Blake and found he was on the autism spectrum with high anxiety issues.

They provided him with regular occupational therapy sessions and play therapy on a daily basis, and it was during one of these sessions that he finally spoke out about his Dad, and how he was afraid of him coming back to hurt his Mum.

He told them his Daddy was 'bad' and always 'hurt his Mum' and 'made her cry.' When Mr Burnsall and his team spoke with Poppy about Blake's diagnosis and behaviour she was devastated, as he had never once mentioned his father before.

Blake felt his job had been to look after his Mother and younger brother and that he should have stopped his Daddy. It was a crazy situation with such a young child knowing that what his Dad was doing was wrong, and yet for the adult to think it was quite normal behaviour.

It seems we don't always give kids the credit they deserve. They are often good judges of what's right and wrong and it broke Poppy into a thousand pieces listening to them. She had not realised the damage Luke had done.

They explained to her that the meltdowns were his way of coping, and that it was just a reaction to any loud noise, or if he felt unsafe. They also confirmed that his previous school and the place where they had been living had all had a very negative effect on him, as he never felt safe or secure. It had all been too much for him to cope with.

Poppy felt so ashamed she had not noticed or understood what was really going on in front of her for the past few years, and how it had affected the boys. She thought she must be the worst mother in the world.

She felt so guilty and suddenly became overwhelmed with grief and started to cry uncontrollably.

Mr Burnsall and his team though were very supportive. They were kind, considerate and caring. They never judged or blamed her, and said most of Blake's behaviour could be addressed, believing that in time she would see a very different child.

She felt so grateful to the staff at that school. They had a belief that all his behavioural problems could be treated and were also the first people to officially recognise Blake's potential as a loving and bright boy.

Poppy was so extremely grateful to them and at the end of their meeting they recommended that Ollie too should also attend therapy sessions, and perhaps he too should see the school counsellor.

Mr Burnsall admitted there was no 'quick fix' and said it would take time to resolve, confirming that the school policy included a holistic approach, confirming they were not there to judge anyone.

He said they would provide the best possible care for all of their children and would support them in any way they could.

Leaving the school that day Poppy felt both happy and sad all rolled into one. She also felt numb, yet relieved, and more optimistic for the future.

Poppy told everyone that she owed so much to Elizabeth and said she didn't know how she would ever repay her. She also found it rather strange that she had not seen or even spoken to her since that initial chance meeting in the rainy street.

Poppy was unsure what Elizabeth might have told people about her, and why she was still helping her out. She thought if she had said anything to them then no one had ever mentioned it.

She knew Elizabeth was still in America trying to set up the US flagship store, but the talk on the factory floor was that many obstacles remained and that she was now wondering if it was all worth it.

# Chapter 11

Meanwhile, some thousands of miles away across the Atlantic, I was still considering the future of the company and my thoughts kept drifting back to the UK.

When you considered, originally everything was in order and that I only came here to sign the final paperwork. But at the last minute, the lawyers found many unforeseen problems in the small print of the contract. They all said that this was all part and parcel of the negotiations. My colleagues have always said that I am normally a very calm and patient person, but I have to admit that all these delays are stretching my patients beyond my limits.

I wanted to return to the UK as soon as possible because I was a genuine 'home bird' and didn't enjoy being away for so long. I hadn't even gone back for Christmas, so my two wonderful girls opted to come out and stay with me for the holidays.

Even though I was away for a long time, I always contacted the department heads at least once a week to keep me posted about everything that was going on.

Isabelle had also kept me up to speed about Poppy and her children, and over the next few months, It was great to hear I heard that Blake's behaviour had settled down somewhat and that his meltdowns had reduced and were now not so intense. He had also taken part in the school play at Christmas.

I was told that Poppy just sat there watching him with pride. He was like a totally different child. He enjoyed a positive school report and the team were surprised at how quickly all the various therapies had worked.

The number of sessions was therefore reduced and it was recommended he join the school's music and drama program, as he had begun to show a real passion for drums

Since starting work at 'Wear with Confidence,' Poppy realised the company had a special relationship with all employees and they seemed to be looked after on a personal basis as well.

Although I had only met her that one time, I still felt a unique bond with her and was looking forward to catching up with her again when I returned.

Poppy, however, was still probably wondering if I would ever be able to explain to her why I had done so much for a 'total stranger,' and I knew that she no doubt had many questions prepared.

Elizabeth was at her wit's end. She had been in Washington for nearly five and half months and little progress had been made.

People often believe that everything moves much faster in America but little do they know, between the lawyers and unions, it had all become a battle of wills and some problems just seemed so petty and small.

There were times when she was certain that they no longer knew what they were arguing about, however, neither side wanted the other to think they held the upper hand.

One time it would be about the name of a product, or they didn't want some material bought from this, that, or another place. For Elizabeth, it was all beginning to feel like she was selling her soul to the Devil.

She confided in Isabelle, "If they have their own way it will not feel like my products or my designs any more. I have seen so many different versions of contracts that it's hard to tell what's new.

It's all a load of nonsense and if it's not sorted out soon it could end up bankrupting me. I thought the hardest part would be finding the right premises for the shop, but how wrong could I have been.

The building has been fully fitted out for eight months. Eight months of mortgage payments and bills, and yet we are no closer to opening the doors.

They seem to think there is an endless amount of money, and if I hear one more time that I need to pay for anything else I will scream. It has become a joke and a very expensive one at that.

Tomorrow's meeting is D-Day. Afterwards, I will have to make a decision. I am so tired of all it. I just want to come home. I am so desperately tired of living out of a suitcase. There is nothing quite like your own home. At first, it was a treat not having to clean and change bed linen or to cook, but that novelty has long worn off.

The following morning I walked into the office of O'Dwyer and O'Toole. They apparently had an update and I thought this might be what they had all been waiting for. For the first time in months, I felt some slight optimism and a hope they had finally reached some sort of agreement.

Ten minutes or so into the meeting though, I could feel myself losing patience. I held my breath and listened to both sides, but could no longer understand what this latest disagreement was all about. After two hours I could take it no longer.

A lengthy call back home to Isabelle, followed by a series of hastily scribbled notes in my diary, later confirmed all of my frustrations.

I confirmed I had enough and just snapped. I pushed back my chair and said, "That's it! Enough is enough! There is only one question I have to ask. Does anyone here actually want this project to go ahead? If so, can we please stop all this nonsense? I have been here for many months and yet it still seems neither side wants to work with the other. Well, ladies and gentlemen, I am not going to invest any more money into the project, until, or unless these contracts are signed sealed and delivered today."

I told them that I had not worked all of my life building a business to see it all go down the drain because of the ego in that room...And I said, with or without the contract, we will set up a shop in another city, where the powers that be will be happy to create new jobs.

I said I would not be wasting any more of my precious time or money on this project. You have until 12pm tomorrow as a final deadline.

Following my surprising outburst, I then just walked out of the room, waved an arm at them all and said, "You all know where to find me."

You could almost hear the deafening silence in the room as no one had ever heard me raise my voice before, or be so annoyed. Normally, I could smooth over each side with a calming comment and to say everyone was in complete shock would be a massive understatement. You could have heard a pin drop.

The only audible sound was that of my noisy high heels clicking on the marble floor as I walked away. Outside the building, I could feel a gentle warmth in the air as I headed back to my hotel, yet my head was in a complete spin.

I was looking forward to changing into my sports gear and getting onto the treadmill to burn away some of the stress. Afterwards, I was hoping for a full body massage and a facial.

I was tired of dining out with lawyers and union reps. The trip was only meant to have taken a month or so, and I couldn't believe how naïve I had been and had somehow allowed the whole thing drag on and on.

Now, back in my hotel room, I called down to the Spa to see if they could book me in for one of their deluxe pamper treatments. To my surprise, they had a cancellation for that afternoon. I was pleased and thought I would also be able to get a run in that day to help clear my head without any further interruptions.

The gym was very quiet. There was only one other person on the cross-trainer, going ten-to-the-dozen. It was the first time in months that I finally felt the strain of this nightmare gradually fading away.

My treadmill started to move very slowly, yet my mind was already racing away and I returned to consider my last day in London. I had not had the time until now to fully appreciate what a strange day it had been.

I still didn't understand what possessed me to act like that. I had never done anything like it before. I kept asking myself why I had gone out into the street in the first place and in the pouring rain just to help a total stranger.

It all seemed a mystery to me and then to take the young lady and her children home was most out of character. I couldn't think of any plausible explanation.

The one thing I did know, however, was to always trust your gut instincts and to follow them without question. It may not have made any sense at the time but it seemed the right thing to do. I knew that it could be many more years before I fully understood the reasons why.

Poppy had never been far from my mind ever since. I constantly wondered how the boys were doing at their new school, and if Blake was improving.

I knew it was a dreadful place they had been staying in and wondered how anyone could ever live in such a place. Poppy was such a sweet girl, doing an amazing job given her challenging situation.

I had been taken aback at just how she had made her flat so homely and believed all she needed was a change of situation. I thought what an amazing Mum she was to her two boys.

I told Isabelle, "Poppy has the potential to achieve many great things, hopefully, she is not too mad at me, or thinks that I have over-stepped the mark, or even worse, that I am an interfering old busybody handing out charity."

"I am still struck by this bizarre connection I have with Poppy. I have never felt this type of connection before, and I'm really looking forward to spending some time with her when I get back."

Isabelle told me that Poppy was well liked by all the staff. She also said she had made great progress and was learning the business much quicker than anyone else. She confirmed, "She is showing a great love for the company and as far as I know the boys have settled into school and are also doing very well."

I kept thinking back to my own troubled upbringing and told myself that the start of Poppy's life had been so different to my own.

Poppy had come from a good loving family. The accident of her sister Daisy was obviously devastating for everyone, but for her parents to turn their back on her, it was so hard to understand what they were thinking, or not thinking.

I believed Poppy's parents had actually lost two daughters that day. I thought It must have been a very hard pill to swallow for everyone, but then for her to have had the pure misfortune to meet that thug Luke, and at a time when she was just getting her life back on track.

I considered that if Poppy had not been so vulnerable at the time she may never have met Luke. I wondered too, if he ever thought about her now, or about his kids. I also wondered how much bad luck could one person have.

It was hard to imagine just how much her life had changed in such a short time. It must have been like comparing chalk and cheese. One minute your whole life is mapped out and then the next, it has all been taken away.

I thought she had coped remarkably well and I acknowledged it felt good that I had been able to help her get her life back on track. She didn't deserve to be treated so badly by such a violent partner.

I told Isabelle, "It amazes me how some parents can turn their backs on their children. Everyone makes mistakes but that doesn't mean you have to pay for them for the rest of your life, the past is the past."

Later, during another long, alcohol-fuelled, emotional and unexpected telephone conversation with Izzy, I finally admitted part of my very own, exceptional story.

I told her, "Poppy and I seem to have a troubled family history in common, as I had not seen my own family for many years. They were unkind and unloving. The real reason for this I do not know, or even if they were always like it.

"I have not given my lot a second thought in such a long time. It's still just too painful to go there. I have spent my whole life trying to forget. I will not allow myself to be hurt by them ever again. I have never spoken to anyone about them.

"I have kept my past a secret from everyone, not even my late husband or my two children have any idea. I cannot allow myself to look back and in many ways, it is easier not to look back as there is a certain comfort in not having to revisit the pain.

"I have told all my friends that I was an only child and that both my parents died when I was young. I met my husband Edward on a warm summer evening in July at a friend's party in Shepherd's Bush. Edward was tall, handsome and very charming. We quite literally bumped into each other on the way into the kitchen to get another drink.

"I was enchanted when he spoke in his deep Welsh accent. It was very strong at times and I would have to ask him to keep repeating what he was saying. But it was his eyes, they were dark brown, and just by looking into them I soon became lost.

"It was love at first sight. From that night we became inseparable. There was no one more surprised by our relationship than me.

"Meeting Edward was totally unexpected, as I never really thought of being with anyone. I always had a problem with trusting people, and many would say that I often came across as rather standoffish.

"Edward was a fourth year intern at King's College Hospital. He didn't like working in A&E as he felt it was hard to get to know the patients, as there was never enough time to spend with them.

"It was a fast-paced environment and the long hours didn't fit into his long-term plans. He wanted to open a small practice where he could treat his patients as human beings, and not just as an illness.

"He believed it was a privilege to be involved in other people's lives and to see people who were sometimes facing the worst outcomes. He also thought it an honour to be with them in their final hours on this earth.

"Edward was full of compassion and had an absolute love for the job. He turned a light on in me that I didn't even know existed.

"When I told him I had signed a contract on some premises, and that I was hoping to open a shop by the end of the month, he got so excited and even offered to come and paint, put up shelves, and move some stock from my flat.

"Sure enough he arrived at the shop at eight in the morning in a pair of blue overalls that were way too big for him. His arms were full of paintbrushes, tools, two coffees, and breakfast.

"He didn't look anything like a doctor. We laughed as much as we painted. It was like we were one person, finishing each other sentences. It was unbelievable when he got down on one knee and asked me to marry him.

"Three weeks later, I was both shocked and afraid at the same time. My heart was screaming yes, but my head said no. It was too soon, it was madness, but every time we said goodbye, my heart would break."

I later revealed to Izzy that Edward had come from a small mining village in South Wales and that he was an only child. His Father was a miner and Mother a baker. They both loved him beyond belief, he was their pride and joy.

They worked hard to provide him with the best education and didn't want him to go down a coal mine like his Father, Grandfather, and uncles. He was also the first in the family to go to College.

When Edward was ten, the mine his father was working in collapsed and he was trapped down there for two and a half weeks along with forty other men.

The landslide that followed engulfed and flattened a local farmhouse, some of the miners' cottages, and the school. It was only luck that there was no school that day as it would have been a miracle if any children had survived.

Many of the men were killed on impact and those who survived received serious injuries. Most of the survivors never worked in the mines again due to the injuries sustained, or the effect it had on their mental health.

That day affected the whole community and beyond. The accident had crushed his father's leg and had left him with a limp and poor mobility, yet he was one of the lucky ones, as after he eventually recovered, he obtained a job in the office.

His father was good at maths and written English and knew the mines like the back of his hand. He took to working in the office like a duck to water.

He started to work on improving health and safety. He worked tirelessly to try to improve the working conditions for all the men.

He also increased the pay and introduced a scheme to look after the men and their families should another incident occur.

He would no longer allow young boys to work underground and insisted everyone had to be at least eighteen to start work. Prior to his role, mine owners had little or no regard for the workers who toiled for hours in appalling conditions for little reward.

Their attitude was that there were plenty of other men to take their places if they were unhappy or complained about their working conditions.

It was the first time the men had ever had someone on their side, to push their case. He fully understood the risks these men took every day. He was the bridge between the workers and the management and eventually, he grew to be respected by both sides.

Needless to say, when they closed the mines it was met with mixed emotions. In some ways, it was a blessing that young men and children were no longer at risk, but on the other hand, there was not a lot of alternative work for the men of the village.

Many people were making do, and surviving before they closed the pits, but afterwards, they were on the breadline, with many having to move in search of a better life for themselves and their families.

# Chapter 12

I explained to Izzy, that when we made our very first trip to South Wales to meet Edward's parents it had terrified me, as until then it had just been the two of us and we were so happy.

I thought what If they didn't like me, I wasn't sure if we could have gotten married as he was so close to his parents, and I didn't want to be the person to change all that, or to make him choose.

I would have had to walk away and the thought of that was breaking my heart. As we pulled up outside their door, I was a wreck. My mouth was so dry I was sure I would pass out. Edward just grabbed my hand and said, "I love you, and they will too." They already know how happy you make me, and if I am happy, they will be too.

I was afraid they would see right through my story of claiming to be an only child and saying my parents had passed away when I was young. My fears though were unfounded and they were amazing.

We hit it off straight away and I was apparently the daughter they never had, and they were the parents I never knew. They really showed me what a family should be like.

We got married on the 30th of November in an 18th Century Methodist Church, in the village where Edward grew up. I was a Catholic but had not practised it since I left Ireland.

It was the same church his parents and grandparents had married in.

The snow was thick on the ground, and I had hand-made my dress. It was draped to the floor in length, with an elegant sweetheart neckline featuring a pearl beaded bodice, and a soft satin skirt with a chapel train covered in a beautiful lace, detailing a vintage finish.

We were surrounded by Edward's parents and close friends. In total, there were about fifty people present. It was clear to everyone that we were totally in love.

We partied the night away in the local hotel but had postponed our planned honeymoon as the shop was inundated with orders and Edward had his finals coming up in the New Year.

Instead, we spent three wonderful days in the Yorkshire Dales in a quaint little hotel. It had been more or less untouched for the past fifty years. It was run by an old couple who were very set in their ways. At times it was a bit strange, when ordering your breakfast they would also ask for your dinner order.

We didn't mind as it was the first time we had been away by ourselves. There was no disturbance from work, no sewing machines rattling away, and no calls from the hospital asking Edward to come in due to another emergency.

On paper, we should never have been matched together as we were polar opposites of each other but in reality, we were a perfect match. I was wild and loved to a party whereas Edward was quiet and loved nothing more than to just sit and watch a movie with a glass of wine. But none of that mattered as we were just very happy together.

When Edward finished his training he decided he wanted to work as a GP rather than stay at the Hospital. He felt that in the Hospital you couldn't make a connection with the patients, so we moved out to the suburbs and he set up a surgery in a small village.

Whilst he was busy getting the practice off the ground, I was equally busy in my shop. There were so many orders coming in for wedding dresses and bridesmaid's dresses on top of pieces for the shop.

We were lucky enough to be able to keep a flat in Kensington High Street due to its location and its great access to transport. It was perfect. If I had to work late I could just walk from the shop, or when we wanted to stay in London for a show.

In the early years it was a struggle to pay the two mortgages and the rent on the shop, but, luck was on our side and somehow we managed, and now I wouldn't want to be without it.

Within a short space of time it became obvious I couldn't do it all on my own, so I took on two members of staff, and then added another two, and so it went.

In the first year of our marriage, we barely saw each other. We would fall into bed at night totally exhausted. We were totally in love and so every minute together was treasured.

A few years later we had an option to buy the shop and all the offices at the back. The landlord was good to me and offered me the place at less than market value, so there was no way I could turn him down.

He didn't want to be bothered by estate agents and people traipsing in and out. He wanted a quick and easy sale. He had suffered a heart attack and wanted to retire to the South of France as he'd had enough of the rat-race.

With the extra staff I had taken on and a new doctor in the

surgery, Edward booked our long awaited honeymoon, so finally, we could take a break. I had never been on a plane before, or been abroad at all for that matter.

I was like a child on Christmas morning when he handed me the tickets to Greece for two weeks. We had not had more than two days off in the past year, so two weeks felt like a month.

We planned to do lots of sightseeing, and maybe some island hopping, and it all seemed so exciting. We went shopping the following day to buy all the essentials for a sun holiday: bikini, shorts, t-shirts, sandals, a dress or two for the evening. If I enjoyed shopping for the holiday this much then I could only imagine what the holiday itself would be like.

As the days passed and it got closer and closer to the holiday, I became emotionally exhausted, as the excitement was overwhelming at times. Edward, as usual, remained calm and reassuring.

He would laugh when I was so excited and I didn't think I could wait any longer. The night before we left I couldn't sleep at all, so I sat up sketching and designing for the shop.

I had so many ideas that my hand struggled to keep up with my mind. Edward got up the following morning as cool as a breeze. I had a quick shower and then we were off.

I was amazed at the number of people at the airport. There were so many flights going to places that I had never heard of before. After checking in, we went through to the departures, had something to eat, and then went for a walk around the shops. We stood in the viewing gallery watching flights taking off and landing with such fine precision.

They just glided past each other. They were so close that at times it looked as if they would crash into each other. I lost count of the number of planes in the sky.

In no time at all they were calling our flight number and hand in hand we walked to our gate and handed over our boarding cards and passports to the lady on the departure desk. On the plane, I was stunned at how tight the seats were but in no time the plane raced down the runway, gently lifting off the ground.

I was terrified. My stomach was in knots. I had to close my eyes and imagine I was sketching a new design. Edward laughed as he held my hand and eased my nerves. After a while, the airhostess brought us some food and drinks and I started to relax.

When we landed and the doors opened, we were hit by a massive blast of heat.

We went to collect our bags from the baggage carousel, and Edward had arranged for a taxi to collect us and take us out to our hotel.

The driver drove like a madman, stopping and starting and swirled precariously around a lady crossing the street, narrowly missing her. As we drove out of town, the noise level soon faded from the hustle and bustle of city life.

We held our breath again as he drove at speed around narrow country roads and then up and along the mountain. He tried his best to speak in broken English and to point out beauty spots and the local history.

We prayed we wouldn't meet any other cars coming in the opposite direction as there was barely enough room for one car, never mind two.

As we got closer to the top of the mountain the road became more like a dirt track. When we opened our eyes the view was breath taking, and built into the mountain were cute little houses, and behind them several small villages all looking out onto the beautifully clear-blue water.

Fifteen minutes later, we arrived at a small guesthouse consisting of twelve rooms, a pool and a restaurant that stretched out on to a terrace overlooking the majestic waters of the Aegean Sea.

It was certainly a sight for sore eyes and looked like a set from a movie scene and it had been untouched since it was first built. This amazing unspoiled place was going to be our home for the next two weeks.

We spent the time in a daze completely in love with each other and that amazing place. Our days included travelling from island to island exploring the many hidden coves, a medieval castle, and hilltop fortresses.

Our favourite place was a small fishing village where we would sit for hours watching the men arriving back from a day at sea. It was also a family affair as waiting for them on the pier were the wives with their arms full of empty baskets who helped them to sort out the catch.

The very same fish would later be available in many of the local restaurants for dinner that night. Sitting there watching the boats coming and going felt like home, and filled me with happy memories of my childhood.

We both fell in love with the place and it was hard to pick out our favourite place. Before we knew, our time here was coming to an end. Our time there had been everything we had needed. It was our Heaven on Earth.

We promised ourselves we would go back as soon as we could get away. We even talked about buying a small house there when funds would allow us too.

Arriving back at Gatwick Airport we were still on cloud nine, full of the joys of young love, even the weather outside could not dampen our spirits.

As soon as we had arrived back home again life was even busier than before. There were long days and short evenings. Not long after our holiday, I was feeling under the weather. I became tired all the time and was violently sick on and off, and was really off my food.

I put it all down to the cold wet weather and thought I must have caught a virus until one evening Edward told me he thought I was pregnant. I laughed as I thought there was no way that could be the case.

Edward insisted I took a pregnancy test, and to our surprise, I WAS pregnant.

The next few months passed quickly between the shop and hospital appointments. My due date arrived earlier than expected. We rushed to the hospital both worried and excited in equal measures. Thank God for Edward, he was calming and reassuring and took control. I could understand why his patients loved him.

An hour after arriving in the labour ward our daughter was born. Just as I began to hold her, the midwife quickly interrupted me and took the baby away, asking me to prepare for another contraction.

In a total surprise, we both shouted, "What?" Before I knew it, the intense pain of contractions started again, but before I could ask any other questions I heard another scream!

The midwife quite casually said, "Congratulations you have another daughter."

We were absolutely shocked, as no one had ever mentioned twins, not even at any of the scans. We were totally dumbstruck.

The midwife then handed me my two beautiful baby girls. The love I felt for those tiny babies was overwhelming. I never imagined it would feel like that. We named them Amelia and Sara. They were two wonderful angels. Life couldn't be any better.

I never believed anything could be that good. I thought these things only happened to other people, I never thought it would happen to me. I had never felt that happy or complete in my whole life and I didn't know you could love anyone that much.

I knew the first time I laid my eyes on them that I would never let anything or anyone hurt them, and that I would do everything in my power to protect them and provide them with all the love and support they would ever need.

When the girls smiled, it melted my heart. The first few weeks and months rolled by in something of a blur. The girls were amazing and were both thriving.

Our unit was happy and we laughed and loved each other a lot. They were our pride and joy. There was nothing else on this earth that compared to the girls.

We were so happy but completely wrecked between the girls, the shop and Edward's patients, so the days passed quickly. Life was so busy and at times, I would forget to eat, and we would fall into bed totally exhausted.

Time passed quickly and in what seemed like no time the girls were no longer the small babies we had first taken home from the hospital. They were now at school.

I worked in the morning, and then after school, I would spend my time dropping them off at drama lessons, swimming, music, and many more varied activities.

I would sit in the car or in the halls with my sketchpad designing, and arranging orders and deliveries. Before I knew it, the years passed and the girls were off to University. We were so proud of them. Edward was delighted that Amelia was following in his footsteps, and they had many a discussion on the pros and cons of life as a doctor.

# Chapter 13

The girls were in their second year at University when all of our lives suddenly took a disastrous turn. Edward's unexpected accident and subsequent death rocked our worlds. It left us on our knees. I was heartbroken and completely stunned.

I was so angry that he had been taken away from me so soon. The darkness I felt at that time was only lightened by the girls. They were my joy and the only reason I kept going. It was why I got up every day and put a false smile on my face and had the strength to get through those horribly dark days.

There were times when even the business could not get me moving or remove the horrendous black cloud of depression that followed me everywhere. I was lucky to have Isabelle as she ran the place like a well-oiled machine. At times, I thought I was drowning in my sorrow. The pain was so bad that at times I couldn't eat, breathe or sleep.

I did everything I could to avoid going back home to an empty house. I put a brave face on and hid the pain that was constantly tearing me apart. I had experienced loss and hardships before, but nothing in my past could ever have prepared me for this excruciating heartache.

This heaviness and emptiness followed me everywhere and there seemed no relief from it.

Those first few years were the hardest of my life. I suppose I was lucky compared to some others. I found my strength in the girls, watching them getting their degrees, and moving through their lives.

Their laughter would lift the dark shadow of gloom and despair, and somewhere along the way, and I am still not sure quite how or why, but the pain gradually started to fade, and each day eventually got that little bit easier than the day before.

On a bad day, however, I could still hear Edward's voice telling me, "I love you, you can do this." I found myself laughing a bit more, and started looking forward to tomorrow. That isn't to say I didn't still miss Edward. I did and still do every day; it's just that the intense pain is no longer there.

Amelia finally obtained her degree in medicine, just like her Dad, but unlike him, she opted to work in the Hospital rather than at a GP practice. She loved the Hospital environment.

She became a junior doctor at King's College Hospital in London.

I still worry a lot about the long hours and the high risk. I get really mad at the long shifts, the overcrowding, the shortage of staff, the lack of breaks and her exhaustion.

This is why the burn out rate is so high. I would love the powers that be, the top management and the government officials who make these decisions to actually work those same shifts in identical conditions for at least three months just to see if they could cope and last the pace.

That is the only way real change will ever happen. My big question is, if it is not OK for lorry or train drivers to work for 72 hours at a time, then why do they expect doctors and nurses to make life or death decisions and provide excellent care to their patients under those same conditions. It stretches them beyond the limit of what any human should ever be expected to reach.

It still makes me so mad when you see them working and fighting to provide the very best care for their patients, who are then often forced to await treatment for hours on a trolley in some draughty hospital corridor.

Amelia laughs at me because I get so mad over the whole situation. I just wish everyone would stand up against the hospital management and the Government and insist on real change and reform.

For now, I have to accept that Amelia loves her job and wouldn't do anything different. It makes her so happy and her face lights up every time she talks about her work. Last year she went to a cottage hospital in Cambodia for six months, fell in love with the place and is hoping to go back again sometime.

Sara completed her degree in drama and is currently working for a small theatre in Soho. She is completely in love with her job and she said it never feels like work.

She also tells me entertaining stories and scandals about what goes on behind the scenes, as there is so much more drama off-stage than on, with some actors displaying some strange personalities.

Sara was only telling me recently about a current leading lady, who as soon as she arrived requested her dressing room be completely re-painted in green, with all the furniture white, and said she would only drink from a certain glass.

Another actor requested a bucket and cleaning supplies so that he could scrub the floors and the walls every day before rehearsals. I guess it's safe to say he would be suffering from OCD.

She loves the camaraderie; the theatre was like a family. She also spent some time on Broadway and more recently finished a pilot show for television with a lot of interest being shown stateside. Currently, she is working on a new series based on a young married couple who are stuck in the middle of a family feud.

She is still waiting on confirmation of funding to complete the project, so at the moment, she is trying to keep it under wraps until the contracts had been signed, sealed and delivered.

Sara has an amazing talent and writing skill, and this was her first attempt at writing and directing a drama. It amazes me at just how different the girls are. They are identical to look at but that is where any similarity ends. Their likes and dislikes are so different and it's hard to believe they're sisters, never mind identical twins.

I must have been still daydreaming and had completely lost track of time when a member of the hotel staff suddenly came to tell me that the Spa staff were waiting. I hastily jumped off the treadmill and into the shower before heading to the Spa. As soon as I entered, I could feel myself being engulfed in a welcome oasis of peace and tranquillity.

I spent the next three hours being totally indulged from the dry flotation bed to the full body massage, followed by a facial, manicure and pedicure, and by the time I left, I felt really wonderful and like a new woman.

When I returned to my room, I quickly changed and then went for a brief stroll in the park before contemplating dinner at an Italian restaurant.

As I turned the corner after returning from the park, I almost bumped into Stuart Richardson, the estate agent who had first sold me my American property. I was taken by surprise, by coincidence I had been thinking about giving him a call to consider putting it back on the market.

"Elizabeth, you look stunning as usual," he said.

Now, I don't really believe in coincidence, so I took this as a good sign. With a new confidence that I didn't feel I had, I surprisingly asked him if he would like to have dinner with me. I didn't think he would, but he readily agreed.

Sitting in the Italian restaurant I was shocked to see how handsome he was and how I had not noticed it before. He was dressed in an Armani suit and Gucci shoes. He was a walking advertisement for success.

I started the conversation by telling him it was great to see him too as I had only just been thinking about giving him a call regarding my American place.

So, I laid my plans on the table by asking him if he knew of anyone who might be interested in leasing the property as the opening of the shop in America looked most unlikely at that stage.

I told him about the difficulties with the contracts and that I was thinking of leasing the property, rather than leaving it empty, as I didn't believe they could resolve the issues quickly.

He said he had a few clients who had been looking for something like that in the area and said he would call them, but couldn't make any promises. Stuart told me he would need to see the building before contacting them, as he knew that I had made a lot of changes to the place since he had last seen it.

He suggested, "Maybe we could have a look in the morning?"

I looked at my watch and was shocked to see it was now one o'clock in the morning. "Oh Stuart, I am so sorry I didn't realise the time. I'm sorry for taking up your time. Thank you so much for a lovely evening."

"The pleasure is all mine, my dear Elizabeth," he said.

We had enjoyed a lovely meal and I had to admit that I was a little sad when the evening came to an end. We walked back to my hotel, and Stuart agreed to collect me early the next morning.

I walked through the hotel lounge to the lift as happy can be and to be honest, I couldn't recall the last time I had felt that happy. I had never looked at another man since losing Edward, and it was a strange feeling, and I was not even sure whether he was married or not, or had any children.

Stuart arrived back at eight o'clock sharp the next day looking as good as he had the previous night. I sat in his car and admired the city as he drove. The conversation was relaxed and easy. I later admitted to Isabelle, "It was like we were old friends. He was amazing and when we went into the property he said it looked fantastic."

He queried, "Elizabeth are you sure you want to let this go? You have invested heavily in this project, are you sure it can't be saved?"

I replied, "Yes, I think it will be better all-round if I cut my losses on this."

"Alright then, I will call my client when I get back to the office and get back to you. Any chance I could buy you a coffee? I hear there is a great coffee shop at the end of the street."

I smiled at him and agreed, saying, "Yes, I would like that very much."

Sitting in the coffee shop, Stuart declared, "I'm surprised you've been here all this time and never called me. Did you forget my offer to show you around the city?"

"Sorry, I never thought I would be here this long and time just slipped away."

"Surely you were not over here by yourself over Christmas?"

With a little laugh I replied, "No, my two girls came over and surprised me on December 23$^{rd}$. I had no idea they were coming. They just knocked on my bedroom door. We had a lovely Christmas. It was great to see them, it is rare these days that we are all together for long periods of time. It was the best gift they could ever have given me, how about you?"

Stuart replied, "I went back to my folks in Boston for Christmas and then a group of us went to New Mexico for the New Year. It was the perfect ending to a very long year.

"Well, I think I had better get back to work to see if I can find you a client for this place! Don't worry, I will get the best price for you. You know I aim to please.  Hopefully, I will have some good news very soon."

I still had a good feeling about this latest development even though the lawyers and the union reps would probably be furious, but as I kept telling myself, as Grandma used to say, 'Follow your gut girl, it will never lead you astray.'

I thought it might not make any sense at that precise moment but knew that time would eventually reveal all, and considered it best to keep my plans to myself until I knew something more definite.

I kept questioning myself, muttering. Surely, they didn't think the situation could continue for much longer. I then thought it was a great shame that Stuart had had to go back to work.

I have to admit that I had really enjoyed his company. It had been the first time in twelve months that I had felt so relaxed and confident.

Later that day Stuart called back to say his client loved the place. They had viewed it from the outside some time before and had fallen in love with it. They had been hoping it would come back on the market.

He asked, "So, we have a deal? They want to move quickly to get this signed up. So, Elizabeth, if you have any doubts now is the time to say."

"No," I replied, "None at all."

"They would like to make a slight change to the contract."

"OK, what is it?"

"They want to take the lease for five years rather than the two you were thinking of, with an option to extend or buy at the end of the lease.

"They want you to know that they are serious about the building option and don't want anyone else to see the place. They are offering an extra $100k if you agree to the extended lease."

I was pleasantly surprised and agreed, adding, "That's great. I am happy with their terms. Stuart, you have done well, much better than I could have imagined."

"All I have to do now is to let my team know that 'Wear with Confidence' will not be opening anytime soon. I'm not sure how they will take it. But here goes."

Stuart replied, "Best of luck with that! I am here if you need anything. OK then, I will get the contracts drawn up and meet you tomorrow, to finalise everything."

# Chapter 14

I had pondered whether to tell everyone back home about my recent change of heart and scribbled out some more words in my diary about closing down the US operation.

I was talking to myself, going through my notes to make sure I had covered everything, and muttered, "I have called the airline and booked my flight home but should I now call my girls and Isabelle? Or maybe I should just turn up and surprise everyone. I think the latter idea sounds fine to me."

I showered and changed and left for the office but phoned ahead to make sure everyone would be there. I walked into the office with an air of trepidation, as I was unsure how they would all react, but knew it was now or never.

In the room, the silence spoke volumes. Based on my previous comments, they now realised that something dramatic was likely to happen.

Clearing my throat, I spoke with authority. "Ladies and gentlemen," "I would like to start by saying that I am very disappointed that an agreement could not be reached.

"As I am sure you are aware, this situation has cost me a lot of time and money. There is no way that this situation can continue, and there is no one more disappointed with the outcome than I am, but I simply cannot allow this situation to continue any longer.

"So it is with regret and sadness that I have to inform you all that I am no longer going to continue with this project, so, as of now, I will NOT be opening a store here.

"I have also found a new tenant to take over the property here and the contracts will be signed tomorrow, as they are in a hurry to move forward.

"I would like to take this opportunity to thank everyone for your hard work and late nights and I can reassure you that everyone will be paid in full for their services. I would suggest you send your invoices directly to accounts and I will ensure a speedy payout".

"Once again, I would like to say thank you to everyone for your input and friendship. I'm sure we will keep in touch, who knows what the future will bring. Now, I would like a few minutes with the sales and marketing team in private."

As they filed out of the room, one by one, each expressed their own disappointment at this unexpected turn of events. I just smiled, nodded and agreed with them whilst biting my tongue.

I really wanted to scream back at them telling them it was all their fault, and that all the squabbling could probably have been avoided.

When everyone had left apart from the sales and marketing people, I deliberately softened my tone and relaxed, telling them, "This bit will be a little easier. Now, I bet you're wondering why I have asked you to stay."

"I have been very happy with your work and I know the collapse of this project has nothing to do with you whatsoever, so, with this in mind, I would like to run a new project idea past you.

"I'm looking at launching some of our products online here in the US. Everything will be manufactured in the UK and shipped over.

"Your company would be solely responsible for the sales and

distribution, and most of the products are almost ready to go. I thought you might be able to utilise some of the work you've already drafted for the shop.

"You might have to make a few changes, but nothing too major. Do you think you would be interested?"

The team members all looked at me bemused but delighted, and one of them even replied with unexpected energy, "Yes, of course we would! We might need a week or two to put a campaign together and to work out a new strategy, but when would you like it to launch?"

I pulled a funny face, asking politely, "Would twelve to sixteen weeks be pushing it a bit?"

They almost replied as one, all eager to intervene, "It might be a bit tight but we could use that as a guide and see how we get on. Leave it with us and we will get back to you in a day or two."

I added, "I need to let you know that I will be returning to the UK tomorrow, but you can contact me on the same number. Don't worry about the time difference. Maybe you might be able to make it over to us for a week or two so you can see at first-hand what we do and to meet the team. It will help you understand the products more."

"That sounds great Elizabeth, I think we will be able to make it work and a trip to London would be wonderful as we have never been and would love to see some of the sights as well."

"Good then, we'd better get started if we are going to make the deadline."

"Goodbye Elizabeth, we will call you towards the end of the week, if not sooner."

I must admit that I left the office feeling a lot happier, as if everything was now back on track. My head though remained in the clouds again as I realised I must get back to the hotel and pack.

I was looking forward to going back home and I couldn't wait to get back into my own bed. I had also missed the luxury of just being able to make a simple cup of tea.

I told myself that I was so looking forward to cooking again in my own kitchen. And how I had missed my own cooking. I'd certainly had enough hotel food to last me a lifetime.

As I was leaving the building, my mobile phone rang. It was Stuart. I wonder what he wants. I hope everything is OK with the contract. "Hello, Stuart, How are you?"

"I'm fine. I was wondering - how did you get on earlier?"

"It went very well, much better than expected."

Stuart confirmed, "I have a draft copy of the contract. I was wondering if you would have a look over it this evening so we can get it finalised ASAP.

"I could meet you at your hotel at five. Maybe we could look at it over dinner.

"Why not", I replied.

"I will pick you up at five. I know this lovely place which is just outside the city."

"Brilliant. See you later Stuart."

"Look forward to it Elizabeth."

At the hotel, I quickly began packing. It was the one thing I liked doing the least. I couldn't believe how much stuff I had accumulated since I had first arrived. There was no way everything would fit into my cases. There was only one thing to be done, and that was to hit the shops, and pick up another bag or two.

I spent the next few hours shopping and picking up bits and pieces for the girls as well as the new suitcases. I nearly lost track of time as I raced back to the hotel to be ready to meet with Stuart.

I decided to go casual for dinner and dressed in white linen pants and a new cashmere jumper, with a little pair of kitten heels to compliment my style. Stuart arrived just after five, but when he saw me walking across the lobby he seemed entranced.

Despite my casual look, I thought I still looked reasonably elegant. Isabelle and the girls always teased me, saying I was always fully aware of my own striking beauty, and the amazing effect it still had on many people, and especially men.

I behaved myself and was very pleasant and polite. I also felt very relaxed in his company. Stuart seemed fascinated by my every word, and hardly ever took his eyes off me the whole time.

My girls claimed I could be utterly enchanting when it suited me, and now I was beginning to wonder if I had been using this supposed charm without actually realising.

I felt some unusual attraction to Stuart but realised he lived thousands of miles away from London and in a different time zone. All that aside, I was still unsure if he was married or single.

As we sat in the taxi, Stuart said, "I'm not sure if you have had a chance to sample some of the fine dining we have on offer here. In case you haven't heard, DC is no longer a city plagued with overcooked steaks, poor excuses for a salad, and overcooked fish.

"We now have some of the finest cuisines in the States. Many would say that we have come a long way from the stiff, stodgy dining scene. We have a new generation of foodies here and some amazing chef's right across the City from posh DuPont Circle to the industrial Chic Navy Yard.

"We have a choice from a wide variety of places to eat offering everything from luxurious tastings to small chic restaurants and bars all over the city. You name and we have it.

"Tonight, I have booked us a table at an incredible Greek restaurant, the food is amazing. I must warn you that from the outside it doesn't look like too much, but it is like walking into someone's home.

"Just keep an open mind and I'm sure you will love it. The staff are all from Greece. They are wonderful and welcoming, and their unique knowledge about the food and wine is second to none."

True to his word, the staff was quite amazing. It was as if we were long lost family members returning home. Upon arrival, we were greeted with a glass of complimentary champagne.

Stuart winked and said, "Cheers to us, and to a successful contract."

He asked, "Have you ever eaten Greek food before Elizabeth?"

I replied, "Yes, but not in a long time, so I am looking forward to tasting it."

**For starters we had:**

*Dolmadkia- Vine leaves, filled with savoury rice, fresh herbs, and extra olive oil.*

*Garides- jumbo prawns, cooked in extra olive oil with a homemade tomato sauce with a touch of Ouzo and Feta Cheese.*

**For Mains we had**

*Kleftiko – Lamb on the bone wrapped and steamed cooked with vegetable's, garlic and fresh herbs, Served with rice.*

*Chicken Souvlaki – Skewered fillets of chicken marinated in Olive oil and oregano. Served with homemade chips and Greek Salad.*


Whilst we were waiting for our starters, I looked over the contract and told Stuart, "Everything is in order. I'm happy to sign it now - if that will speed things up."

Stuart added, "Let's toast to your success, Elizabeth."

"And to your negotiation skills, Stuart."

"Now that business has been taken care of, we can relax."

"I second that," replied Stuart.

I was determined to find out more about Stuart and asked him, "Stuart, tell me something about yourself."

"That's easy, as there is not much to tell. I moved here from Boston when I was about twenty-five on a year's contract with a law firm. I love this place, so I ended up staying and opening up my own business.

"I didn't stay in law for too long as I didn't really enjoy it. I ended up as a realtor by default really. In the law firm, I was responsible for finalising the property contracts, so it seemed like a sensible move at the time.

"My parents were not too happy after all the money they had paid for me to get my law degree, but in time they accepted it, as they could see how happy I was, and not to mention that I proved to them I could make a darn good living from it.

"I never married, although I came close once, things didn't work out, and sadly I have no children."

We talked for hours, and to my complete surprise, he had been so open and honest about his life. I could now feel myself melting a little towards him.

# Chapter 15

I had always spoken very little about myself, preferring to repeat the same old story that I had always told everyone. At one stage almost told Stuart the truth, but just stopped myself in time, then I suddenly thought, I don't know what came me over me.

I had never come that close to telling anyone before – with the exception of part of it to Isabelle - but I guess it had been playing on my mind. It had been a very long time since I even allowed my mind to go back that far into my past.

Stuart seemed genuinely disappointed when I said I was going back home the next day. He became a little quieter for a while, and then said, "Well, that's just my luck."

On the way back to the hotel, he asked if I could change my ticket and stay for a few extra days so that he could show me the sights and the best Washington had to offer.

I can't lie, there was a major part of me that wanted that too. I liked being in his company.

Outside the hotel, he took me by surprise when he took me into his arms and kissed me passionately on the lips. My body reacted as if this was a normal everyday occurrence.

The kiss left us both breathless and speechless, until Stuart said, "I can't believe I have been waiting my whole life for a woman like you and then when I find her she leaves before we even begin."

I pulled away, embarrassed and red-faced, unsure as to what to say or do. The words rushed out of my mouth, "I must be going now. I still have a lot to do before my flight tomorrow."

I told him, "Thank you again for a wonderful evening and all your help with the contracts. I feel the place is in safe hands under your watchful eye. Goodbye, Stuart."

He kissed me again, this time on the cheek. "Goodbye, my English Rose, I will miss your wonderful smile."

I walked into the hotel with very wobbly legs but it had nothing to do with the wine at dinner. I was confused as to what had just happened.

I kept asking myself what all this means. I have never looked at another man since Edward. I had never even been interested in another relationship. That is not to say I have not had plenty of offers, I had, but always declined them gracefully.

Why did I meet him now? It would never work as we lived on opposite sides of the world. I didn't know if that was a good or a bad thing.

I was actually thankful to be going home the next day, so that I didn't have to deal with any of those potentially awkward questions or feelings now. There was no point in wondering what if.

I arrived back in Heathrow to a very busy airport on a very dark and dreary morning. The weather was almost identical to the day I had left. I felt I could have been in a time warp.

Walking outside, I hailed a taxi and headed home. Sat in the back of my taxi I picked up my mobile, went online and logged in to a home delivery service. I ordered the basic: milk, bread, eggs, bacon, etc.

As I was going through the list, I thought it looked more like a full shop as I was quite unsure when the girls had last been home and what food they had left, and thought, 'Better safe than sorry.'

Along the way, I asked the driver to pull over so I that could grab a take-out coffee and breakfast. Stepping back into the taxi, I handed the driver a coffee as well. He was really thankful and said it was very thoughtful of me.

The hot coffee was like liquid gold. I was just about to call the girls to let them know I was home when my phone rang. It was Stuart. I answered, saying cheekily, "Missing me already?"

He replied, "How did you guess! Are you able to read my mind?" And then he let out a very loud laugh. In an effort to reach more comfortable ground, I asked, "Is everything OK with the contract, did they sign?"

"They did, and yes, they are very happy. They have already paid the deposit and fees into your account. I just wanted to say again thank you for last night. I really enjoyed your company. I am sorry if I made you feel uncomfortable, that was not my intention."

"No, not at all," I replied.

"How was your flight? Are you home yet?"

"The flight was long, and no I am not home yet, I'm still in the taxi."

We talked easily for a while, before saying goodbye. When I turned the key in my front door, I felt like a child on Christmas morning. Home, Sweet Home!  Stepping into the hall though, I was suddenly hit by just how cold the place was, and it sent a shiver down my spine.

I thought, "Right, first let's get the heating on." I set it to high and then I went into the sitting room and turned the gas fire on, full blast.

# Chapter 16

I took my cases upstairs and hastily pulled out a thick jumper and pulled on some comfy tracksuit bottoms from out of the cupboard in an effort to warm up. Next stop was the kitchen, to make a piping hot cup of tea. I had just turned the kettle on when the doorbell rang. It made me jump out of my skin.

Opening the door, I was surprised to see it was the home deliveryman. He had arrived very quickly. He put all the shopping in the house and by the time I finished putting most things away, the kettle was singing.

I then went into the sitting room and just flopped in front of the fire. It was a great feeling to be back home. "Oh God, how I had missed a good cup of Tetley's tea." The tea in the States is nothing like the tea we have here. I was savouring each drop as it warmed me up.

I turned on the television set just for some noise. I couldn't remember the last time I'd watched daytime TV. It was so peaceful just sitting there, and this room was definitely my favourite room in the house.

It was filled with so many happy memories. It had been my safe haven after Edward's death. Many people had suggested I should sell the place after his passing, as it was a big house for just one person, but I couldn't imagine living anywhere else.

When we first bought the house, it was a wreck. There was nothing in the house but bare walls. We had to renovate all the electrics, the plumbing, heating, and insulation before we could install the new kitchen and bathrooms, never mind the painting and decorating.

It was a genuine labour of love and love had provided us with this fabulous home. It had also been a great place to raise the girls.

The rain was getting heavier by the minute as it pelted against the window, and the wind had picked up.

Without any notice, there was a sudden roar of thunder, followed by a flash of lightning. The thunder was so loud that I couldn't even hear the television, so I turned it off, and looked out towards the window so that I could watch the lightning flash.

I loved a good thunderstorm. It had been ages since there had been such a massive one. It also reminded me of being in my parent's house when I was young, being huddled around the fire, and my father running around unplugging all the electric items.

My Mother would run around at the same time with a bottle of holy water, spraying it everywhere, and saying 'Hail Mary' at rapid speed. She was asking for protection from the Devil, or something like that. She would bless herself after each flash. If God himself had been knocking at the door, no one would dare move to let him in.

Thinking of all this brought a brief smile to my face. I don't have too many happy memories from that time in my life that ever made me smile, so I still cherish the ones I have.

I never allowed myself to go back to that time in my life, and even today, I still find it very painful. It was easier to block it all out, the good and the bad. Now it all feels like they belonged to someone else and are not really my own memories.

Thankfully, no one ever asked me too many questions about my childhood. Sometimes, I regret I never told Edward, but to be truthful, it was not something that had entered my head in many years.

It still unnerves me a bit, when I find myself looking back. It makes no sense. I wondered if it was seeing Poppy on the street that day that somehow triggered a reaction somewhere at the back of my mind, and understood there were some bizarre similarities in both of our lives.

My Grandmother, Lord have Mercy on her soul, was a wonderful woman, kind, caring, hardworking and as honest as the day is long.

All the neighbours in our village had a great time for her, she was highly respected. How she ended up with a daughter like my mother I will never know. I would say she took the wrong baby from the hospital, but it was a home birth, the case for all the women in our village.

The thought of not having the twins in the hospital makes me have so much more respect for women of my grandmother's generation. I couldn't have imagined having the girls at home without pain relief. I thought it was no wonder that infant mortality was so high.

All they had was their faith and a bottle of holy water. How they managed to say the rosary in the middle of childbirth was still a mystery to me. It sounds crazy nowadays, but that was good old Ireland!

I can still hear my grandmother's voice in my head, her calm tones and wacky sense of humour. My Grandmother would say they were real women in those days and would roll with laughter afterwards, saying thank God the times have changed.

I miss my grandmother the most. She was my rock. I never knew my grandfather; he died of a sudden heart attack about a year or so before I was born.

My mother never spoke about her Dad, and would always tell me to be quiet if I asked any questions about him. My Grandmother, on the other hand, would speak of him often. By all accounts, he was well loved in the village and was a hard-working family man.

He was also a great provider for his family. They had a small farm in the West of Ireland. It was said he had a rare gift with horses. If you ever wanted your horse trained, or if your horse was sick, then he was the man to see.

He was known as a gentle giant, as he was well over 6ft tall. The others in the village called him the 'horse whisperer.' People apparently travelled from all over the country asking him to train their horses.

Gran would look at his photo and a tear would escape from her eyes when she admitted she still loved the bones of him, and still missed him every day. She confirmed he was the only love of her life.

She said it was love at first sight, from the very first time she saw him in the yard with her father. He started working on the farm when he was sixteen.

My grandmother had recalled, "He was so keen to learn as much as he could about horses and farming from my father. He was a natural with horses, right from the beginning, and if they were having a problem when birthing a foal, he would sit in the shed with them all night, sometimes there for days on end. "

"He was like the son my parents never had. Needless to say, they were over the moon when he asked if he could marry me. We had their blessing and were married in the local church in Ballyconneely when we were just seventeen."

"We just laughed at the priest when he said he felt it was best for us to wait. Your grandfather smiled and said, "There was no point in wasting time, Father."

"We were married on a beautiful warm sunny day in August", my grandmother said, "And we never looked back. We were just babies when you think back. We moved into the house with Mum and Dad until he finished building this house."

"We didn't have to wait too long for your mother to arrive. We were so happy. We always wanted a large family. Sadly, due to complications with the birth, I was never able to have any more children."

"We were heartbroken, but your grandfather scooped me up into his arms and said he had everything he ever wanted right here in this room."

"Afterwards he would say it was for the best as he didn't think he would be able to watch me being in so much pain ever again. He would have tears rolling down his face when he said he couldn't bear the thought of losing me."

"He joked and said he would have to go first and get the place ready as he couldn't stay in this life without me."

Once a month my grandmother and I would walk the three miles to the graveyard where he was buried. She would pick fresh flowers from the garden to place on the grave. She would stand beside his headstone, looking out to sea. She would sing his favourite songs, the 'Galway Shawl, Low Lie the Fields of Athenry, and Muirsheen Durkin.'

There were many more but I can't remember them all now. She would have tears in her eyes as she would say, "Oh, dear Michael, you left me far too soon, I wasn't ready to let you go, but, I know you're still with me, even if I can no longer see you. I guess you're busy up there getting the house ready, making everything just right for me."

"My love, when I close my eyes, I can see you dancing. When my time here is up, make sure you are the one that calls for me, or else you will be getting a piece of my mind, and I do believe there will be no way to escape, all the Saints and Angels will not be able to save you.

"Then we would head off to the local pub for a glass of red lemonade and a pack of Tayto crisps. We couldn't leave out the chocolate; my grandmother had a fierce sweet tooth, something I have inherited."

She would often tell me that I was the light of her life and that I was a blessing to have in the house. I spent much of my time with her. I loved being with her. She was always happy. She was also a great cook and taught me how to sew, knit and croquet. She was a very patient lady.

She made my Holy Communion dress from scratch. She sat up night after night hand stitching each section of delicate embroidery on the linen fabric, with the gaslight flickering away and her glasses hanging off her nose. She would be gently humming away to herself. With each stitch, she placed all of her love. It was intertwined into the thread. She had a real talent.

You would never know to look at the details on the dress that her eyes were failing. On the day of my Holy Communion, she beamed with pride. The dress was the talk of the town as no one had ever seen the like of it before.

The dress made me feel like a Princess. She was a happy-go-lucky lady. She lived a simple and happy life. The day I loved the most as a child was Friday as she would take me into Clifden to get the shopping and afterwards, we would always go to the pub for Oxtail soup and a sandwich.

In August every year, we would go to the pony show in Clifden and afterwards, as a special treat she would take me to O'Grady's restaurant, which was a very posh place, for chicken and chips, but my favourite was a small piece of fish, which I now know is called scampi.

Afterwards, we would head down to the showground to watch the horses being paraded around the ring. We could easily spend the day there sitting watching the horses. It was her favourite day of the year, and the day she would miss my grandfather the most, as they had always attended it together when he was alive.

She would remember going there with her father as a very young girl. They both loved their horses as Grandad used to breed the Connemara ponies and had won several prizes over the years. He had gained a reputation for producing the best Connemara ponies in the country.

People travelled from all over the place to buy one of his horses, or if they were having a problem training them, they would come to him, and in no time at all, he would have the horse as gentle as a mouse.

He would often refuse to sell a horse - regardless of the price - if he felt the owners were not going to treat the horse well. He would be heard saying that you could tell a lot about a man by how he treats his horse.

They both loved their horses and treated them like their children. He would often be seen shedding a tear when a horse would be leaving the stables.

My grandparents were known to be good people. They loved each other dearly and would often finish each other sentences. They would also be able to communicate with each other by just a look; there was no need for words.

They were soul mates for sure. My grandmother would say there was never a cross word spoken between them, and there were not too many couples that could say that.

She would talk about angels and fairies, how they were her own personal helpers always on hand to help. She would never cut the flowers in the garden unless she'd asked permission from the fairies first.

You would often see her placing a drop of whiskey and some porridge around the trees, to thank them for all their hard work. She would say, "All you have to do is ask my dear", and God knows I need all the help I can get with that mother of yours.

"Your parents think I'm talking rubbish, but what do they know? I am beginning to think that they do not have a brain cell between them anymore."

She would mutter to me, "It was a bad day when she got mixed up with that yolk of a man. Your poor grandfather begged her not to marry him. We could see he was a bad egg from the very beginning."

My grandmother used to read tealeaves for people, at the time I didn't know much about it, but there would always be someone dropping in for a cuppa, and it would nearly always end with, "Well then, what do you see?"

According to the villagers, she was never wrong and would be able to tell women, if they were pregnant, whether it was a boy or a girl.

When someone was close to death, they would often ask her to visit them too. I heard people talking about her healing abilities and predictions at her funeral.

I was so intrigued to hear more, but it made Mum mad, saying, "She would tell them she was sick in the head, and that they were all a bit loopy as well to believe in all that nonsense!"

A fight broke out once when one of the old ladies told her, "It was her that was sick in the head, and she should be ashamed of herself and all the trouble she had caused over the years. "You broke your mother and fathers' hearts, yourself and that Gombeen.

"God bless your poor father, he must be turning in his grave at the carry-on of you. The only thing you ever got right was that sweet little girl of yours; she was your mother's pride and joy. She is a little Doteen."

I miss my grandmother beyond belief. I miss her laugh, her warm hugs, and her voice, but thinking about her still makes me smile. When she was alive, there wasn't a day that went by that I didn't see her.

I was lucky as we only lived across the road and it was after her death that my life took a turn for the worse, and day by day, the life I once knew and loved slipped away piece by piece. At first, it was small things that you would barely notice, and to the outside world, life looked rosy.

It was a true statement that no one really knows what goes on behind closed doors and often the signs of suffering and torment are not always visible. The signs are not easily read and many people are simply not interested, or they are too busy wrapped up in their own lives.

People only see the mask you wear and at times only see what they want you to see. School was my only sanctuary. It was a safe space where I could laugh and play, and I was not a nuisance there.

I loved school and had a good mix of friends. I loved learning and was a model student. I might not have been the best in the class but I always did my best.

My parents would, however, always would mock me over this, 'Oh Miss butter would not melt, you just wait until they see the real you.'

It was a small village school so everyone knew everyone and we all knew each other's parents, and had a fair idea of what it was like at home. Some children had it good and others not so good.

Some would come in hungry and unkempt looking like they might have been in the fields beforehand, or they might not have had any food in the house to eat. In our small community, there was always a job to be done and no member of the family was too small to take part.

Thankfully, we all looked out for each other and would try to help. It was not unheard of that we would share our lunches with the children that we knew had not eaten. We would try our best to keep our spirits high and would focus on what we would do when we left school. We all had our dreams

I am not sure what turned my mother into such a cruel and bitter woman, and sometimes, I queried whether she had always been like that, and I hadn't noticed before.

She had a tongue sharper than a sword, and never stopped complaining about this and that, and how good everyone else all had it. She was a terrible woman for talking about people and to listen to her you would think she was a Saint.

Dad was not home very often and that was a good thing as the house was a little calmer when he was not there. Mum wasn't so bad when she was by herself. You could easily stay out of her way, and I would be fine, as she would only look for me if the dinner was not ready or she needed some tea, or the house was not clean.

So I learned very quickly to do it all without her asking and spent the rest of the time in my bedroom, or if the weather was fine, playing down at the stream.

When Dad was home they would fight constantly. In the beginning, they would just be shouting and arguing but over time it turned into one or the other of them breaking furniture. On more than one occasion, however, one of them threw a chair through the window.

They could go out for hours and come back late at night ossified*, hugging each other again as if nothing had happened. At times I thought my mother was afraid of him, and at other times I thought she enjoyed all of his antics.

Everything was a drama. It was so hard to know what was going through her head. Dad was often drunk with a temper and was well known in the local town for all the wrong reasons.

Locals would say, "What else would you expect with his red head? It's as if he has the head of the Devil on him."

As a young child, he was always in trouble for fighting or causing trouble and even my grandmother used to warn people to sometimes stay out of his way.

*Very drunk.

Most of the time there were no warning signs that he was about to explode, and he could be laughing and joking one minute, and the next he would be like a raging bull.

He could turn the house upside down in a matter of minutes. At times there wouldn't be a dish left on the dresser. That was life and you learned very quickly to adapt in order to survive. Thank God for school.

In the words of my grandmother, he was 'Creacáilte,' saying sure that 'Auld fella would lamp you one as quickly as he would look at you. He could do with someone giving him a good clatter. Maybe someone will one of these days and it might knock some sense into him.'

At school, I was the same person I was before Granny died. I hid the tears and the pain of isolation I felt. It was good to get away from home where I could laugh and plan my future just like everyone else. I wanted to head to the 'Big Smoke' to train as a nurse or maybe a teacher. I was not quite sure which one I liked more.

Peader O'Malley was in the class above me and he lived just over the road from us. He would often help carry the water from the well up to my grandmother's house. He and his mother would be regular visitors at my grandmother's place. We would sit down by the stream doing our homework.

He would say he was stupid as he struggled with schoolwork, so I would help him. He was brilliant at making things and he could turn his hands to anything to do with the building trade. He would be working in town with the local builder.

We would normally walk home from school together and he would often carry my bag. Then one afternoon we were walking home as normal, laughing and messing about. The only thing different was that Dad was home and he was never usually home at this time.

He was sitting on the hill at the side of the house. I did not even see or hear him, but sadly, he had seen us. I went into the house to start my chores just like any other day.

Dad walked in with a bottle of whiskey in his hand and a belt in the other, he was completely smashed but before I had a chance to move he lunged at me striking me hard with the belt. I fell to the floor and then he grabbed me by the back of my neck and threw me across the floor.

He was 'effing and blinding' and was kicking me in the stomach and screaming at me saying, "You dirty bitch, you are nothing but a slut, you thick bitch, have you no shame? You think you are so much better than anyone else."

He was relentless, only stopping to take a swig of the whiskey and to catch his breath. I tried to get up but I couldn't find the strength. He just kept on lashing into me. Then Mum came into the house carrying the shopping.

"Mother of God, what's going on?" she screamed. He turned to her and said it was about time I got taken down a peg or two. Mum laughed. She put the shopping down on the table and came over to me crouched down on the floor and said, "You deserve this, your grandmother spoiled you. It's time you found out where your place is. Fancy College, my arse! You are nothing but a total Gombeen. Your grandmother has filled your head with nonsense."

I pleaded with her, "Mum please help me."

"Help you?" she replied. "Why would I do that you ungrateful bitch!" She joined in helping him. I could hear something crack. There was blood all over the place. I think I passed out once or twice.

I am not sure how long this went on for but it felt like hours and hours. I could not understand why they were so angry with me, I had not done anything.

Then I could hear my father shouting, "if he ever saw me with the bastard O'Malley again he would kill me for sure". This was completely nuts as Peadar had done nothing either.

At this point, I closed my eyes. I could hear my grandmother saying, "My love, you know what to do."

I cried out to her and my angels, demanding, "Please come and help me, make this stop, for all that is Holy please make this stop."

I thought I could hear a knock on the door, and then I passed out again. I could faintly hear a familiar voice calling out my name. It sounded like Mrs O'Brien.

When I opened my eyes she was on the floor beside me, "Holy Mary Mother of God what have they done to the poor child."

Her two sons had to pull my father off me and were having difficulty holding him back. She turned to my mother and said, "I think you have killed the poor child, she is barely breathing."

My mother said, "If I'd had any sense at all, I would have drowned her years ago, I knew she would be nothing but trouble. She's been a curse on my life since she was born."

"Jesus, woman, are you mad? It's you and that madman that's caused all this trouble, not this poor innocent creature on the floor."

The O'Brien boys turned to my father and told him he needed to leave now or they would kill him where he was standing. Hearing this, both my parents high-tailed it out of the house. The O'Brien's wrapped me in a blanket, picked me up and carried me out of the house and into the car and took me straight to the hospital in Galway.

They stopped in town at the doctor's so he could bandage the cuts and try to stop the bleeding. At times, I could hear Mrs O'Brien's voice as she prayed, "Please Maeve, wake up!"

She said, "Thank God, your grandmother is not alive to see all this. She must be turning in her grave. That yoke of a so-called man has ruined your mother. He is a complete and utter headcase.

"He was only ever after the land and your mother's money, but he has a sweet tongue on him and your foolish mother fell for his patter. God rest your grandparents, they begged her not to marry him but she was 'Gombeen.'

"At first he was as sweet as pie and put on a good act, but after your grandfather died, he started to show his true colours. He didn't get his own way and he underestimated your grandmother.

She put him in his place and he was afraid of her.

"He was quiet for a while but now with your grandmother out of his way, he is often out of control and your mother is no match for him. This time he's gone too far."

When I got to the hospital, they must have given me something to put me to sleep. To be honest I don't remember how I got there. When I opened my eyes, Mrs O'Brien was sitting in the chair beside the bed with the rosary beads in her hands.

When she realised I was awake she started to cry and called the nurse. Before I knew it, the room was full of doctors and nurses. They moved around the bed making such noises. The Doctor spoke softly and gently, saying, "I was a very lucky girl to be alive."

He laughed when I replied, that, "I didn't feel very lucky."

Mrs O'Brien laughed too, and said, "Thank goodness they had not taken my sense of humour from me."

I tried to laugh, but it was just too painful, the Doctor explained that I was unconscious when I arrived, so they decided to sedate me to allow the swelling in my brain to go down. I had been in an induced coma for two weeks.

He told me my ribs were broken as well as my arm, and that I had lots of cuts and bruises, but were healing nicely. He also told me that I would have to stay in hospital for another week or two so that they could run some more tests. Overall, though, they seemed happy at the way I was healing.

After the Doctor left the room, I turned to Mrs O'Brien to ask her what had happened and why.

She had tears in her eyes and said, "There's no need to worry about that now, there is plenty of time. We must make sure you are better first."

The next few days passed in a blur and there was a constant stream of other doctors and nurses in and out, with test after test. About a week later, they decided I was strong enough to try to get out of bed.

'Mother Devine,' I thought my body was being ripped apart as the pain was excruciating. It felt worse than the beating itself. Thankfully they supplied me with painkillers and over the next week I was able to move about more and more, with less help.

That was a great sign, but it also filled me with dread as what was I going to do when they discharged me. I was only thirteen and a half years old.

I was afraid I would have to go back home as there was nowhere else I could stay. I had no aunts or uncles. The only visitor I had during my time in hospital was Mrs O'Brien and her two sons. The doctors told me that she never once left my side and it was her that had saved my life. If she had not arrived when she did, there was no way I would have survived as I had lost a lot of blood.

Mrs O'Brien arrived again later that day just in time for the doctors to say that they would be sending me home in the next week, all going well.

She must have read my face or else she was a mind reader, she looked at me and said, "She will not be going anywhere near that place, she will never set a foot inside that house while those evil monsters are there.

"Your grandmother had a gift for talking to the dead. She always said that if he ever stepped out of line that she would haunt him.

By Jesus, I say he wouldn't be able to sleep for the rest his life after this. I would say she has a hot poker wrapped around his back.

"Don't you worry pet, you will be coming to stay with me and the boys where you will be safe. You will never have to go back to those two while I have a breath left in me".

Two days before I was discharged, Peadar came to see me. He apologised he had not come sooner, but Mrs O Brien told him, 'no visitors allowed.'

He had tears in his eyes. He couldn't believe all the bruising and marks. I told him that he should have seen them before as they were getting better every day and didn't hurt so much anymore.

He asked if it was true that it was his fault he had lashed out at me. He explained, "There was talk in the town that it was because he had seen us walking home from school together."

I tried to tell him it was not his fault, and that they were both unstable most of the time, and that Dad had been drinking homemade Poteen before he had started on the whiskey.

He said he never wanted to cause me any trouble and if he had known that Dad would have lashed out like that he would never have left me in the first place, but seriously, how could anyone ever guess he would do this?

He added, "I just want you to know that if you ever need anything, I am here for you."

I said, "Thank you Peadar, you have always been a good friend to me. I will be home in a few days, maybe you could come and visit me? I will be staying with Mrs O'Brien until we work things out."

"I will, you can count on that!"

Peadar left soon after and said he was getting the bus back into town. I was surprised at how much I had enjoyed his visit. I found it funny he would think this had something to do with him.

D-Day arrived two weeks later when the doctors said it was time to be discharged, as there was nothing else they could do for me, and that the best medicine now was time, and plenty of rest, rest, rest!

True to her word Mrs O'Brien came to collect me, she told me that I would be staying with her for the foreseeable future, and not to worry about anything.

As we walked away from the hospital, she said, "You must be starving as the hospital food is dreadful. How do they expect anyone to make a full recovery on it?

"Let get some food here before going home."

I tried to tell her I was not hungry, but it fell on deaf ears.

It was a warm sunny day and I was enjoying the sun warming my bones. It is funny how it is the simple things you miss the most when on a normal day you do not give them a second thought, and just take them for granted.

We went to the 'chipper' to get fish and chips. This was such a treat. I couldn't remember the last time I had eaten fish and chips. It was not the norm in our house. I covered the chips with a ton of vinegar and some salt.

Each bite was like a trip to heaven, and even though I was not hungry, to my surprise I had eaten everything and there was not a scrap of food left. Seeing the empty wrappers made Mrs O'Brien happy.

She was smiling like a Cheshire cat. "Good girl, we will have you as right as rain in no time." The bus ride home was painful. I could feel every bump and turn in the road. Thankfully, I later managed to fall asleep. When we arrived in Clifden the O'Brien boys were waiting for us at the bus stop, their hands full of Tayto, Cadbury's chocolates and red lemonade. The Irish cure for all ailments.

# Chapter 17

Sitting in the car on the way out of town the three of them talked non-stop, I was not sure if they wanted me to answer or not, but you couldn't get a word in edgeways.

As we approached the narrow laneway towards home, I was terrified. All kinds of thoughts were now running through my head, and I wondered what would happen if I saw my parents.

Once again, it was as if they were reading my mind as Mrs O'Brien turned around and said, "There's no need to worry about those two bastards. They are cowards when they have to deal with adults. They would not dream of coming near you. We have already warned them off, and they are afraid of the boys.

"They are also afraid of their shadows at the minute and are deliberately keeping a low profile, as there is no one in the village happy with their antics.

It took about another three months for everything to heal and for me to feel a lot better. To be fair to the O'Brien's, they treated me like Royalty. I had not seen or heard a thing from my parents and I was now a lot more relaxed and less anxious. I was hoping they wouldn't just turn up and cause trouble.

It was now the end of April and I was itching to get back to school. I had missed my friends and although they had been great at sending me letters, it was not quite the same as being at school. One evening after dinner, I decided to broach the subject with Mrs O'Brien.

Let's just say she was not happy, she thought it would be best to wait until September to give me a chance to fully recover. I said I was missing my friends and didn't want to fall behind any more, as I had already missed so much.

"Nonsense!" she said. I have spoken to your teachers and they say you are as bright as a button and will have no trouble at all in catching up. It's far more important for you to get better."

The idea of me going back to school seemed to upset her, so I let the subject drop. To be honest she might have been right when she said it was too soon, as I had not left the house since coming out of the hospital.

I was still afraid to see my parents as I was unsure how I would react.

One afternoon, when the O'Brien boys were out on the bog and Mrs O'Brien had gone into town to do the shopping there was a loud knock on the door.

I just froze! I could see a shadow through the window and it looked very familiar but was not sure if it was my father. I quickly and quietly ran into my bedroom and sat on the bed. I asked myself what should I do, but just covered my ears and hid under all the blankets.

When Mrs O'Brien came home, I told her about the knock earlier, she said not to worry, as it could have been anyone. Later that night though, my father approached the O'Brien boys in the pub to say that, "Both himself and my mother feel it's time for me to come home." There were no apologies and no excuses.

The lads soon sent him on his way with a flea in his ear. We all thought that would have been the end of the story, but no, he would not leave it be.

Later that night he came back banging and screaming at the door. He nearly took it off its hinges. Mrs O'Brien told him he'd better go before she called the Gardaí, to which he replied, "go ahead", as he said he would have her arrested for kidnapping.

He told her, "Your insults mean nothing to me, but I'm a fair man, so I give you warning that if you don't send her back home soon, I will burn your house to the ground with both of you in it while you are sleeping. It would serve you well to have minded your business in the first place."

She replied. "Don't you threaten me, you big oaf! You are in no position to threaten me. Wait until the boys get their hands on you, you will not be such a big man then, coming here trying to frighten an old lady and a young girl. Is that what makes you feel like a man?"

"Listen here you interfering old Biddy, that's a promise, not a threat!" With that, he walked away, leaving Mrs O'Brien visibly shaken and unable to talk. Neither of us spoke the rest of that night, for fear of breathing the poisonous dread still hung in the air.

I said to her, "I will have to go back Mrs O'Brien. You have done so much for me, but I couldn't let him hurt you too."

After a while, Mrs O'Brien said it was time for bed and told me not to worry as there was no way I would be going back there, and that it would all work out in the end. Early the next morning, I could hear the O'Brien's talking, they were saying that there was no other solution but this.

At breakfast, Mrs O'Brien told me about her sister-in-law from Dublin, who was a widow. She never had any children as her husband had been killed whilst serving in the army not long after they were married.

She started working for a wealthy family as housekeeper not long after his death. They had been very good to her over the years. She said she had spoken to her last night and they had agreed you can stay with her and help with the housework in the evening and on the weekends.

She explained, "This is on condition that you will attend school every day. I know this is not what you want, but it is the only way to keep you safe for now."

I was heartbroken at the thought of leaving Mrs O'Brien and everything that I had known for my whole life.

I had only been to Galway once in my life and that was when I was in the hospital. Dublin was as alien to me as was America. So for the rest of the day, we made plans for me to go to Dublin in a few days. I was not allowed to say I was going to any of my friends just in case my father heard.

Later that night the boys came back from the pub visibly upset. Apparently, my father had been in there earlier and he was told to leave when he was heard saying he was going to kill me and there was no one to stop him.

I was bemused and asked, "Tell me, Mrs O'Brien, why does he want to hurt me so badly?"

"Well, we are not too sure but he has always had a chip on his shoulder and has never been too stable. It's well-known that your mother and Peader's father used to go out before they were married.

"He has got it into his head that she was still seeing him on and off over the years. When they had a skin-full of drink he would always question your mother and ask if he was your real father.

Mrs O'Brien said it was all nonsense and none of it was true, and that my father didn't have too many brain cells to begin with, but whatever he had,  had long since died.

I thought, God forgive me, but it would be easier to think he was not, and that the kind and good hearted Mr O'Malley was really my dad. He was a hardworking family man, who loved his children and was always praising them.

Mrs O'Brien started to pack my bags and said that the sooner I left the safer I would be. She said that first thing in the morning the boys would drive me to Galway to catch the bus to Dublin.

It was a quiet journey into Galway. The boys and Mrs O'Brien barely spoke. There were no words that could fully describe how we were feeling that day.

I looked out the car window to admire the scenery and to take it all in for I didn't know when I would see them again. When we arrived in Galway and got out of the car, and the reason we had all been so quiet now became obvious, as all our eyes were as red as blood.

We hugged each other warmly as the tears rolled freely down our faces. Mrs O'Brien handed me a packed lunch and an envelope with money, saying, "My darling Maeve Lynch, your life from here on will only get better. Patsy will look after you and you will never want for anything, all I ask is that you work hard at school and do the best you can."

I said, "Mrs O' Brien, how will I ever be able to thank you for everything you have done? I am so sorry if I have caused you any trouble."

"Maeve, you must promise that you never come back while those two are alive as you will never be safe. Your grandmother would be very proud of you and she will be watching over you every day of your life, so you will never be alone."

As the bus started to move, I could see the boys holding their mother up. She was overcome with grief. I waved goodbye to the three people who had saved my life and protected me when my own family had failed me.

I put my head down and cried all the way to Dublin with a large part of me wishing the bus would never arrive.

# Chapter 18

When the bus finally reached Bus Aras, the fear of the unknown became all too real. As I stepped off, I was overcome with how big everything was and how quickly people moved.

I was to meet Patsy Flynn outside the bus terminal at 6pm, but it was then only four o'clock so I had to wait for another two hours, so I went for a walk along the river.

I just walked and walked until I saw some massive ships. I had never seen the likes of them before. There were buses, cars, and trucks, all going on and off them. I was unsure how this was possible so I walked a little closer.

Somehow, I got caught in the crowd. There must have been hundreds of people there, young and old. There were also lots of children running about laughing and some crying.

I was moving with them and before I knew it, I was pushed onto one of the largest boats in the world. I had never seen anything bigger than a currach. I was amazed at the size. There was a bar, a restaurant, and even shops.

I could hear a horn blowing and was startled. Children started to shout hurray, and I overheard someone saying we were about to move. I ran towards the exit door but it was now closed. I told a man in uniform that I needed to get off, but he only laughed and said it was too late as we had already set sail.

I asked myself, how did this happen? How come no one asked me for a ticket, or what was I doing there. It was like I was invisible! Shit, shit!

I thought, what I am going to do now?

I walked around and around until my legs hurt. The smell of food started to attract me as people passed by with trays of delicious food. I was suddenly overcome with hunger.

I went to the restaurant and got fish and chips just like the day in Galway with Mrs O'Brien. Sitting there eating my feast, a strange sense of calm came over me. Nobody would have guessed that I was all alone and completely lost.

I gazed out the window and you could see nothing but water. For a time I had almost forgotten the predicament that I had found myself in. Finally, I found a quiet corner to sit. I must have fallen asleep because there was a lady now tapping me on the shoulder to say we had arrived at Holyhead in Anglesey, North Wales, and it was now time to get off.

It was now pitch dark outside. I asked the lady asked me, "How long have we been on the boat?"

Truth be told, I had no real idea, or even where Holyhead was. I said I wanted to go back to Dublin but she said it was impossible, and that I quickly needed to get off and buy a return ticket from the box office.

Reluctantly, I left the boat and went in search of the office. Once off the boat though, many people that I had seen earlier just seemed to have disappeared into thin air. One minute the place was full, and the next it was completely empty.

The few people I could see weren't speaking in English, or Irish for that matter. When I eventually found the office it was closed. There was no-one in sight. They began turning off the lights. I ran towards the toilets as I was not sure what is else to do. I thought I would just stay there for a minute to make a plan. It was very dark and cold outside, and I had nowhere else to go.

I wondered, what in the name of God was I going to do?

As I sat there, I could hear the keys being turned in the door. Eventually, I gained the courage to go and check the door, but it was locked. I guess that answered one question, I would have to stay there for the night, which was a blessing as I didn't really want to go outside, as it had just started raining heavily.

The next thing on my mind was how much trouble I was in. Patsy Flynn would surely have contacted Mrs O'Brien by now and they would be worried out of their minds. All the calm and courage I had had earlier just drained away from me until I became so frightened. The realisation that I was all alone in a place where I knew no one and didn't understand a word of what they were saying.

I knew for sure that I could not go back to Ireland as I would be in too much trouble. I would write to Mrs O'Brien and let her know that all is well even if it was not. The one thing I was grateful for was that it was warm and dry in there.

I locked the cubicle door just in case anyone came in, and whispered, "Welcome to Holyhead." I told myself that tomorrow I would look for someone that speaks English, and to try work out what to do next.

I also believed I should look for a job, as the money I had will not last long.

The following morning, I was awoken early by the sounds of people coming and going. I was too scared to move. Then I heard the familiar sounds of home. It was two Irish girls chatting away excitedly about how great it was to be away from home and to be finally free of their overbearing parents.

They spoke about going to Manchester where there was plenty of work for everyone. They had the address of a boarding house where all the Irish girls stay when they first come over.

As they were leaving, I decided that I would follow them to Manchester as they seemed to have it all worked out. It was easy to follow them as they were the only ones with strong Cork accents.

I was careful not to let them see me as I didn't want them asking me any questions. I followed them on to the train and copied everything they did, I even managed to pick some food up from the shop as I was starving.

I was sitting a few seats behind them when my heart stopped. They were talking about the Gardai looking for a 14-year old girl from Galway who had gone missing.

They said they had been stopped several times by different Gardai in Dublin, asking if they had seen a young teenage girl. Suddenly I froze again. Maybe it was not a good idea to go and book in at the same place they were staying.

I told myself I would follow them to see where they were going so that I knew what to look out for, and what to say when I got there.

When we got off the train in Manchester, I was again bewildered by how big and strange everything looked. The buildings were so much bigger and more impressive than Galway, or anything I had ever seen in Dublin.

I could not get over the speed people moved at, no one would look at the next person, never mind to speak to each other. This was a strange place, and I was frightened beyond belief. It was not long before I lost the girls.

I looked around but could not find them. As I walked around the city I was surprised by the number of people sleeping in the street. I had never seen anything like this before.

I walked and walked around for hours until I was exhausted. I was so scared. It was getting dark and I was very tired and urgently needed somewhere to stay. I still had most of the money Mrs O'Brien had given me but I knew I would need to be very careful as it wouldn't last long. I walked down the street just as all the shops were closing.

I noticed a building with a door that was slightly broken and ajar. I went inside and closed the door as much as I could. At least the place was dry. I sat in the corner and prayed to everyone that could hear me including my grandmother.

I asked that they would guide me out of this nightmare and to keep me safe, 'Oh Lord, do you hear the irony in that?' I started to laugh so loud that I could not stop.

The one place I should have been safe was where I nearly died. It was the place where I was in the most danger! I fell asleep that night thinking about all that had happened in the past few months and what to do next.

The first thing on my list was to send a letter to Mrs O'Brien to tell her to stop worrying, as I doubt my parents even knew I was missing and wouldn't care less. My dreams were full of so many happy memories of my grandmother and my friends.

I was awoken early next morning to the sound of a bus and cars driving past.

I stretched my aching bones and my stomach began to rumble. I decided to pack my bag and go for a look around my new home. I was feeling hopeful, so I explored my new surrounds and was full of delight at what I could see.

I wrote down the address of all the places of interest to help me find my way. As each day passed, I was becoming more confident in this strange city.

Each night I returned to the place I had found on the first night. I would visit the local swimming pool most days so I could have a shower and wash my hair.

I promised myself that one day I would buy a swimsuit and learn to swim properly. It seems hard to believe that I lived with the sea on my doorstep for fourteen years and I didn't know how to swim.

Occasionally, my friends and I would go to the beach and attempt to swim. I thought I was the bee's knees because I could do the doggy paddle, but now I could see other people gliding through the water like fish, I realised how daft I would look doing the doggy paddle there.

I was always careful to look clean and tidy so no one would have ever guessed that I was homeless. I kept my clothes clean by taking them to the laundry shop at the end of the street every second week.

As I explored the city, I never felt alone. I could feel my grandmother's hand on my back and her voice in my head. It must have been a month or so later that my money was nearly all gone.

I was trying to think what I could do to make money and try to find a flat before the winter really began to set in. The nights were beginning to get colder and I was not sure if I would be able to stay where I was for much longer.

It was with all these thoughts running through my head that I inadvertently took a wrong turn and found myself walking down a street to a small market where everyone was busy selling something. You could buy all your fruit and vegetables or meat for your dinner, as well as all sorts of cleaning and household products.

There were plenty of clothes for sale but I must say they weren't very fashionable or well made. As my grandmother would say, 'you wouldn't wear that to the bog.'

After a while, I found myself at a stall selling all types of material including wool and needles. Without thinking, I took money from my bag and bought some material and sewing needles, some thread as well, and knitting needles, plus pink and blue wool.

I hadn't a clue as to what to do with them as I was not the best at knitting or sewing, but I could hear my grandmother saying, "Good Girl, I will show you all you need to know. Trust me and follow my instructions."

Jesus, I thought if I ever told anyone about this, they would have me locked up for the rest of my life.

That evening I went back to my little bolt-hole and sat near the door so I could use the street lamp to see what I was doing, and believe it or not, I made a couple of baby dresses and a boy sailor suit with a cute cap.

I was impressed with myself, as I had sewn bits for my grandmother but they had never looked this good. Over the next few days, I knitted a shawl in blue and one in pink, some little baby jumpers, hats and mittens.

I used every scrap of material and wasted nothing. Now that they were completed, I went back to the street where all the markets stalls were, and nervously approached the lady that I had bought the material to see if she would buy them from me.

She took an age looking at each item, checking them again and again.

I was just about to cry when she said she wouldn't buy them but agreed I could use the space next to her to set up a small stall. At the same time, she handed me some more material and wool and said. "As you're standing there you may as well be busy."

I was embarrassed, as I didn't know if she was just making fun of me. I told her I didn't have any more money to buy the material until I had sold what I had already made.

She roared with laughter, "You will have those sold before we have time to eat breakfast. You can pay me as soon as you sell your stock, and I will only charge you at cost price."

I said, "I do not want to come across as rude or anything, but why would you do this for me?"

"Good question," she replied, "It's simple, what you have made is great quality and the people around here will snap it up. It will be good for me in the long-run, as if they want something in a different colour you can get them to buy the material from me, and that way I will also make a living.

"You see you have a gift and the people around here have no imagination of what goes with what, or how to make anything as grand as this.

"These days I don't sell a lot of material but I get the feeling that with you here that is about to change. My name is Olive, so what's yours, young lady?"

I thought I am not sure where this name came from but knew I couldn't use my real name after hearing the two girls from Cork talking about the police interest in finding me.

***This was also the first time since I had arrived here that anyone had asked me for my name. Today was the day 'Elizabeth Reid' was born, and Maeve Lynch was no more!***

Please to meet you Elizabeth, "Now, do you know what you are going to charge for these items?"

"Ah, no I don't!"

Olive kindly told me what to charge and advised me not to take anything less.

"If you have any contrary customers, I will be right here. As the folks around here will try and get them off you for nothing, as special as you are, you're new to this area."

Within an hour, everything had been sold. Olive laughed and said, "I told you so, didn't I?"

I had even taken an order from one lady who wanted to get something for a neighbour's baby. She ordered a full set, a hat, coat, gloves, and a blanket to match. She was very persistent that she would be back in the morning to collect them.

# Chapter 19

I went home with my arms full of material and my head full of whatever else I could do that would be quick and easy to make. The best bit was, I had some money in my pocket. It was great to be able to put some money back as my funds were getting scarily low.

The next few months passed quickly. It was now the beginning of December and the frost was thick on the ground at night. Everyone on the market was still talking about a white Christmas.

As much as I would love to see a white Christmas, if I was still living in a nice warm place, but at that moment I had still not saved enough for a flat, or even a room share.

The next morning was particularly cold, so as soon as the last item sold, I packed my bags and headed towards the 'Greasy Spoon' for a hot soup and a bite to eat. I would often sit there and do a bit of knitting or sewing.

Ted, the owner, was not there that day, it was a much younger guy called Brian, who looked rather harassed, as if he didn't want to be there. The place was also very busy so I was just happy to wait, as I was not in any hurry.

He eventually came and took my order and apologised that I had had to wait so long, explaining that his young waitress had not turned up.

"Can you believe it," he queried, "She sent her flatmate in with a note to say she's quit as she has found something better, can you believe her cheek?

"Dad has been in the hospital for the last week, he has had a heart attack, so there is no way of knowing when, or if he will be back."

I went back to my sewing and he went back to serving his customers. I was just getting ready to pack up my belongings when I saw him putting up a sign which stated, 'HELP WANTED IMMEDIATE START.'

Before I knew it, I asked him what the job requirements were.

He just laughed and said, "You just need to be able to handle hard work and not to expect too much in wages for the privilege."

"Well, I could start now if that would be any help." I said.

With that, he ripped up the advert, saying, "Well, no time like the present!"

"My name is Brian, what's yours?"

"I'm Elizabeth, Elizabeth Reid."

"Well Elizabeth, I am very glad to meet you, let's get started in the kitchen."

He told me to start with the washing up. I thought, sweet Jesus, I had never seen so many pots. There were dishes everywhere. I was unsure as to where to start. Part of me was saying sorry that I had agreed to do this, but it was certainly better than going outside in that horribly cold and wet weather. At least in there, it was warm and dry.

I spent the rest of the day washing dishes, clearing table, and running in and out of the kitchen with plates of food. It was six o'clock when Brian finally declared, "I think that's enough for today. Let's sit down and have some food before we clean the floors."

I was exhausted, but I was so grateful just to sit down. I was really tired and didn't think I had the energy to eat. That was until he placed a cottage pie and salad in front of me.

We both sat in silence while we ate. I was ravenous! Brian later got up and returned with two steaming hot cups of tea and some chocolate cake.

He said, "We deserve it. It was one of the busiest days we've had in a long time. I don't know what I would have done without you."

I replied, "I guess it was fate that I was in here today. I only came in by chance, as it was so cold out there. I had finished early as I had sold everything in record time. I thought I would come in and get a head start on the orders."

"What is it you do?" he asked.

"I make children's clothes and sell them on the market. It only started as something to make some money from and until I found something better, but then I found people were putting in orders, so now I have more orders than I can keep up with.

"A few months back I was asked to make a christening gown, so now I make them to order along with communion dress and suits for the boys. I was surprised that there was such a demand for them here, so I now spend less time on the stall, and more time making the clothes."

I asked Brian, "What kind of hours would you need me for, as I would still need to be available to do the stall in the mornings. I normally finish there around 10-ish, so I can come straight here afterwards if that's OK."

He said, "That sounds great to me, Elizabeth. Why don't you head home, as I feel I have worked you to the bone today, so I will see you tomorrow. Thanks for all your help, I hope you have a good evening."

"Goodnight, Brian, see you in the morning."

I walked home feeling better than I had in many months. I was delighted with myself, as now I could start saving and get a place sooner rather than later. I had a good feeling that life was now on the up. The best part was, I would be in a warm place for most of the day and did not have to worry about food. This was a win-win for me!

I was looking forward to tomorrow for the first time in a long time. The days that followed passed by in a haze, it was just work, work, work! The mornings were very busy on the stall, and sometimes I would arrive early at the café as Brian was always glad to see me.

There were other days when I would give him an additional hand, and other times when we would just sit and chat. He was a funny guy, always in good humour.

The days in the café passed very quickly, as each day seemed to be busier than the one before. I was now leaving later and later in the evenings as it was getting harder and harder to go back to my awful hovel.

Sometimes though, I thought it was getting harder to accept, as I felt warm and cosy during the day, which made it more difficult to adjust to the bitter cold later. It had also been raining almost non-stop for the past week.

I kept looking on the bright side that at least I nearly had enough for a deposit on a flat. That night I was not only knackered but very wet and cold. Thankfully, I fell asleep as soon as I lay down. I was awoken, however, at one o'clock the next morning by the rain pouring in. Everything was now drenched and I realised that I couldn't stay there anymore, so I just packed everything up in my rucksack.

I was very, very tired and shivering as I finally left my 'safe haven.'

I had nowhere else to go, so I started walking as it normally helped me to think, but there were no bright lights coming into my head that night. I was just about to walk past the railway station when I went in to use the toilet.

Inside, I used the hand dryer to warm my hair and tried the best I could to try to dry my clothes too. It was the second time in my life that I'd had to spend a night in ladies toilets. I was feeling very down and felt I had hit rock bottom.

I made a promise to myself that this would be the last time I would ever spend a night like that, as I knew for sure that I couldn't continue living that way. I needed to have my own space, and somewhere where I could lock my door and it would be mine. Once again, I sent a silent prayer to my grandmother.

# Chapter 20

I was so tired the following morning, as I had not slept a wink. I had also been so stiff and uncomfortable. Needless to say, my humour was not great. Fortunately, I quickly sold all the clothes and bought some more material.

I decided I would look in the local newsagents to see if there were any rooms available that I could afford. My spirits didn't lift very much as at each number I called, I was met with the same response, 'Sorry the room has already been taken.'

Thankfully, the café was so busy that it took my mind off my own problematic situation. At least for now, I was warm and dry and there was food in my belly, which was a lot more than some people had.

I thought, I just have to be positive and believe it will all work out. Even the rain had now stopped, so I thought, not all might be lost.

At the end of the evening when Brian and I were eating our meal, he told me that Ted was no longer coming back. He had apparently decided to retire as his heart attack had given him a real wake-up call.

Brian explained, "He is selling his house and moving to the South of France. He is tired of the rat race. He has worked all of his life and now he wants to enjoy the rest. Good luck to him, I say. I hope he will be very happy."

I was just about to tell him about my predicament when his phone rang and by the time he had come back, the moment had passed. I was not sure if this was a good thing or not, then he asked if I could finish and lock up as he needed to get home as one of the kids had fallen off his bike and was now on his way to the hospital."

I quickly replied, "No problem, you go and I sort things out. I will also come in early tomorrow to help you to set up just in case it's a late night in A&E."

When he left, I locked the front door and went about cleaning our table, then I washed the floor and turned the light off. I went into the kitchen to finish the washing-up and to tidy away the remaining dishes.

After I finished, I made myself a cup of tea and started cutting and sewing a pattern for a dress. I couldn't believe just how much I'd done and by the time I looked at the clock, it was then 1.30am!

I tidied my work and packed it safely away. I turned off the light and was just about to close the door, when I suddenly had an idea that I might be able to stay there for the night, and then tomorrow after work, I could go back and perhaps check my old space.

I battled with this prospect for a while before deciding it would do no harm. As I had already said I would come back early in the morning, so, I made a bed in a back storeroom and settled down.

It was nice to be warm and dry for a change. I will never again take for granted what a privilege it is to have a roof over your head. The following morning I awoke bright-eyed and bushy-tailed. I cleaned up after myself and started with the food prep for the day. By 6.30am, the place was ready for action.

I was sitting in the kitchen having breakfast when Brian arrived. He was surprised that everything was ready and all he had to do was start cooking. I left at 7 am to head to the market. It was a bright, dry day, and everyone was in great form.

I had just set up when a neighbour of Olive's came over to her. She was in an awful state, but through all her tears, I couldn't hear what she was saying.

Olive called me over to tell me that she was getting married in two months and when she went to the shop to pick up her dress, she found a notice to say the shop had gone bust and the place was empty.

The best they could do was to say, 'sorry for any inconvenience caused.'

There was no way she could afford another one. Olive told her, "Shush, dry your tears. Elizabeth does some amazing work, and she will able to make one for you."

I was shocked, and replied, "I'm sorry but I don't make wedding dresses."

"Nonsense!" said Olive, "Of course you will!"

Before I knew it she was buying the material and I was measuring her. She gave me a detailed description of what the dress she had bought was like, then handed me the material, and said I will see you in three weeks for a fitting.

I thought, Mother Devine, what was I going to do now? There was no way I could make a wedding dress and certainly not in that timeframe. It was the most important dress of her life and her whole day could be ruined if it wasn't up to standard.

I asked myself, what if I make a complete mess of it! I don't want to live with the guilt of ruining somebody's day. This was looking like a total disaster. I relayed my fears to Olive but it was like the woman had suddenly gone deaf and dumb!

She started laughing at me, telling everyone who would listen that I was making Nora's wedding dress and said, "There's not a better woman in Manchester to make it!"

Adding that, "It will be the talk of the town."

Not only, was there the pressure of making the dress now, but I didn't have anywhere to make it.

I queried, how in the name of God did I get myself into this predicament, and more importantly, how the hell do I get out of it? If I got this wrong it could be the end of me. I would not be able to show my face again. I couldn't let her down.'

I walked into the café and it was packed. There was not a seat to be found. It was a blessing in disguise, as I didn't have time to think about this pending wedding disaster. It was close to eight o'clock by the time we finished cleaning up. I was deep in thought when Brian asked, "I will give you a penny for them."

I had never heard this expression before so had no idea what he was talking about. "Tell me what's going on in that head of yours? As you have not been yourself all day. It can't be that bad now?"

I wondered what I should tell him. I thought, I can't say I'm homeless, as I am too ashamed, so I decided to start with the fact I had been given the task of making a wedding dress for a lady called Nora, and that it was now freaking me out, as it was way beyond my skills.

He laughed, but I got so cross, so I wondered what was so funny? I told him, "I don't find it a laughing matter!"

"I'm sorry, It's just that you don't know just how good you are. You have a real talent. I have seen some of the stuff you have made and you would not be able to buy that in the shops. You just need to believe in yourself and look at this way, it's an amazing opportunity, so grab it with both hands and never give up."

I burst into tears and couldn't talk.

He added, "You'll see it will all work out for the best, it always does."

Through my sniffs and tears, I blurted out that he didn't understand, and said that where I was staying, there was no place to make a dress like that.

He scratched his head, "If that's your only problem, I might be able to help, follow me."

I followed him out to the back of the kitchen and up the stairs. He said, "This place is in an awful state, but I am sure we can do something with it."

When he opened the door onto the landing, it opened out into a large sitting room with a small kitchen to the side. There was a small bathroom and a bedroom.

He said, "I know it doesn't look like much but once I take out all this rubbish and give it a lick of paint, it will look as good as new."

I hadn't a clue as to what he was going to do next, but, never in my wildest dreams had I ever imagined what he was then showing me.

I was so stunned that I couldn't even move or talk. I was stuck to the spot. This was unreal, and now I couldn't hear a word he was saying.

This was too good to be true, but there had to be a catch. Finally, I whispered, "There is no way I can afford such a place."

"You fool," he said, "I don't need any rent. You've earned it with all the extra hours, now go downstairs. You can have it instead of extra wages.

"Dad had planned to clean the place out before his heart attack but never got around to it."

Without thinking, I threw my hands around his neck, "Now, now, don't get too excited, as there is a lot of work to be done. I will empty the place and get the paint but you will have to clean and paint it all yourself."

I was like a child, "When can I get started?" I began hopping up and down.

"Now, if you want. You could start by moving things into the hall and I will take them down and bin them, as I can't imagine there's anything of much use here. Dad had a problem with throwing anything out. Mum used to go mad."

With that, he handed me the key and said, "Welcome to your new flat," then left me standing there.

For the rest of the night, I moved bags and bags of stuff into the hall. I picked up the hoover, mop and cleaning products from the kitchen downstairs.

I worked right through the night. In fact, I had not realised it was morning until Brian knocked on the door.

"WOW!" he said, "I can't believe the difference already. I have not seen half the furniture in years. I had even forgotten it was here.

"Did you get to bed at all?"

"No," I replied, "There is so much that still needs to be done." I was as happy as can be. I made a list of all the things I needed, like bedcovers, towels etc.

# Chapter 21

My life became a non-stop dash. When I was not working at the café, I was upstairs sewing away. The wedding dress was eventually finished just a few days before the wedding. I had never been as nervous as I was in waiting for Nora to come in for her fitting.

I thought, please God that she will love it, but I shouldn't have worried at all as she really LOVED the dress. She said it was so much nicer than the one in the other shop and fitted her perfectly. She danced around the room and announced loudly that she didn't want to take it off.

 "Thank you so much, Olive said you were good, but she didn't say you were this good. You have really saved the day." She danced her way and down the stairs.

After that, wedding people came into the café on a regular basis asking for me to design their wedding dress or bridesmaids dresses and before I knew it I was not really working in the café anymore, as I was just too busy sewing.

Then one day a whirlwind appeared in the name of Ruby Daniels. She was at a wedding where I had made the bride's dress and the wedding party's outfits. Needless to say, she fell in love with them, and when her boss, who worked in London was looking for an evening dress for a charity gala, she told her about me.

Before I knew it, I was on a train to London to meet her boss to get an idea of what she was looking for. Ruby met me when I arrived at King's Cross.

She insisted we went for lunch before going to the office. She explained, "Once you get in there, there will be no time to stop or even go to the toilet, never mind food, as Rita doesn't know what the word 'stop' means. She does everything on fast forward."

I liked Ruby, she was full of beans and had a great sense of humour.

She wasn't lying about Rita. She knew what she wanted and was very happy with the sketches I had done. It was hard to keep up with her. By the time I left, she had ordered six dresses for a month's time.

She asked Ruby to sort out payment. Ruby handed me a cheque as we were leaving. I couldn't believe the amount on it as we had never discussed a price.

When I said to Ruby that it was too much she just laughed and said that was the deposit, and that the rest would be paid in full when the dresses were finished. I was shocked!

Ruby admitted that was the going price in London and said I could probably get even more once my name was out there. Rita became a good customer and would regularly place orders.

Ruby was also a regular visitor to the flat and it was not long before we became good friends. She finally convinced me to make the move to London.

Manchester had been my home for the past four years, and it had been good to me. It was hard to say goodbye to all that was so familiar to me.

When I first arrived in London, I stayed with Ruby as both a friend and a flatmate. I could not have asked for a better friend. Moving to London was the best decision I ever made. It became my second home within a very short space of time. I loved everything about the place. It was where my dreams finally came true.

Over the years I would write to Mrs O'Brien and send her copies of some of my designs. I would write once a month giving her an update on how I was getting on. I was living in the flat before I told her I had changed my name, as I was afraid that anyone from back home in Ireland could find me, and let my parents know where I was.

I only gave her my address. I was over the moon when she wrote back, at first, I was unsure if she would, I knew how deeply upset she must have been when I first ran away.

She told me she was delighted to hear that I was doing so well and she really looked forward to my letters. She also thought it was a great idea that I had changed my name, as my parents had been really mad when I disappeared and claimed that if they ever got their hands on me they would wring my neck.

She found it entertaining they could be driven mad as they wouldn't be able to find me. She replied, "I always said you were a clever one."

I also looked forward to receiving her letters to tell me what was going on over there. Sometimes I would close my eyes for a few moments and could soon find myself transported back, sitting by the lake, my favourite spot in the whole world.

Ruby eventually got engaged and moved back to Manchester to be closer to her family. When she left, I missed her terribly but we still kept in touch.

Life in London was wonderful. It was everything my small village of

Ballyconnelly was not. It was fast-paced with more people than one could ever count. There were bright lights, and everything was so much bigger and better.

At the beginning, I found it odd, and yet reassuring in a strange sort of way that no one really knew who I was. Most of the time in London you would never make eye contact with anyone, despite the fact you would probably see the same people day-in, day-out, just going about their daily lives.

At home in Ireland, you would never pass anyone without saying hello and getting the latest update on everyone in the family. I worked day and night. The more garments I produced, the more orders I secured.

I even started sketching jewellery and researching different materials, and there were times when I didn't have the time or strength to bless myself, and often went without sleep just to get an order out on time.

Then when Edward and the girls came into my life was complete and Ireland never entered my head, and it just became a distant memory. When the girls were about four or five they came home from school with a project on their family tree.

It was the only time anyone had really asked me about my past. It was like an omen as two months later I received a letter from Mrs O'Brien. She said she was unwell and due to go into hospital within a few days for some more tests.

It was the only time I felt drawn to go back home. Later I found out that things were far more serious. I would call the hospital to get regular updates

It was on one Friday evening when the nurse told me Mrs O'Brien didn't have a lot of time left. She said all they could do was to make her comfortable. I travelled on the next available flight to Shannon. I booked it on impulse before I had a chance to change my mind.

I told Edward I was going over to talk to some suppliers and to talk to a shop owner in Galway about stocking my designs. I knew it was short notice but that if I didn't go now, I might miss the deal as there was a great demand for Irish linen and lace.

I explained that I would like to get there before anyone else who might push the price up. At first, he wanted all of us to go, saying we could take the girls out of school for a few days.

He was really excited at the thought until I told him I already had a full diary and couldn't take time off at the moment as there were too many orders to be filled. I promised we could go at another time when we could both organise our diaries better.

With sad puppy eyes, he hugged me tight and asked, where would he be without me, adding that I was always right.

# Chapter 22

Seeing Mrs O'Brien after all that time was a sight for sore eyes. She looked so peaceful just lying there. It was only after a while that I realised how lifeless she really was. It became heartbreaking to see her like that.

She had been my saviour. I owed her everything. My life would have been nothing at all if it wasn't for her. She was always kind and generous. I sat there silently watching her.

She looked much the same, except that her hair was greyer, and she had a few more wrinkles. It was an hour or so before she woke up.

I was lost in my own world when she spoke, "Jesus, I must be dead if I can see who I think I can."

I nearly jumped out of my skin too. Our eyes filled with tears. So much had happened since we had last seen each other. She said she was so proud of me, and that she had been the talk of the county wearing a beautiful blue satin dress and some gorgeous pieces of jewellery that I had sent her for Oliver's wedding.

She claimed, "I felt like a Queen. Nobody had ever seen the likes of it before."

We spoke about my husband Edward and the girls, and I showed her some pictures of them. She was like a doting grandmother, and we spoke about her boys and their wives and children.

Eventually, the conversation came back to my parents. I thanked her again for everything she had done for me all those years ago, and that I was so sorry for running away. She explained that she had made a promise to my grandmother before she passed to make sure I would be looked after. And that if those two horrors ever tried anything, I was not to leave you alone there.

She confirmed, "Let me tell you, that was an easy promise to keep. You are a real joy, Maeve Lynch. Your grandmother knew they could not be trusted, anyway, I won't be afraid to meet your gran on the other side.

She was smiling like a Cheshire cat at this. It was obviously a joke between the two of them.

"Wasn't your grandmother a very wise woman making sure she taught you how to sew and knit? It was a blessing in disguise."

As we were talking about her and the old days, I could feel my grandmother beside me humming away as she darned the needles and gently sewed delicate stitches.

Maybe Mrs O'Brien felt the same as she turned to me and said, "You know she is never very far away, she is always watching over you. Your grandparents were very good to me and Jimmy and especially after Jimmy died.

"I don't think I would have made it through those dark days only for them. They were great neighbours and friends to me and everyone in the village."

She told me that my parents hadn't mellowed with age, adding that if anything they had got worse. They were barred from nearly every place in the village and the town. So, there was nothing left for them to do but make their own drink and to rot their brains drinking it.

The Gardai raided the place several times but never found their stash.

She said, "You did well to get away from them, they would have destroyed you."

Then I asked about Peadar. She winked her eyes and said, "The poor lad had it bad."

I told her I didn't understand, "Had what bad?"

With a twinkle in her eye, she cheekily replied, "You, my dear, he was so in love with you! It was very nearly the end of him when you left."

I said, "Get out of that Mrs O'Brien, no way!"

"Maeve he did! He would often come over and ask about you and where you were, and if I knew anything at all. He blamed himself for what had happened to you.

"No matter how many times I told him that it was not his fault and that your parents were not right in the head. Six months after you went missing he left and went to Australia and the last I heard, was that he got married to an Australian girl and had three kids.

"He has only come back a hand full of times. He is happy out there and is doing very well for himself. He said there were too many bad memories here for him. His brother Frank has the family farm and is still single. He is interested in the matchmaking no less. It would be a lucky woman that would catch him.

"Tell me Maeve, do you ever miss the West of Ireland?"

"Yes, Mrs O' Brien, I still do even to this day. I also miss your baking, there is no one that can match it. The smell of the brown bread, and my favourite: the treacle bread - not to mention your scones and Victoria sponge.

"You would have made a fortune in London. They would have sold out in all the expensive shops. You would have had them lined up in the street.

"I miss not being able to go to Granny's grave and just to be able to sit there and talk to her just like we used to do when she would visit Grandad. And sometimes if I close my eyes, I can still imagine being there, and that's almost as good."

"Are you really happy Maeve?"

"Yes, I am. I was really blessed with Edward and the girls. They are my life and I am theirs. Somehow, I think my parents probably did me a favour in the way they treated me. If they had been different then I would never have had Edward or the girls. And my life would be completely different."

She asked me what Edward had to say about my parents and with a strange look on my face I had to admit to her that I had never told him, as I was too ashamed or afraid, in case he came over to Ireland and had them arrested.

It was just too hard to block them out of my life completely, and I just didn't want to give any more thought or energy to them.

She said to me sternly, "My dear girl, there is nothing to be ashamed of. You have never done any of this, and it was not your fault in anyone's language. Got that?"

I could see she was getting tired, but she didn't want to go to sleep. We had been talking for hours and hours.

I told her, "Mrs O'Brien, I don't think I could ever thank you enough for all that you have done for me, and I am truly sorry for running away. I never planned it and I certainly never wanted to hurt you."

"Shush now girl, no need to go over any of that. I was glad I could help and I would do it again in a heartbeat if I had too. I have enjoyed all of your letters over the years and you have made an old lady very happy.

"I am glad you got away and your life has turned out so well. Your happiness has been the best way to say thanks. As your teacher said all those years ago that you have a good head on your shoulders and were very bright. They were not wrong, and if only they could see you now."

"Mrs O'Brien, are you tired? It's OK if you want to get some sleep."

She said, "Maeve, I want to look at you one more time. You have given me my final wish. I had prayed that I would see you one more time. For that, I have to thank you. When my time comes, I can now go with a happy heart. I have had a happy life and now I am tired, very tired!

"When I get to the other side I will give your grandmother a big hug from you, she would be very proud. Maeve, can you make me a final promise?"

"Yes, of course, anything."

"Promise me that you will never look back and will always move forward."

"That I can do, just for you," I confirmed.

With tears in both of our eyes and a hug that had to last a lifetime, we said our final goodbyes. By the time she had laid back down in the bed, she was almost asleep.

I was in pieces as I walked out of her room. I walked out backwards as I wanted to see her for as long as I could. I stood outside the door for a very long time just watching her sleeping. She was my 'Guardian Angel', that was for sure.

Eventually, I had to leave, as I was an embarrassment to myself. I was uncontrollable. I collapsed on the floor, heartbroken. I had never experienced a pain like that before. The floodgates to my inner emotions just opened up and I could no longer stem the flow.

The nurse came and put her hand on my shoulder, and said, "She has been waiting on you, you know. She spoke about you all of the time. You made her very proud.

"Why don't you come and sit in the relative's room and allow yourself some time. I know this must have been a real shock for you. Let me get you a cup of tea. You need something a bit stronger but I am afraid tea is all we have."

Without a word from me, she had me wrapped in her arms and was walking towards the room. Before I knew it, she handed me a strong cup of tea with enough sugar in it to cause diabetes.

She spoke in a calm, soothing voice. Sometime later, she left the room telling me to take as much time as I needed, and to call her if I wanted anything at all.

I had not even noticed she had left the room, or how long I sat there but I knew that I had to find every ounce of strength I had - and even to borrow some more - just to walk away from the ward.

I knew I had done the right thing in going back to say goodbye. I then wished Edward had been there to help me. I should have told him the truth from the beginning. If I had, then I realised that I wouldn't be in that mess then, and wouldn't be there on my own.

I thanked the nurse for the tea and her kindness and walked out of the hospital with a heavy heart.

As I was walked across the car park, however, I could hear someone shouting, "Maeve Lynch, is that you?"

I put my head down into my coat and kept walking as fast as I could, as I thought they couldn't be talking to me, surely?

Before I knew it there were two fine men stood in front of me. One of them giving out orders to the other. "Maeve?" he queried, "Jesus we can't take him anywhere." It was Mrs O'Brien's two lads, Gerry and Oliver.

Next thing I knew they had their arms wrapped around me, squeezing me so tight that I thought I would pass out. They swung me round like a rag doll.

"You're a sight for sore eyes."

We were standing there staring at each other and out of nowhere; there were tears in my eyes again. I was speechless. I could not possibly have had any more tears left at this stage.

"How the Devil are you?" One of the men asked.

The spell was broken then the sky opened and the rain came bucketing down.

Gerry said, "Let's get to the pub before we get pneumonia and we will be in the bed beside herself."

There was no time for asking questions there, the three of us headed across the road to the pub. It was a wonderful sight to come into a big roaring fire in the corner. We sat in the seat closest to it, took off our coats and then Gerry made a beeline to the counter, shouting across the room, "What can I get you both."

Oliver laughed, and said, "He's not changed much. Any excuse to get a pint in."

Settling into our seat with drinks in hands, Gerry said he had ordered some soup and sandwiches, as we needed something to warm us up on such a miserable day.

It was like a comedy act. They both spoke at the same time. "We thought we were seeing things out there. It's a bit mad as we were only talking about you on the way in.

"Jesus Maeve, you must have given the old lady a heart attack." With that, the two lads elbowed each other and laughed loud and hearty, sounding like hyenas.

His brother added, "Would you shut up you big eejit, you always had a big mouth. We can always count on you to put your big size thirteen into it."

"Oh shit! I didn't mean that Maeve. Mother would be over the moon to see you. She never stopped talking about you. She loved getting your letters and parcels. She would be as proud as punch marching each item around the town."

I couldn't believe how they could be so relaxed with their Mother so close to the next world. But it was good to be with these two gentle giants. They looked like bears with beards. They would also roar like bears but behind it all, they were really as soft as kittens.

We sat there for hours chatting, my flight forgotten, recalling the good old days. It was as if there were no missing years between us.

We laughed and cried in equal measures. It was great to hear about their wives and children. Sitting there was easy. I had no mask to hide behind as they knew me inside out.

Apart from Izzy, I had never spoken about my life so much to anyone else since I had left my hometown. As we sat there it felt good to feel that free and easy with no one judging me.

It was also very refreshing to hear the stories from back home and to hear how everyone was doing. It was then late into the evening and many a flight had left Shannon, so it was with a heavy heart that I said goodbye to these amazing men.

They hugged me tight again and made me promise that I would not come back to the funeral when the time came. They said, "Mother wouldn't want you to be there."

I told them she had said as much to me just before I left.

Oliver said, "Just by you being here today would have made her so happy, happier than you could believe. It was her biggest wish to see you one more time so she could tell you in person how proud she was of you and how happy you made her.

"She prayed for you every night without fail. She would laugh and say that the only way God could prove to her that he existed was to see you again. You made her very happy on so many fronts.

"You made her day. We could never compete with your visit. Thank you from the bottom of our hearts."

I told them, "Well, I'm glad to hear it, but for years I have felt so guilty at running away like I did and for all the upset I caused her."

"She never was upset or angry with you. She was glad you got away and that you have made something out of your life. You were the daughter she never had."

After I left the boys I rang Edward, to let him know that I was OK and would be getting a different flight back. My wonderful Edward never questioned me about how I missed my flight as he trusted me completely, which made me feel like a bad person.

I should have been able to share this part of my life with him and I know he would only love me more because of it, but I just couldn't get the words out. Part of me was still afraid that he would go back to my parents and create war with them, and if I am honest with myself, I just don't ever want to see them again. If I never see them, it would be too soon.

I just do not have the strength to relive that part of my life again. After all these years, I never really think about them as anything other than strangers.

I am a firm believer there is no point in looking back as you can't change the past, the best thing to do is learn by it and never go back. Move forward one step at a time even when you don't know where or what you are going to do or how you can turn your life around.

On my way home, my head was in a spin. I knew I should talk to Edward when I got back and yet I didn't know how to. I would just hate for him to know how vulnerable I had been, and still am in so many ways.

I knew that I had been blessed with him and the girls. They are the shining light in my life and make every day worth living. I would be lost without them.

# Chapter 23

Sitting in Shannon airport waiting for my flight home, I was filled with sadness and grief, for I knew I could never come back. My protector would no longer be there waiting for me. As the plane lifted off the runway, I could not hold back the tears any longer. For I knew in my heart and soul I was saying goodbye for good.

I never imagined that leaving Ireland would ever have made me feel like that, or realise how hard it was leaving my birthplace again. I guess for me that it was closure of a sort, for that part of my life. I had moved away and now I had outgrown it even though part of me still yearned for it.

My whole story was bittersweet. My home now was then in London with Edward and my girls. I believed my grandmother had sent him to me, as she would have loved him to bits, and as for the girls, she would have doted on them both.

They were lucky that Edwards's parents adored them and they were treated like royalty. There could not be better grandparents in the world. They were generous with their time and energy.

They would come to visit regularly and the girls would love going to stay with them during their school holidays. It was not unusual for them to call in the evening just before bedtime so they could read a story to them as they were being tucked into bed.

When I awoke, I was sweating and kept shaking. I was quite unsure of where I was. I felt frozen to the spot. It felt as if I had been transported back into the past and I was terrified.

It has been a long time since I had thought about that part of my life. I was so was shocked at all the details I recalled. I had deliberately wiped much of it from my memory as I had trained myself to only remember the goods bits and the happy days.

I must have been out of it for hours and now I was absolutely starving. The only indication of time was that it was now dark outside, so it must have been late in the evening. I still found it hard to move due to the fear still flowing through my veins. I summoned up all my strength just to walk to the kitchen to make a quick sandwich.

After eating, I must have drifted off again. When I woke up much later I jumped into the shower as I really stank and thought, thank God there is no one else in the house as the smell would have knocked them out.

I loved my house so much. It was full of so many happy memories. It had always been my security and had been my haven over the years. Opening the front door was like wrapping a cosy blanket around me.

I went outside to sit on the decking. The rain was still falling as hard and as fast as it was that morning. I was unsure if it had been raining like that all day or not. I loved sitting out there especially when it was raining. It was soothing and calmed the mind after a hectic day.

I sat there eating my sandwich and rocking in Edward's former chair. I always felt so close to him in that very spot. It was as if he was still sitting there with me talking about our days just like old times. It was always our favourite spot, and in winter or summer, we would sit there in the evening to catch up and exchange the stories of the day.

I was feeling very content with my belly full. I could feel my body beginning to relax, and my heart filled with joy for I am very lucky. I had achieved so much.

I allowed myself to question why I had never felt any anger towards my parents. At the time I was so frightened, and afterwards, I suppose I felt really sorry for them as they were stuck in a cycle of anger and misery.

It seemed that nothing could ever make them happy. They could not enjoy anything. I believed that no one could have helped them once they got involved with each other.

Their biggest crime was that they were wrong for each other in every way and had the misfortune of not admitting they were unhappy, but mostly I felt for my mother as she had a bright future ahead of her until she met that evil man.

She was clever and was stunning, everything he was not, but how she fell for him is still a mystery to everyone. It was like a real-life 'beauty and the beast' story. One word would sum up my father and that was a 'brute.'

He was built like a "brick shit house" as the old folks at home would say. Anger never really came into it until now. Now looking back at it all, I was very angry, but why?

My life is so much better now than I could ever have expected. If things had been different I would have gone to college in Galway, to study nursing. I had it all planned out and wanted to become a midwife and return to Clifden to work in the local hospital, or as an outreach midwife as part of the community.

I would be in a place where I knew everyone and everyone would know me. I would have married a local man and lived in a cottage by the sea. I would have been very happy with this life. Yes, I would have liked to have travelled a bit before settling down, but never in my wildest dreams did I see my life as it is today or the journey it has taken to get me here.

There was no real comparison in our two lives, it was like chalk and cheese. Over the years I often wonder which life my grandmother would have preferred.

The hardest part of not been able to go back is not being able to visit my grandmother's grave or to place flowers on it, or on Mrs O Brien's.

Over the years, whenever I was feeling sad or unsure of what to do I'd close my eyes and would pretend that I was sitting there asking my grandmother for her advice. I could always hear her voice in response to my questions or at times my cries for help. I could feel her sitting beside me, her soothing voice encouraging me all the way and highlighting my strengths

I allowed my mind to wonder what it might have been like to go back to Ireland. I could imagine the trip from Galway City on the N59 bus to Clifden with the wonderful view of the Twelve Bens and the lakes along the way, and the windy roads where sheep appear from nowhere, and the ever changing scenery.

The traffic jam in Maam Cross on Mart Day. You would never tire of seeing it, as every time you look at it you discover something new. It's always like seeing it for the very first time. It is just so beautiful.

I was angry, very angry, again. To say I was in a rage was an understatement. I had never lost my temper in my life, to be honest. I didn't even know I had a temper until then. How dare they?

What gave my parents the right to treat me like they had? What had I ever done to deserve it? Nothing, nothing at all. How come they got away with it? How come the Gardai were never called? I can't believe I never asked any of these questions before.

Maybe it was because I was too busy focusing on the future and putting as much distance between me and the past as possible, but I was shocked, this was my life, my past, my history. It was also history that I could never really share with anyone, not even the good bits. It was like watching a movie where I was the leading lady.

I would have loved to have been able to walk the Old Boreen to the graveyard where my grandparents rested and to sit on the stone beside their graves and to rest against the headstone looking out to sea with the mountains as a backdrop.

I would have loved to watch the ever-changing landscape, talking and dreaming of the future with them, to share stories of the girls growing up, and later after Edward's death, there would have been no better medicine to help me heal.

I would often lie in bed at night with the longing and a yearning to be in that most peaceful spot on earth. The place has the ability to heal the soul. His parents wanted him to be cremated and his ashes spread along the hills at the back of his childhood home where he played as a child.

I was happy to agree with them as the only other place I would have wanted to lay him to rest was with my grandparents, if things had been different, as they would have loved him for the man he was, and for the way he loved the girls and me.

Over the years I became a dab hand at being able to place myself there with them whenever I was struggling with a decision, or if I needed to hear her advice. I would be able to hear her voice again and to hear her soothing tones, her straight-talking no-nonsense approach to life, saying, "there is nothing you can't do if you have everything you need to make it work."

Occasionally I could see her stamping her feet and when I could see this I knew without any doubt that she was not happy and it would be best to walk away from the deal. She was always my biggest and best supporter.

She was a firm believer in life after death, and that the other world was always there for us. She never made any decision without talking to her Seamus. If you didn't know any better you would never have guessed he had died many years before. She had some great wisdom in her words.

I never believed in any of this as a child but I later discovered that she had never spoken a truer word. Since the day I left home, I have never felt alone, not even on the first night that I arrived in a strange place sleeping in a bathroom, or on lonely night's when I was sleeping on the streets.

She was always right beside me. She would even sing to me when I was scared and afraid. I am certain that she placed all of my opportunities in front of me, and carefully crafted my path. All I had to do was follow.

She was my 'Guardian Angel.' Without her support, I would never have survived, and I certainly would not be doing what I am today without her dedication and patience, passing on her skills and her love for creating something beautiful from nothing.

The hours she spent teaching me stitches, the butterfly, cross stitch, chain stitches and running stitches, just to name a few. She would spend hour after hour helping me to make hairbands for my friends and me.

I also had the best-dressed dolls in the country as we would make all their clothes from a very young age. We would also make dolls from scratch and my favourite teddy, which I still have to this day, we made together.

I would not be the woman I am without her. We all need that one person who believes in us and puts us first. My grandmother was my champion. I firmly believe that it was her that sent Mrs O'Brien to the house that day. She sent her to save me from my nightmare. I still find it very hard to believe it ever happened. It sometimes feels like it happened to someone else.

I have never forgotten all that she did for me, she saved my life. She nursed me with so much love and care in the weeks and months after that dreadful day. I will be forever indebted to her. She was selfless in her actions.

She intervened without any thoughts of her own safety. Even when I think about it today I still regret leaving the way I did, for all the worry I put her through. I was very thankful that I got to see her before she passed, just to have the chance to say sorry, to be able to tell her how much I appreciated all she had done for me.

I was blessed to have these two amazing role models in my life. As a result, I have always tried to be fair and kind to everyone I met as you never know what's going on in their lives, and one kind word can make their day a little bit easier. It costs a person nothing to be pleasant.

I have also found I have been blessed as a result with my staff as they have never let me down or given me any hassle. They have always gone above and beyond the call of duty.

If I take a deep breath, I can see myself walking down the Boreen with the grass growing in the middle of the road that leads to my grandparent's grave.

I can see myself as a child again on a warm summer day running through the fields or jumping into the lake at the back of the house. It is the most peaceful place on earth. With a short walk, I would be on the local beach.

I would often spend all day on the beach and didn't see another human being, it would be just me with my dreams and a bottle of tea and a Tayto crisp sandwich, the sheep munching away on the grass.

Occasionally during the summer months, I might meet the odd tourist that would be camping on the beach. They would be in awe of the place, as they nearly always found it by accident, as the beach was like a local secret, you definitely wouldn't spot it on any map.

It was miles apart from the busy streets of London - always surrounded by people no matter how hard you try to find a quiet place.

Yes, we are blessed with the amazing parks that are dotted around the city - they certainly help to clear the mind, but they will always be full of people day or night. Even after all these years, it is the sitting by the sea that my heart yearns for, and to breath in the fresh scent of the water.

For all the misfortune I have encountered as a child, I still believe that I was very lucky to have lived in such a beautiful place. It is a shame that my girls never got to experience any of it.

It's no wonder people travelled from all over the world to visit dear old Clifden and the surrounding villages, of Ballyconneely, Bunowen, Roundstone, Cleggan, but to name a few, as there is no place like it in the world.

It's Heaven on Earth, and Edward and I often talked about moving to the coast one day, but it was never the right time with the practice and with the shop, and then when you wake up one day, you sadly find you have run out of time.

For many years now, Isabelle and sales and marketing had been wanting to set up a shop in Dublin, or Cork. as we have a large client base over there that often travel across to us and are always asking if we would think about opening up something there.

But I was always afraid, even after all these years, that someone might recognise me. I am not sure why this should bother me as Mam and Dad had both long since passed.

At times I would read the 'Connacht Tribune' online, just to be nosey more than anything else, it was here that I noticed the headline - MAN DIES AS A RESULT OF A BAR FIGHT.

They were talking about Dad. Apparently, he was in a fight one night and got a bang on the head and never went to the hospital. As a result, he died from a slow bleed to the brain, which sounds just like the man I remember, as he would often come in with cuts across his face and bruises.

Some would say it was only a matter of time before it happened, as he had many a lucky escape! He would have been too stubborn to get help. I don't think he ever went near a doctor in his life, and as for Mum, she drank herself into an early grave a year or two later.

After he died she became a bit of a recluse. It was heartbreaking really. They both died very young. What a waste of life! I often wondered what happened to my grandmother's house and the farm. Whether they sold it before they passed to buy more drink, or whether my father could have lost it all in a card game.

He was always in debt between either the cards or the bookies and he never had a penny. He collected his dole on a Thursday and wouldn't have anything left by Saturday evening. He never gave my Mother a bob or two for food or something else.

I was not sure where she was getting her money from after Granny passed, I know my grandmother used to pay her bills in the local village shop, but she would only pay for the food. She would ask the shop to take off the charges for the drink and cigarettes and tell them not to give her any more of them on tick. I am not sure if my mother ever asked the shop who paid the bill, or if the bill was ever paid.

When we went to Clifden the first thing my grandmother used to do was go into each of the shops to see if they were owed anything. I now ask myself did my mother ever acknowledged all that my grandmother did for her without ever saying a word.

I don't remember them talking much or my mother going to visit Granny's house. She would send me over to her as soon as I came in from school.

During the school holidays, I would more or less live there. I don't remember either my mother or father ever coming looking for me. I think my mother resented our relationship, and I dare say she was jealous.

I wondered who was living there now. Did they love the place as much as I did? Do they know how much love my grandparents poured into the place? Does the front garden still bloom in the summer? Do the daffodils still line the path from the road to the door? Do the neighbours still call in as they are passing the door, knowing the kettle was always on.

I hope they didn't change the outside too much as the area is now filled with lots of holiday homes. My grandparents would hate that as they would want to see a loving family growing up there - to hear the children's laughter, and for sure they would be doing their best to help them in any way they could.

I was suddenly startled back to reality with loud music coming from next door and the banging of car doors. I could not believe it was 10.30pm. Jesus, where did the time go? It was like I was still stuck in my time warp. I got up and went to the kitchen and poured myself a large glass of wine, before calling for a takeaway and then going upstairs to hop into the shower.

Stepping into the hot shower I sent a silent prayer out to anyone that was listening that neither of the girls would come home tonight. I can't believe that I actually said that but I am just too shaken to talk to anyone yet. I have to pull myself together. I need time to try and work out what had just happened and why. Why now? And what does this mean?

I didn't have the strength to tell the girls about my past just yet. I would be afraid they would be ashamed of me when they found out I was homeless and they would be so mad that I had lied to them for all these years.

They might never be able to look at me in the same way again. They might see me as a fraud. I could only imagine how they would feel about me if they knew. I could not risk losing them over this and anyway it all happened so long ago. I could no longer imagine my life without them, as they were my life.

The old fears of the past were suddenly very real and alive, not only the fear of it all coming to the surface and having to relive it again but the fear of being found out, and to be labelled as a runaway and homeless liar.

These things happen to other people. You never expect that person to be your mother. I didn't understand why all this was coming up now as I promised myself a long time ago never to look back and until today I had lived by that promise.

It's a sad state of affairs when a person is safer on the streets than in their own homes with their families. It speaks volumes. I wonder if anyone knows how many people do not feel safe in their home for one reason or another.

Now I need to put this back into the past and leave it there. 'Let sleeping dogs lie,' as the old folks back home in Ireland would say. No good will come from digging it all up, it serves no purpose.

After I had finished in the shower, I put on my PJ's and went downstairs just in time to take delivery of my Chinese takeaway and to pour another glass of wine, then I sat in the kitchen eating my wonderful food and giving thanks to being home.

I had a feeling that today was just a blip, so tomorrow would be a good day. The following morning, I woke up bright eyed and bushy tailed ready for whatever the day had in store.

Determined that the past was the past and the best place for it was to stay there. I had no idea what all that was about last night or where all those memories came from. Putting on the coffee, I called the girls to arrange to meet for lunch, and to my surprise both were free.

To say they were ecstatic that I was back was putting it mildly, and afterwards, I headed into the office. I was looking forward to getting my life back again. It was a return to the routine I knew and loved, surrounded by my girls and friends. It was a place where I felt safe and in control.

I was excited to be home, and being back again, it felt like I was being given a new lease of life. Suddenly I had loads of new ideas and couldn't wait to sit down and put them on paper.

The morning flew by. I never had a chance to check my desk. I never even opened my laptop to check for emails. By the time I went around to each department to say hello, it was time to rush out and meet my lovely ladies for lunch. I was also looking forward to catching up with Poppy, but she was on holiday and was not due back until later in the week.

I couldn't believe that I had not spoken to her since that first day we met. I have to admit that I was a little nervous to meet her again, as I was not quite sure what she would think of me. But on all accounts, she has proven herself to be a very efficient and conscientious worker. Isabelle and all the other managers were always singing her praises.

It was just as well that Isabelle was also off that day, as I had not even had time to grab a coffee all morning. I called her on route to let her know I was back home again. She would be happy to have me back at the helm.

She was a great business partner and an even better friend. She had been my rock since the first day we met. We had been there for each other in every way possible. Our families were so close, her children and the girls are like the cousins they never had. I arranged to meet the girls at the Italian in Covent Garden, it was our favourite place to eat.

It was wonderful to see them again in person and to watch them chat and see their facial expressions. Before we knew it, it was 4.30pm, so there was no point going back to the office. No one watching us would ever think we had spoken on the phone nearly every day over the past few months.

As we headed home, they filled me in on what had been going on in their lives over the last few weeks. It was hard to keep up with them as they moved at an incredible pace. We all laughed like crazy!

# Chapter 24

When Poppy returned to work after her holiday she seemed in a bit of a state when she was told I was back. She just didn't know what to think, or what she was going to say to me as she had not spoken to me since the day I first helped her out, and then took her home.

It was likely to be a very strange reunion. Poppy's head was all over the place. She had spoken with Isabelle on many occasions to ask what should she say to me, and asked how could she thank me for the opportunities I had given her.

What would I think of her now, and seeing her as an employee? Would I be happy with the work she had done so far? Would I tell her that she must return to her old place, or that I needed the flat back, or that I had made a mistake and it was now time for her to go?

Poppy's mind must have been in overdrive. She was apparently turning herself inside out, driving herself crazy, and in the process driving everyone else half-batty.

No matter how many times people tried to reassure her that all was well, Poppy couldn't settle. She said she owed so much to me and now she was afraid it was just a dream, and she was about to wake up, only she didn't want to wake up, she loved her new life, all of it, and her boys were also very happy.

It seemed that Poppy didn't know what to do if all this turned out to be a dream after all. Where would she go? The only thing that kept her half-way sane was the fact she had somehow managed to save a large chunk of her wages.

She thought that would help to tide her over until she found another job and a flat, but there was no way she could ever afford anything as nice as the one she now had.

The thought of another move, however, and placing the boys in another school filled her with dread, and so much pain that it was unbearable. They loved the school so much that they would be completely heartbroken if they had to leave it now. Poppy thought, she didn't know how she would tell her boys, and told her colleagues she loved her job, her flat and her new life and didn't want anything to change. She prayed, 'Please God. I have never asked you for anything before, so please let things stay the same. I promise I will never ask for anything else again and will even start going to Church on Sunday.'

By the time I contacted Poppy to ask if she could come up to the office she was nearly on Valium. If only she could have got her hands on some she would have probably taken the whole bottle! She was so close to fainting on the way. Her body was shaking and you would swear she was awaiting execution on 'Death Row.'

Her knees banged together and the sweat was rolling down her face. She had to stop in the bathroom on the second floor just to throw up and to try calm her nerves.

She stood there for a few minutes looking back at herself in the mirror and trying to talk herself into a more relaxed frame of mind, muttering, "I can do this, I can do this. It will be OK. She is a kind lady and is happy with my work. You can do this, you are a strong woman and can deal with anything."

I'm not quite sure how she managed to pull herself together and suddenly found the courage to continue to my office, Poppy later claimed it felt like the longest walk of her life.

Opening the door Poppy sent out a final prayer for everything to be OK, and a hope she wouldn't mess it all up. She still seemed a little tongue-tied and hoped she didn't sound like a fool.

Poppy needed not to have worried though, when she entered the office, I was so happy to see her that I just jumped up and hugged her tightly. I then looked back to admire her and then threw my arms around her again. I was so pleased to see her and I could see a vast difference in her appearance and manner.

I confirmed, "Poppy my dear it's so lovely to see you again. I must say you're looking a lot better than the last time we met. So thank goodness for that! I hope you are happy here as I have heard some great things about your work, so please don't be worrying.

"I just want to catch up. I just feel awfully rude that I have not been able to meet up with you since that dreadful day. I hope you do not think I was interfering in your business, or trying to take control of your life. But your situation left me feeling that it was all wrong and that the system had let you down badly."

Poppy replied excitedly, "No, not at all Elizabeth. I am very grateful for everything you have done for me. I will never be able to thank you enough.

"At first I wasn't sure if any of this was for real, but now I don't have the words to say just how much it all means to me and the boys. I will never be able to repay you, or understand why you went out of your way, as you did."

I smiled and acknowledged her, "As I said, I felt the system let you and the boys down. That was no place to be living for any human being, and I was lucky enough to be in a position to help, so why not offer someone an opportunity?

"That's enough talk about all that, now tell me, how are your handsome boys? How have they settled into their new school?"

Poppy then updated me on everything that had happened since we last met with all the pride of a very contented mother. A smile finally broke out across her face and her eyes lit up with emotion when she spoke about her loving children.

She explained, "They are like two different children now. They are getting on like a house on fire and at school, they have both made lots of new friends for the first time in their lives. They even go on play dates.

"The school have been amazing with them. They said they respond exceptionally well to all the counselling and therapy. In the beginning, progress was slow at times, and I wondered if it was working at all, but then one day it all fell into place and I have never looked back since.

"The school is amazing Elizabeth. I would never have found it if not for you. They are both so happy now, and so easy-going since they started there. Their outbursts are much less and are much easier to handle now I know how to respond to them."

Poppy tried to thank me again for everything I had done for her and the boys, but I simply replied that any decent human being should have done the very same thing.

I then explained, "Poppy my dear, we all need a helping hand at some stage in our lives. You are the brave one when you showed up here and trusted us and what we were offering. So, my dear, you are responsible for the changes, not me."

I later asked her if she had had any further contact with her parents, to which she replied, "No, they still don't want anything to do with me or the boys."

"That's a terrible shame, but people can be awfully stubborn."

"The boys often ask about them since they had to do a project on their grandparents for school and it's hard on them, more so than me, as they do not understand why they can see them."

After spending an hour or so talking about the boys, I asked, "How are you finding working here?"

"I love it, I really love it. Everyone here has been so good to me."

"Everyone loves you too Poppy. They have all said that you're an exceptionally hard worker and have a great flair and passion for the work."

Poppy beamed from ear to ear.

"I am sure Isabelle has told you that after working in each department you can then choose which one suits you best, and which one you would like to stay in? Have you had a chance to give that any thought?"

"To be honest, I'm not sure, as I have enjoyed working in each department, but I know for sure that design is just not me as my brain is not a bit creative.

"I am fascinated at how you can create the most amazing items from nothing, you throw a few lines on a piece of paper and the next thing you know it is an amazing piece of work. I guess if I had to choose right now I would like to spend some more time with marketing."

I smiled with pleasure, "I'm glad you said that Poppy, as the girls said you had some great ideas on how to increase our brand awareness. I would like to suggest that you spend the next few months with them and see if any of those ideas can become a reality.

"I would really like you to consider going back to College and to get a degree in marketing and online business. If you choose to go back I would be happy for the company to pay for the course in full, and also offer you a day release to study. How does that sound Poppy?"

"Elizabeth, there is a lot to think about. It is an amazing offer but I am not sure if I would be able to do all that study at this stage in my life."

"Nonsense, nonsense! The first time we met you said you were on your way to University. Now, I understand a lot has happened since then, but you have the brains. You may as well put them to good use. Now is the perfect time.

"And if you think this is just another of my charity stunts you would be wrong. I offer the same options to all my staff. In return, I get them to sign a contract to say you will not leave the company during the term of the degree and you must be willing to work here for a minimum of two years afterwards.

"Of course, if you wanted to leave before that you can, but the catch is you would have to pay the company the cost of the degree. Apart from that, there is no other catch. So you see it is a perfect opportunity for both of us.

"Why don't you think about it for a few days and then get back to me? And of course, once you're qualified you would be entitled to a pay rise, which is always nice. I will ask Nicola to send you the details of the course so you will know exactly what's involved. Once you see the course content you will soon realise it will be no problem for you."

Poppy left my office completely stunned.

Poppy later thought, where did this woman come from? She knew Elizabeth was not a woman you could say no to easily. It was like she'd cast a spell on her, and you were unable to say no, yet making Poppy feel like she could do anything.

Poppy had been told by Isabelle and nearly everyone else that it was like being part of a large family, but this was far better than most families. Here they really did believe in you and encouraged you all the way.

She thought that it's as if they can see something in you that you don't know about yourself. It's was a wonderful feeling to be accepted for who you are.

A few days later Poppy sat down at her kitchen table reading the course overview. She was terrified yet excited in equal measures. She was not sure which one was more dominant, so she slowly continued to read:

**Year 1**

- Accounting Fundamentals

- Introducing the Modern Workplace

- Marketing Essentials

- Business Research, Learning and Professional Development

- ICT (Information and Communications Technology) for Business
- The Global Business Environment

**Year 2**

- Digital Marketing
- Entrepreneurship
- Management Accounting
- Managing People
- The Human Resources Professional
- The Legal Framework

**Year 3**

- Contemporary Issues in Marketing and Management
- Dissertation
- International Financial Management
- Leadership and Management Theory and Practice
- Strategic Management & Sustainability

Poppy's head began spinning with all this new information. It looked like an unachievable volume of work. It was a huge commitment but she could feel the excitement growing. The more she told herself it was impossible, the faster her heart would beat. She knew by the time she went to bed that she would be signing up. She remained apprehensive but excited as she picked up the phone to call Elizabeth to give her the good news.

She knew it was going to be hard but somehow she would have to make it work, as the opportunity was just too good to miss. As expected, Elizabeth was over the moon. The next few months passed in a haze, between getting ready to return to University, work, and the boys.

The first evening Poppy attended College she was very nervous. It was as if she was back at school again for the first time. Everyone looked so young, and some of them looked barely seventeen! She believed she must be the eldest by a long shot, and considered she was probably the only one there with two young boys, so she remained uncertain as to how she would relate to them.

The first few weeks were mind-boggling, but she had an advantage over all the others in her class thanks to her work with 'Wear With Confidence.'

Most other students were just out of school and so had no practical work experience and had no idea what the lecture was about most of the time, and so struggled with key assignments.

By Christmas of the first year, Poppy was surprised at how much of the course she had covered. She was loving the course and found that she easily fitted in with the group.

Most of the time they ignored the fact she was much older than most of them.

When they broke up for the Christmas holidays, she was quite sad as she really looked forward to her classes. Sometimes she found herself daydreaming about the lecturer.

He was charming with the most amazing blue eyes she had ever seen. Sometimes she got lost in them and at times, her imagination ran wild.

The months rolled past and she passed each term with flying colours, then one night after college they all went for a drink. The others eventually left one by one, until it was just Poppy and Mr Russo. They sat chatting until it was closing time. She really enjoyed his company and he was very open and honest about his life and answered any questions.

His father was a second-generation Italian and his Mother a Londoner. He was one of four children and in his own words, he was the favourite. Over the next few weeks, they began seeing each other more and more. Poppy was reluctant at first to enter into a relationship with anyone else, especially after Luke, as he had instilled in her a lack of trust in any man.

She had never ever been semi-interested in anyone else since Luke. He was her first boyfriend but had nearly destroyed her, and she was not sure whether she could ever let anyone into her life after that. There was no way she would ever bring another man into her children's lives either unless she was one-hundred per cent certain.

Ian Russo was patient, kind, and slowly broke down all of her barriers. When she finally introduced him to the boys they all got on extremely well.

Ian later became a very important person in their lives, so much so, that he asked Poppy to marry him after the graduation. He became upset when she told him about her family. She had never really intended to tell him the full story about Luke, but one evening it all came flooding out. To be honest it was such a relief for her to finally have everything out in the open. It was as if she had suddenly become a new person, and a large black cloud suddenly lifted.

Graduation Day arrived in no time at all and Poppy managed to finish with a first. She could now say that she had a BA Degree in Marketing. Ian had planned a celebratory dinner afterwards.

Isabelle and I also attended along with Ian and Poppy's children. The boys were so excited to see their Mummy dressed in a spectacular gown and a funny hat.

I'm not sure who was more pleased, me or Poppy. She beamed with pride as she walked up to collect her Degree Certificate. Afterwards, they were standing around talking to some others in the class, when out of the corner of her eye, Poppy thought she could see her parents, but she wondered how? And why?

She thought they would have had no idea of where she was, and it had been a good few years since she had last called to try and reconcile, to no avail. Maybe she was just seeing things and thought perhaps the emotion of the day was getting to her.

She always hoped that when she finally graduated they might be standing there beside her, but it seemed an awful state of affairs when parents turned their backs on their own children for no logical reason at all.

Poppy continually told herself that she would never do the same to her boys and would always be there for them no matter what. As Poppy and her boys turned to walk out of the hall, she nearly had a heart attack as her parents were now walking towards her. She didn't know what to do and was too shocked to run, so just became frozen to the spot.

The words would not come out of her mouth. She stood there like a statue as they approached. She was simply frozen in time. No one really knew what was happening.

Finally, her father spoke to her in his familiar low voice and said he was so sorry and was very proud of her. Poppy's mother too stood there with tears in her eyes. She then realised that she too had also become emotional and tearful.

Poppy's mum put her arms around her, followed by her dad, and the three of them just stood there crying. I'm not sure who broke the circle. Finally, her mum and dad spoke and told her that I had been around to see them a few months back to let them know how well she was doing, and just how proud they should be of her.

Mum explained, "Elizabeth told us all about the boys and how wonderful they were. She made us see just how much we were missing. She clearly pointed out to us that we have been very unreasonable and have let you and the boys down very badly in the past.

"That we have been totally irresponsible and that it was horrendous to have lost one daughter to the unfortunate accident, but totally unforgivable to lose the other just because their grief was so strong.

"We have always known the accident was not your fault but we found it hard seeing you as you were a constant reminder that we had lost Daisy. You two were so close and look so alike. Somewhere along the way, we lost sight of you. We forgot that you lost your sister your best friend. That your life was also turned upside down. We were drowning in our grief we could not see you were also grieving."

"We are so sorry for everything. We have let you down so badly and it is unforgivable. Your boys are the only grandchildren we will ever have and we would very much like to be part of their lives if you would let us.

"I know there is nothing we can do to make up for the past, but if you would like we can build a great future. We know we do not deserve your forgiveness, and if you choose you don't want us in your life we will respect your decision.

"We just hope we have not left it too late? We will not put any pressure on you either way. We just wanted to let you know we are truly very sorry for everything we have said and done.

"We will never let you or the boys down again and to be honest we were relieved when Elizabeth came to see us, as we were unsure how we could get the courage to come and see you. Without her, we would not have had the guts to come here today."

Out of nowhere, Ian and the boys came across and asked Poppy's Mum and Dad if they would like to join them to help celebrate the occasion. Ian looked back at Poppy with eyes that said it would all be OK.

Poppy said, "Sorry, Mum and Dad, this is Ian, my fiancé, and these are your grandsons, Blake and Ollie."

Ian shook the hands of her parents and commented, "That's sorted then. Let's get some food into these two or there will be all hell to pay."

Poppy bent down to her boys and introduced them to their

Grandpop and Grandma. The boys immediately grabbed their hands and said, "Come on, we're hungry!"

Ian then asked everyone if they had seen Elizabeth, as I had made myself scarce since Poppy's Mum and Dad had arrived. Poppy said mischievously, "So I wonder where she has got too?"

He replied, "Not to worry, Elizabeth and Isabelle have probably gone straight to the restaurant to wait for us."

The five of them then walked across to the restaurant like any other family. They chatted easily and the boys were happy to have someone new to tell their old jokes to.

No one would have ever believed the family had not seen each other in so many wasted years.

When they entered the restaurant, there were loud cheers and clapping. It took Poppy a few minutes to realise they were all clapping for her. So many people were there from work. She was shocked that they'd all made an effort to attend.

Ian had previously told Poppy it was going to be a small affair with the kids, plus Elizabeth and Isabelle. A small affair indeed, but before she could say another word Ian took her in his arms and swung her around whilst kissing her hard on the lips.

He said, "Congratulations baby, you've DONE IT! After greeting everyone, Poppy finally approached me.

I probably looked uncertain for the first time since I had met her and felt a little uncomfortable.

I was stumbling for words, and said, "I'm sorry if I have upset you, and I promise it is the last time I will interfere in your life. I hope you are not too angry with me. But, I had to speak with them.

Someone needed to get them to see sense."

She replied, "No, Elizabeth, thank you! I could never have gone back, and never did I think they would ever come looking for me. You have done so much for me but this leaves me speechless.

# Chapter 25

Life gradually returned to normal for me and by the end of the week, the constant stress and strain of my American adventure just seemed like a distant memory.

I was happy to be back in every way and to be able to meet the girls for a coffee at lunchtime or after work. It was this special time that made me so happy.

I have always believed it's the small things in life that make me the happiest, big gestures are wonderful but the effects wear off much quicker. It's the most wonderful feeling in the world when one of my girls, or both, would arrive home unexpectedly with a takeaway and/or a bottle of wine.

It must have been a week or two later when I received an enormous bunch of flowers. The sight of them made my heart skip a beat. Isabelle was in my office in a flash wanting to know where they had come from. It was only at this point that I realised I had never mentioned Stuart in any way except as a realtor.

I loved Isabelle, she was like the sister I never had. I was very lucky to be working beside her every day. She has a great sense of humour. She is quick witted and funny. She has a great way with people and could always be counted on to lighten the mood or to calm any situation.

Isabelle could restore order with just a look. She has always been much better at dealing with people than me and I can get quite frustrated, as I prefer to work with my pen and pad designing and planning.

I'm just as happy behind the machine as I am in the boardroom. People seem surprised to hear that I still make a lot of the designs myself. I love nothing better that trapesing around trade shows looking at new material and new techniques. It gives me such a rush. Many would say it's how I get my highs. I am like a child on Christmas morning. It's a feeling that I never get tired off.

Isabelle soon came bouncing into my office. "Elizabeth Reid, what are you not telling me? Have you got a secret admirer? Who are they from?"

Before I could say another word, Isabelle had picked up the card.

She demanded, "Spill the beans now. You have been keeping me in the dark! Who is this mystery, man? And don't tell me it's just a bunch of flowers and he is just a friend or a happy client? You do not get flowers like this from a friend."

Isabelle sat on my desk. She was like a schoolgirl and had no intention of letting up until she knew the full story.

I tried my best to shew her out the door, but I should have known better, that once she gets started there is no stopping her until she gets to the bottom of something.

Isabelle insisted, "Come on, you can't keep me in the dark on this. I have never known you to be remotely interested in anyone other than Edward, and it is about time that you had some fun. He wouldn't like to see you living like a nun."

I replied, "Izzy, you can hardly say I live like a nun! That would be a bit of stretch to anyone's imagination"

"Well, my dearest friend, you can hardly say you have been painting the town red. Now, stop trying to change the subject and spill! I will not leave here until you do. Tell me, is he tall dark and handsome? Where is he from?"

"Izzy, you're a real pest, do you know that?"

"Yes, I do, but you still have not answered any of my questions".

"What do I have to do to get you to explain yourself? You must be interested in him, otherwise, you would have mentioned him."

"There is nothing to tell. The flowers are from Stuart the realtor from the States who was looking after the building. We met a few times for dinner and that's it. We met up again a few days before I came back and to be honest he was great company but there is no way anything more than that could be possible as, I am not sure if you have noticed, but there is a great big ocean between us, not to mention the time difference, so when I say it's nothing, I really mean it."

Isabelle wasn't satisfied by my rather clumsy explanation, and said, "There is a flaw in your approach, so its time you told me everything. Oh My God Ms Reid, I do believe you are blushing. I have never seen you blush before. So it's a good attempt to get rid of me but you will have to do much better than that. You could start by telling me all about this mysterious man of yours, or do you have more than one hidden away?"

I frowned back at Izzy and knew it was now hopeless trying to dodge her questioning, I said, "Yes, I did dream for a bit and wondered what if we had met sooner, or if we lived in the same country whether it might work out? As you know I am not very good with affairs of the heart, as I have only ever had one boyfriend, and that was my Ed.

"Since he died, I have never even been remotely interested in anyone else and I never wanted anyone else. I am very happy on my own. But Stuart did make me stop and think that it would be nice to have someone. So maybe sometime in the future, someone might come along who knows?"

Izzy said, "Well I guess Liz that's a huge step forward for you? Does that mean I can start setting you up on blind dates? And maybe get you registered online?"

"No! Don't you dare. I will never speak to you again! That's one of the worst ideas you've ever had. That would be totally unforgivable, especially coming from my best friend."

At that stage Izzy was nearly on the floor with laughter, she added, "I can see you now all dressed up and raring to go."

We were behaving like two innocent, excited teenagers, then Isabelle asked, "Liz, what are you going to do now?"

I replied rather surprised, adding, "Not quite sure, there's not a lot I can do."

"Well, for starters, you might want to call him and thank him for the flowers. You cannot keep the man waiting, and then see where it goes."

The only way I could get Izzy out of my office was to agree to dinner with her after work at her house. My thoughts were topsy-turvy inside out. I had no idea what to think. Yes, Stuart was a really nice guy, but this was ridiculous. Long distant relationships never work and besides, I have no clue if he feels the same, or if I am reading too much into just a simple flirt.

But It was too early to call him, I knew that if I had not called him before dinner, I would be afraid Izzy would pick up the phone for me and God knows what she would say.

I guarantee it would be along the lines of 'When's the Big Day then? I have a new hat that I would love to wear.' Izzy is a ticket. She is as mad as a brush. I have no idea how Duncan, her long-suffering husband, has put up with her at times, as she is always at 90-miles per hour, whilst the rest of us are just trying to keep up.

Izzy had me bombarded with emails for the rest of the day, each one funnier than the previous. I could just see her behind her desk laughing her head off. I had tried to stop opening them, but as usual, I would give in. I sent her one back asking if she had any work to do.

After an hour or so, I said stuff it! I couldn't concentrate on anything, so I picked up the phone dialled his number and waited for Stuart to answer.

I thought, if he doesn't answer after three rings I will hang up. and then I could at least say that I tried. I told myself that I would take that as a sign that it's best to leave this on a strictly professional basis, as my head believes this might be the best for everyone.

This was all new to me, when I met Edward, everything just fell into place, and there was no what if, or I wonder.

I was surprised that he answered before I even heard it ring. He must have had the phone glued to his ear.

"Good Morning Stuart. I hope I didn't wake you. I just wanted to call and say thank you for the wonderful flowers, they are absolutely beautiful."

"Good Morning my English Rose. I am happy to be woken by such a beautiful lady."

We continued to talk about God knows what for an hour and a half, and the time just slipped away. By the time we finished, I was still none the wiser about what was going on, or if there had been anything going on in the first place.

There was definitely no real update for Ms Nosey Parker! There was no juicy gossip for dinner tonight. I hoped she would not be too disappointed, as by now her imagination would probably have run away with her. I guessed the best way to put it, was that we were just good friends.

The next few months passed very quickly. The shop was so busy that it was hard to keep up and all the new designs were flying out of the door.

We had a huge increase in sales Stateside and it could not have been better if we tried. Once again, Izzy was talking about a growing number of inquiries coming in from Ireland, and people were asking if we would consider opening a shop over there. For now, I had deferred that decision, as we were far too busy to even think about opening up somewhere else.

I thought that perhaps we could look at it next year and write it into our business plan going forward, thinking that should keep everyone happy for a while, and hopefully, then they might forget about it altogether.

The twins were coming over later that day so they could plan a holiday to Mexico. Their schedules were in sync for once in their lives since finishing University and they were planning to travel for about six weeks. At the end of this time, they were hoping to meet up with me in Hawaii.

Ever since I was a child I wanted to visit Honolulu and Maui, and I must have seen a movie at some stage years before with people being welcomed onto the island by ladies in grass skirts and with the flowers draped around their necks.

I fantasised about the place for years and now could hardly believe that I would finally get a chance to go there.

We were up half the night planning. The girls had a list as long as your arm, from Tulum, the ancient seaside walled city, to the Mayan ruins, and from the climbable pyramids to Cancun.

They had friends working with an NGO in some of the poorer areas and we're hoping to link up with them and work in a few disadvantaged areas for a few weeks.

They were so excited but it was hard not to get carried away with them, yet there was still a small part of me that was absolutely terrified, as some of the areas they intended to travel to were not the safest in the world. In addition, some places were so remote, that there would be little or no communication. I consoled myself that at least they would be together.

I wondered how they would get on without all their mod cons all the things they are well used to having over here. I think the hardest thing will be the fact there are no toilets or running water in some places. There will be no place for all their gadget and hair straighteners, make-up will the last thing they will need. I couldn't imagine them hand washing their clothes, or not being able to shower at least once a day.

I thought that I would just have to 'watch this space,' and considered that I was going to find the next six weeks very long especially without any adequate communication every day. I convinced myself just to focus on our forthcoming holiday to Hawaii.

# Chapter 26

A week after the girls left for their trip of a lifetime, I began using the time very wisely and working a little longer and harder each day. When at four o clock on Friday afternoon, I had a call from reception to say I had a visitor who didn't have an appointment.

I was surprised as I had not been expecting anyone and had no appointments booked. I asked if they could make an appointment but my receptionist said he was a friend who was passing and just called to see if I was free.

I had no idea of who it could be, but feeling a little frustrated at being interrupted, my curiosity got the better of me, so I told my colleague that I would be down in a few minutes.

I finished the last few touches to my sketch, tidied my desk, and checked my make-up before going down to reception to see who was waiting.

I nearly fainted with the shock of seeing Stuart standing there as cool as can be. I had to look twice to make sure I was not seeing things. I became rooted to the spot, and it was only when he spoke that I finally snapped out of my daze. We hugged each other and kissed.

He said, "Well, well, Elizabeth! I don't think I have ever seen you speechless before. I guess it would be safe to say I have surprised you."

I just stood there mesmerised for a few seconds with my mouth wide open.

"I was hoping to take you to dinner tonight, if you are free."

I asked him, "What are you doing here? Why didn't you call to say you were in town?"

"Why would I do that, and miss that look on your face, it was priceless."

I told him, "You're lucky I'm in good health. You could have given me a heart attack!"

"I just wanted to surprise you"

"Well, you've certainly done that alright."

"Do you want to come up to my office while I tidy up and then we can go to dinner?"

"That sounds good to me."

Before we reached my office, would you believe it, Isabelle was already there waiting to greet us. I thought, she doesn't miss a trick. It's like she has an inbuilt radar for gossip.

I introduced him to Izzy, "Stuart, I would like you to meet Isabelle, my business partner, and a very good friend. Izzy, this is Stuart the realtor who looks after the building in the States."

"Well, Stuart, it's very nice to meet you."

"The pleasure is all mine, Isabelle."

"So, what do we owe this pleasure too?" Isabelle asked.

"I am on a business trip and whilst here, I decided to check in and to see if I could meet up and take Elizabeth to dinner. You would also be very welcome to join us if you're free."

She screwed up her face and replied, "I would love too, but I am afraid I have already got plans for tonight. Maybe another time?"

"Sure thing Isabelle, we can make a date."

She replied. "Well now my lovelies, I will love you and leave you, Have a lovely evening, and I will talk to you later Elizabeth."

With that, she disappeared almost as quickly as she had arrived.

"Stuart, you do know she will be on the phone in no time at all wanting to know all the details. She has a nose for gossip."

"Now, if you could give me a minute. I just need to send this email and then I can close down for the evening."

"No problem, take your time. I'm not in any hurry."

"Would you like a coffee while you're waiting?"

"Sure, if you point me in the right direction I will make it."

"Ok then, the coffee machine is just over there, help yourself."

"Would you like one Elizabeth?"

"No thanks, I just finished one before you arrived."

Whilst Stuart made the coffee, I rapidly typed a response to a few emails. My heart was in a spin. It was so hard to concentrate when he was just standing there as cool as a cucumber.

I had so many questions and didn't know where to start. The main one was what was he doing here, and since when did he do any business in the UK? It just confirmed that I really didn't know very much about the guy.

I honestly thought I would never see him again. If I had known, I would never have kissed him before I left. I thought what in God's name am I going to do now. Jesus, it was so hard to focus on the email and my eyes kept roaming over to the coffee stand.

I had forgotten just how handsome he was. I decided, sod this, I can't even pretend to answer any of these emails. Just as I was about to log off, true to form Izzy sent me about ten new emails ranging from 'who is a dark horse, to what is Mr Mac dreamy doing now? I knew you were holding out on me! What's on the dessert menu tonight? You need to come clean and fill me in, first thing in the morning or better still call me when you get home, that's if you get home alone!'

My face felt as red as a beetroot. I closed down my computer at a rapid speed and prepared myself for what might come. I told myself, here goes, in for a penny in for a pound!

I kept repeating, it's just dinner, right, and said to myself, I am glad the girls are away, otherwise I would be getting the Spanish Inquisition from them too.

"OK Stuart I'm ready, where shall we go?"

"Right then, does this mean I have your complete and undivided attention, Ms Reid?"

"I guess you could say that, so where are we going?"

"Well my lady, this is your town so you can be my tour guide."

"What would you like to eat?"

"Somewhere where I can sample the finest British food."

"There is the perfect place not far from here. We can walk if you wish."

"Let's do that. You lead the way."

With that, we headed out of the office and walked up Kensington High Street. It was a lovely evening for a stroll. We walked and chatted with ease as if we were two old friends, and there were no awkward silences.

Once we were seated in the restaurant, with the food ordered and a drink in hand, Stuart said, "I guess you're wondering why I am here?"

"You could say that. You're a very long way from home."

"Well, cards on the table. I have been looking to do something new for a while and wanted to get away from all the hustle and bustle of Washington. I am tired of the fast-paced, cutthroat deals and being just a face in the crowd.

"I need a break from all that, and then this unusual opportunity came my way and I thought why not, if I don't do it now I might never get the chance again.

"I have hired extra staff to manage the day to day running of the office and I will keep in touch on a regular basis. If I have to, I will go back once a month, to begin with, but I am hoping that won't be for too long. I feel it will all work out, in the end, I have a good bunch working for me."

"That sounds great, but what are you going to be doing whilst you're over here. What is your new job?"

"I used to do a lot of work for Guy James in Washington. He was a building contractor who made a fortune in building and redeveloping run-down condos all over the States. He was a big developer over there. Any building he ever touched used to fly off the market in record time.

"Over the years we became good friends and when he left Washington about ten years ago to return to Ireland to raise his young family we remained in touch. He always said he would return to Ireland to retire a rich man.

"Well, he returned alright, but not so much as retired. He still does a lot of building work both in Ireland and all over the UK. He has recently started a few projects in Spain and Bulgaria with others in the pipeline.

"He has asked me to help set up and train staff in sales and marketing, but first I need to familiarise myself with the legal jargon, for each country.

"Thankfully the UK and Ireland are not too far apart, but it will still take a while for me to get to grips with all the loose ends. It will involve a lot of travel around the place to start with, but once I have recruited a team I will be able to settle down. For now, I will be based somewhere between London and Dublin, but I am hoping to spend more time here when everything is up and running.

"I believe it's the perfect time, as I have always wanted to travel to Europe and this way I will get to do that, and get paid so it is a win-win for me. Guy was delighted when I finally came on board as he has been on my case for a few years now.

"He calls it broadening my horizon. He would say you can't live your whole life in America, you need to get to see the rest of the world. I think he would secretly like me to find a nice Irish girl and settle down.

"He's a real character and definitely has the gift of the Irish charm. My parents weren't so happy when I told them about the move, but in the end, they just wanted me to be happy, and I have not been too happy in Washington for a long time, and deep down they knew it just as much as I did.

"I was just afraid to admit it. I knew as soon as I admitted it, then I would have to do something about it and there was part of me that seemed so comfortable in my misery. I guess many would refer to it as an addiction, in that you can't recover until you admit you're an addict.

"Meeting you made me realise I was on a treadmill, and it was time to get off. I know this sounds a bit mad but after you left, I became lost. You have been on my mind a lot. I missed you. I wanted to hear your voice and to see your smile and to watch you play with your hair just like you are doing now.

"I know we don't really know each other but I would like to get to know you. If I'm moving too fast, I am sorry, I do not want to frighten you off.

"I'm not even sure if you feel the same way, or if you need some more time to think about it. I can live with that, but I would love to see a lot more of you.

"Elizabeth, you have gotten under my skin and into my heart. I know I must sound like a complete head case, but, before you answer promise me you will think about it."

"I don't know what to say, Stuart. You certainly don't beat around the bush, do you?"

I told him, If you want me to be honest, I have certainly thought about you too. I did wonder what might have happened if we had met sooner, or if I didn't have to leave so soon after meeting you.

"You're right, it does sound crazy, we hardly know each other at all, but, I guess it could be fun."

"Does that mean you would like to get to know me better Ms

Reid?"

"I guess it does."

"Well, let me tell you. I will not disappoint you, but I must warn you that I am an open book, what you see is what you get."

"Surely, that's not totally true?"

"I'm afraid it is."

I then queried, "Tell me did you ever get married? Do you have any children?"

"The short answer is no, to both, but I was once engaged and when it ended I was heartbroken for a long time. Since then I have had a few girlfriends but nothing serious. After the engagement, I was left with a trust issue."

"Do you want to talk about it?"

"Yes, I think it would be best to start as I mean to go on. The full disclosure is best to be upfront, so then you can make your mind up straight away.

"Her name was Claudia and she always wanted to be a model for one of the top fashion houses. We were together for three years before I proposed.

"Up until then everything was perfect, or so I thought, then a month before the wedding I came home to find a note saying I was not good enough for her and couldn't provide her with all the things she needed, and that she felt I had let her down. She claimed that I had not been honest about my intentions and had led her to believe there was more money in the bank account than there actually was.

"So with regret, she told me she was leaving to start a new life with a guy who worked in the stock market, and that I was not to contact her ever again she had made her decision. She also said 'by the way,' she intended to keep the engagement ring, as it was the least she deserved after all the pain I had caused her.

"Now I can see that the warning signs were there ever since we got engaged as she turned into a bridezilla almost straight away. To be fair to my parents and friends they had said from the start they didn't like her. They thought she was just a gold digger. She left me on the floor.

"It was an absolute nightmare cancelling all the wedding arrangements at short notice too, and most places had insisted on being paid up-front and in full.

"So that is the sum total of my unsuccessful love life. Now I can safely say, I had a narrow escape."

I must have looked stunned, and commented, "WOW! That must have been terrible. I can't imagine why someone would want to do such a thing. It is a really cruel thing to do to anyone. What a bitch! I can't understand why anyone could be so vile. Have you ever heard from her since?"

"Yes, she kindly sent me an invite to her wedding with Mr Stockbroker. A few years later, she sent me a letter and photo with her and her three kids. She said she was sorry for everything and claimed she had made a big mistake and would like us to try again.

"I thought it was a joke at first until my mother contacted me and said she called her to ask if I had received her letter as she'd not received any response.

"She told her the same thing she had written within her letter, saying she made the worst mistake of her life, and that I was her only true love, and would do anything for us to be together again.

"I believe Mum witnessed the full works, tears and all! Mum told her in no uncertain terms that I would not have her back and thanked her for showing her true colours before the wedding, as none of my family or friends had ever liked her in the first place. Secretly, they were relieved when the wedding was cancelled.

"For my sake, they had been willing to accept her into the family, but Mum said she had a nerve, to call and to think that I would ever want her back. She told her that I had had a very lucky escape.

"She also asked her, why? If she had felt that bad, why didn't she pay for her half of the wedding costs. She said, no, my girl, you've made your bed, so now lie in it.

"My mother is a very quiet person who normally wouldn't say boo to a goose, but Dad said she really let rip at her that day. After she got off the phone, he had to pour her a large gin and tonic to help calm her down. He was sure she would have a heart attack."

By now, I was in stitches, there were tears coming down my face.

"I'm sorry but I couldn't help laughing, although it's not very funny. It really is a dreadful thing to happen, but I can only image your Mum – a woman I have never met - jumping up and down like a mad woman. I wonder how I would have reacted in the same situation if it was one of my girls."

# Chapter 27

We spoke about the girls and my upcoming trip to Hawaii until we noticed that there was no one else left in the restaurant, and the staff were hovering at the back waiting for us to leave.

"I guess we have out-stayed our welcome. How about I pay and we can go back to the hotel for a drink?" said Stuart.

"Let's do that then."

After leaving the restaurant, I was surprised at myself when I suggested that we could go back to my place. The words came out before I could stop them. Talk about 'foot in mouth syndrome.' I thought I must get that looked at as surely some genius has already invented a cure.

Stuart jumped at the chance and before you could say hocus pocus we were in a taxi heading back to my house. To say I was nervous as I turned the key in the door was an understatement.

He must have sensed it as he put his hand on my shoulder and said, "It's OK if you have changed your mind. We did agree to take things slowly. I can assure you, I will be the perfect gentleman. Your honour is safe for tonight at least."

We both chuckled like kids. We talked well into the early hours and Stuart was the perfect gentleman, much to my disappointment. I was shocked at myself when I realised I had wanted him to kiss me again.

For the next few weeks, we spoke regularly during the day. We even met nearly every evening for dinner. I have to say I loved having him around and I missed him when we were at work.

I looked forward to his texts and calls throughout the day, but best of all was when he would collect me after work. That night, I was planning to cook a special meal so I left work early and Stuart said he would be round at about 8.00pm. He was bringing wine, so it was one thing less for me to worry about.

As I walked around the supermarket, I must have changed my mind several times about what to cook. In the end, I settled on a smoked salmon salad for starters, followed by steak with peppercorn sauce, served with garlic rosemary potatoes and vegetables. For dessert, homemade pavlova with fresh cream topped with strawberries.

Since Stuart had arrived on the scene, I'd not had time to worry about the girls, but they were scheduled to call that evening around 7 pm. I considered that I needed to tell them about Stuart, but was at a loss as to what to say.

It seemed crazy that as an adult, I would be in the position of having to worry about what my kids will think when they are told Mum has a boyfriend. If indeed that was what we now were! I had to tell myself to stop daydreaming and to hurry up, or I would never be ready in time. I dashed around the shops at rapid speed, thinking the sooner I got home, the easier my life would be.

Once home, I was like a woman possessed. I started with the Pavlova base, then the salad. I got the vegetable ready and finally marinated the steaks.

By 7pm I was already downstairs waiting by the phone. Thankfully, I didn't have to wait too long as a few minutes later the phone jumped into life so I grabbed it quickly in anticipation.

It was great to hear them sounding so excited about everything they'd been getting up too. They spoke non-stop for 15 minutes before they took a breath.

This was my chance to spill the beans. I took a deep breath and the words came flowing out of my mouth. Suddenly I told them everything about Stuart. They were screaming with delight. "It's about time Mum. When will we get to meet him?"

In no time at all, it was time for them to go. "Don't worry, I will give you all the details in Hawaii, we will have loads of time then."

When Stuart arrived, I was on a high as the girls now knew, and they were happy for me. I know they will fall in love with Stuart just as much as I have.

Dinner was a huge success. Stuart loved everything, he just stopped short of licking the plate. Later that night when we were sitting down to watch a movie with a glass of wine when Stuart suddenly turned to me and declared, "Elizabeth, I feel that I really do not know all of you. You have not told me anything about your childhood or your family.

"I have told you everything about me, warts and all."

He looked into my eyes and said, "I love you and there is nothing about you that I can't love. You can tell me what it is that you have kept locked away."

With my head down and my eyes staring at the floor, the most I could say was that there is a lot in my past that I am not proud of. He gently placed his hands on my face and lifted my head so he could look into my eyes.

Stuart said, "I know there is a lot of hurt in your heart. Your eyes reveal everything."

The tears came streaming down my face. It was like a never-ending waterfall.

"I am here for you my darling. I love you, but I need you to be as honest with me as I have been with you. I am here for you."

I was drifting into a strange place that I had never visited before. He was the only person in the world who seemed able to see deep into my heart and soul. I believed that now I had been found out there was nothing else for me to do but talk.

I guess I had been running from the past long enough. There is a saying that you can run from the past but you can't hide as it always catches up with you. And after all those years it finally caught up with me.

"Stuart you have no idea how hard this is for me. I have never ever spoken about my past. I have told everyone including my late husband Edward that my parents were dead, and although that is true now, it was certainly not the case when I first met Edward.

"It was easier to say that than face the horror of my reality. I'm afraid when you hear everything you will not like the person standing here in front of you, and that you will see me differently, and I'm not sure I can cope with that."

"Elizabeth Reid, I will love you no matter what. I have never in my life loved anyone the way I love you. I know you might find that hard to believe since we have only known each other a short time, but, I have a hunch that you feel the same way about me.

"So you need to trust me when I say it will not change the way I feel about you. But you need to understand that our relationship will only be stronger when we know the real person and not just the person the world sees.

"We need to be able to share things that we cannot share with the rest of the world and know that we are totally safe and loved. Your past has made you who you are today, so you should not be ashamed of any of it. Please, Elizabeth trust me."

I closed my eyes thinking there is no way I could ever explain all this, even if I wanted too.

I wouldn't know where to begin, then from nowhere, slowly I could hear a small voice speaking to me, and over the next few hours, I talked about my life from the earliest memory right up to the present day.

It was as if I was having an out of body experience. I spoke with a sense of calm and matter of fact. There were no tears or emotional outbursts. I am not sure where my strength came from and I didn't even recognise my own voice. It all sounded very alien to me. I may not have recognised the voice, but I knew the story.

Not once did Stuart speak or ask questions he sat there in silence. I had forgotten that he was in the room until I opened my eyes to see him also with tears rolling down his red face. Before I could speak he jumped up and wrapped me in his arms, it was a while before either of us spoke.

Stuart was then the first to speak with a croaky voice.

He finally commented, "Elizabeth, or should I say Maeve, thank you for telling me. I'm so sorry you had to experience such things, and I am so sorry your childhood was taken away from you, and that your parents couldn't see you, or love you the way a parent should.

"I'm so sorry you were so alone. You're amazing! The way your parents have treated you is wrong in so many ways. I don't know where to begin. They can't call themselves parents. It makes me so mad. They didn't deserve to be parents in the first place.

"How come they were not prosecuted? How they got away with it is beyond me. You must believe that you are a very special person. You have nothing to be ashamed of, but everything to be proud of.

"The shame you feel belongs to your parents. You will never be alone again. I am here for you for now and forever. You should be very proud of yourself. You are an inspiration. Look at everything you have been through and what you have achieved.

"Look at how you have turned your life around to be the success you are today. You are a wonderful person you should always stand tall and proud.

"I am glad you have told me and I love you even more now. Thank you for sharing your past with me. You share your story with other people to give them hope that they too can turn their lives around starting with your girls.

"They will be so proud of you because of how you have overcome everything.  They will love you even more than they do now. Let them see how strong you are. Your relationship will be even closer than it is now once you tell them and let them into your world.

"Show them the whole you, believe me, you will be amazed. It will help heal you and make you complete again. It's time to heal."

My body started to shake. He pulled me closer into his arms as he whispered into my ear. "I am here for you, lean on me if you need too. I can be with you when you tell them if you want me too."

I have never appreciated him more than I did at that moment but I needed to tell them by myself. We just sat there wrapped in each other arms and remained speechless for the rest of the night, neither of us wanting to move in case it would break the spell.

I felt happier, lighter and more content than I ever had before. I was loving my life. In fact, I would say that I had never felt so alive before.

On the night before flying out to Hawaii to meet up with the girls I was frantic, as I had left all my packing to the very last minute, something I never normally did. I would generally pack at least a week in advance.

As I finished, I could feel the excitement building. I had no idea what was going on. When they asked me at the airport security if I had packed the bags myself, and if I knew what was in them, I struggled to keep a straight face.

This was a trip of a lifetime. All of the excitement that I first felt when we booked it had now multiplied. I was looking forward to meeting up with the girls; I had missed them terribly. It had been a long time since I had last seen them and most of the time it was near impossible to talk as communication was either poor or non-existent.

We had never gone so long without speaking to each other. Stuart took me to the airport in the morning, and it was strange to think that I was going to miss him so much considering the fact we had only known each other for a short time, yet it felt like I had known him all my life.

We had spent nearly every evening together since he first arrived at my office just a few short weeks before. We spoke daily on the phone. I was surprised at how quickly we had connected, and we had fallen in love with each other so quickly. Yet, there was no doubt that I was totally head over heels in love with him.

I never expected to fall for anyone else. I thought Edward was to be my one and only love. I can't explain or even understand fully but what I do know with every fibre of my body is that Stuart is my soul mate. It's now like he is the other half of me. He compliments me. It also surprises me that I do not feel like I am betraying or forgetting about Edward in any way, quite the opposite, it's like he has given me his blessing.

I think he's very happy for me. I can't say that I love Stuart the same way that I loved Edward, it's just different, maybe because we are both a little bit older or it may be due to the fact I have no secrets and there is nothing to hide.

Since that night when Stuart put me on the spot, I have been astonished that I didn't freeze or run like I had done so many times in the past. I didn't feel like a rabbit caught in the headlights. I had started to tell Edward so many times but in the end, I just couldn't get the words out.

But, something changed when he looked into my eyes and he said, "Elizabeth, it's time to tell your story, to let someone in. You are not alone." I can still hear him saying "you are not alone, I am here for you. I am totally in love with you. Nothing you could say would change that, my dearest Elizabeth. I would knock down the doors of heaven and hell for you!"

Then he just sat and waited. It was like he already knew something, somehow!

Stuart took me to the airport even though I wanted to get a taxi. I was afraid to admit it, but it was hard to say goodbye to Stuart. I was going to miss him so much. As we kissed goodbye outside the departure gate he said he would be there in a heartbeat if I needed him.

He said, "Call me day or night, I will be waiting."

Reluctantly I passed through the security section both happy and sad at the same time. Part of me wished that I had asked Stuart to come along too, but I knew it would be best to talk to the girls alone.

I was really looking forward to seeing them and to catching up as so much had happened in our lives since we were last together. I know they are adults but I still love holding them in my arms, I was not sure how I would tell them about my life.

I now saw my life in two distinct parts; the one I had pushed so far to the back of my mind as Maeve Lynch, that it no longer felt as if it is was ever a part of me, and the second is the life of Elizabeth Reid. I'm not sure how they will feel about being lied to all this time, but, I did know they would be happy to hear about Stuart.

For years they had been on my case to find a man and have some fun. They would laugh and say, "Go on Mum, you only live once."

Sitting on the plane I could feel myself beginning to relax. It was not long before the steward was handing out drinks. I sipped my glass of white wine and took my book out. I read about ten pages before drifting off to sleep. The next thing I heard was the pilot announcing that we would be landing in Los Angeles shortly.

I had a two-hour stop-over in Los Angeles before catching my flight to Honolulu. In the airport, I grabbed some food. I was starving, as I had missed the meal on the way over. In no time at all, I was sitting at the departure gate again waiting to board. I was so excited. I was like a child.

When the wheels lifted off the ground, I nearly screamed with delight. My stomach was doing somersaults. You would have thought it was my first time on a plane. The next five and a half hours passed slowly so I had a chance to finish the book I had started on the previous flight.

It felt as if the flight would never get there and I was not disappointed when the plane finally landed in Honolulu. As we disembarked, we were greeted by beautiful local girls with fresh flowers. It was everything I had imagined.

I walked through to the luggage reclaim area and collected my bags. I had just gone through into the lounge when my two girls jumped out of nowhere and grabbed me. We stood there for ages hugging and crying in equal measures.

We got some strange looks from other passengers so we quickly made our way outside to the car the girls had hired. We went straight to the hotel. As the girls had arrived a few days earlier they had already had a chance to check out the place, and made a list of things to do and places to see.

We chatted like mad. Any tiredness or jet lag that I might have had soon disappeared. In the hotel room, I had a quick shower and changed into something a little more comfortable.

They were both so animated and had so much to tell me. We headed down to the bar to get some food and they ordered three Margaritas. As soon as the waiter left, Amelia was the first to say, "Mum you look so different," followed by Sara, who confirmed, "You have a bit of a glow."

"What have you been up to Mum? Is this to do with your new man, Stuart?"

The twins both looked at each other with that secret communication they 've had since infants. They both turned and spoke at the same time.

"Have you something to share with us? Tell us more about Stuart. Is it serious? What's he like? Mum, you're blushing, your face has gone as red as a beetroot, so you do have something to tell us."

I knew that once these two were on the case and sniffed out some gossip there was no way of shaking them off.

"OK, OK, I'll tell you all about him. I couldn't tell you too much on the phone."

With a grin on my face, I gave them a brief update about my new love life. As I had expected, the girls were thrilled.

"Mum, if he makes you happy then that's all that matters but that will not stop us from grilling him. We are very happy for you. We are looking forward to meeting him, and if you think he is someone special then we are going to love him too."

After I had answered all the when, where and how, I found myself, slowly telling the girls that I also needed to  tell them something about my childhood. I was shaking as I spoke.

With my head lowered, I explained my predicament, saying, I am sorry, as I should have told you before now. Please understand that this is not easy for me. I never even told your father about this. For a long, long time I had buried all this and had hidden some things from my past, but the truth was that for the most part, I had been hiding it from myself.

We sat there in our own world as if time had stood still. I told them, "Girls, I love you both so much. I hope you can forgive me for not telling you sooner, but I was ashamed, and I never wanted you to be ashamed of me."

The girls rushed forward with tears in their eyes. "Mum, we love you. How could we ever be ashamed of you? The shame is not yours to carry."

They then asked question after question about matters that had never even entered my head. Some of them I could answer and some I had no answer for.

It's safe to say they were both shocked and upset on my behalf. I told them I was afraid that when I told them they would see me differently, and more of a fraud. This made them somewhat cross.

Amelia said, "Mum, are you insane? How could you ever think this would change how we feel about you? You are our Mum and a fabulous one at that. We could never have asked for a better one. We love you more than words could ever explain."

Sara began shaking her head, adding, "Mum, you are an amazing mother and now you have told us everything it just makes you an even better mother. You have always shown us that we were loved and cherished and could achieve anything.

"When you have never experienced this love or support, you could not have done anything better. We love you now and always. We are so proud of you and that will never change.

"Mum, we have no idea how you survived any of it, from the betrayal from your parents, or from sleeping on the streets."

# Chapter 28

I was relieved that the truth had finally been told. I realised I must have had a fire in my belly that filled me with grit and determination to make something of my life.

I told the twins, "It was that same feeling when you girls were born. It was like the fire had been lit again to make me strive to be the best mother I could ever be.

"I never really knew where I was going. I never planned any of my success. There were times in the beginning that I thought I was just dreaming about the life I was living, half-afraid that someone would pinch me and I would wake up to find out that none of it was actually real.

"That is why I have always appreciated all the good things in my life and would give thanks daily. The only thing I know for sure is that my grandmother has been beside me all the way, leading me to where I am today.

"It was her protection that has kept me safe during my darkest days. At times I believe I am living a life that she would have loved if she had enjoyed the same opportunities we have today.

"She had a real knack for creating garments from nothing. She had such a creative mind. It was like she flipped my world around to get me here. She would have loved you girls, that's for sure."

"Mum, you are not only the best mother we could have ever dreamt of but you are talented and beautiful."

I never thought it possible but somehow we seemed even closer than before. I had been worrying over nothing. My girls were amazing. They just took the whole thing in their stride.

The rest of our holiday soon went and before I knew it, we were all packing for our return flights home. We laughed a lot and ate a lot, and it didn't take long for me to realise that I would need another holiday to recover from this one.

Every day we were up at 6.00 am exploring all Hawaii had to offer, from the island hopping to my failed attempt at surfing, which let me tell you is a lot harder than it looks; to the helicopter rides over the Island. It was utterly thrilling.

We visited Pearl Harbour, and Hanauma Bay, where we had the most amazing time snorkelling, plus Hawaii Volcanoes National Park, to scuba diving in Waikiki, to a wonderful trip to the waterfall on the road to Hana.

There was so much to do and not enough time. This was definitely a trip of a lifetime. It had lived up to my expectations and had so much more. It was a truly beautiful country.

I had spoken to Stuart almost daily to keep him up to date with our adventures, and the girls spoke to him most days as well. I really missed him but he had been here before so knew the places we spoke about, and in a way, it was like he was here with us.

All of my life I knew I had been lucky, and that I had so much to be thankful for. I have been truly blessed by meeting some amazing people who have formed part of my life's journey, but most of all I have been blessed with two amazing daughters.

As we left the island, we promised we would have to come back, and agreed that once a year we would take time out of our busy lives to take a trip like this.

I was really looking forward to seeing Stuart again. The girls too were in high spirits and teased me to no end, saying they had very high standards and needed to set him straight and to confirm he was taking on all three of the Reid's, not just the one!

As promised, Stuart was waiting for us at the airport in Heathrow. He was looking exceptionally handsome. My heart was in a spin when I saw him standing there with his arms full of flowers for all three of us.

He simply said, "A bunch for all you ladies."

When we wrapped our arms around each other and kissed the girls were whistling and making up rhymes. The girls loved Stuart almost as much as I did, which was a relief, as I couldn't imagine what I would have done if they didn't get on.

Life returned to normal once we were back. I went back to work and Amelia was busy at the Hospital. Sara was getting ready to move to America for nine months to work on producing a play she had written.

She was also working behind the scenes on a script for a pilot movie. As for me, the office was manic every day and seemed busier than ever before. At the rate we were going it, I knew that it wouldn't be long before we had to take on more staff.

Stuart was spending a lot of time in Ireland and Europe, so with all of our schedules, it was so hard for us all to be together again in the same place at the same time.

It was Christmas by the time we all met up again. It had been about four years since Amelia had been off on Christmas Day. Last year, myself and Sara even went to the hospital to spend a few minutes with her.

Christmas Day was extra busy this time as Isabelle and her family were coming for dinner, and both Amelia and Sara's boyfriends were coming as well as Stuart's parents. I was a little nervous as this was going to be my first meeting with them. I had asked them to stay here with us but thankfully, they booked into a local hotel.

Christmas was a great success. We had a fabulous day and everyone chatted easily, and we were all slightly worse for wear as we said goodbye to our guest.

Stuart took his parents back to the hotel and would return later. They were lovely and we got on really well.

He returned just as the final load of dishes were loaded into the machine. We were each having a nightcap in front of the fire when Stuart asked if I would like to join him at the wedding of Guy James's daughter in Dublin.

I had never been to an Irish wedding but heard that you have never lived if you've not been, as there is no other country in the world that can party like the Irish.

All this sounded exciting but suddenly I froze. I started to mumble that I didn't think it would be a good idea.

"Why not, Mum?" the twins echoed.

I told them, "I've not been back since I went to see Mrs O' Brien before she died."

Amelia said, "Mum I was thinking it might be a good idea for us to visit Clifden. We would love to see where you came from. We could go before Sara heads off Stateside.

"You have not told us very much about the area you grew up in."

Before I could speak, Sara chipped in and agreed, saying, "That's a brilliant idea. We should definitely go. This way you will be able to put the entire ghosts of the past behind you.

"You did say you missed not been able to visit your grandmother's grave. This way, we would be able to put flowers on her grave, besides, it has been so long no one would even know it is you! I bet you look a lot different these days."

I put my head into my hands and started to shake, and explained, "I don't think I can go back. It would just be too much to deal with. Did I tell you that the Gardai were looking for me at the time? They had me registered as a missing person."

"What's the Gardaí?"

"They are the police."

"Well, why can't they just say that?"

I laughed a little, "Girls, Gardaí is the Irish word for the police."

"Mum, do you speak Irish?"

"Yes, a little bit. I have forgotten most of it. There are still different parts of Connemara where they speak Irish as their first language. My grandmother's brother only used to speak Gaelic.

"He didn't have a word of English. I doubt there would be too many like that today, but I do know there seems to be a new interest in learning the language, which is good, I guess?"

"The Girls are right," said Stuart, "It would give you some closure and healing if you were to go back. It would be very different this time, as we would be there with you.

"You never know, you might even feel better about the place and listen to Isabelle about opening a shop over there.

"We could go over for a few days and if you want we can leave at any time. We would be there to support you all the way. We love you. We only want the very best for you, and, you know you need to go back, if for no other reason than to get closure. Besides, we would love to see the place where you were born, and spent the first thirteen years of your life.

"Are you not interested to see if the place has changed, or if it is still the same?"

"I have often wondered about that on and off over the years, but not enough to go back and see for myself."

After, a lot of debate and explaining that my fears were still real, it was finally agreed that we would go over for a week and travel around the West spending a day or two in Clifden.

We talked and talked until there was nothing else to say. I felt exhausted. I was still very unsure as to how this would all work out, or how they had finally persuaded me to go along with them.

Before I had a chance to change my mind, however, Stuart was online booking the flights from Gatwick to Shannon for the 2nd of February at 2 pm with Aer Lingus.

In what seemed like no time at all, we were all soon heading out towards Gatwick Airport. The flight only took about an hour and twenty-five minutes, and yet somehow it felt like the longest flight of my life.

My nerves were all over the place. The girls and Stuart did their best to try to take my mind off everything. They talked non-stop about all the local tourist spots.

We all agreed that we would like to spend some time in Galway City, but agreed that it might be best to head straight to Clifden in the hope that once we had that part of the journey out of the way then I would be able to relax and enjoy the rest of the trip.

As the plane wheels struck the tarmac, I am not sure if I was relieved or terrified. Once we left the plane, however, Stuart took control, and I for one was very happy that someone else was in charge so that I could just follow their instructions without thinking of anything else.

We stopped off in Ennis to get something to eat before heading West, and strangely enough, I was now feeling very hungry. After a lovely meal, we continued our journey. The drive would take us just under two hours.

Sara had booked us all into the Riverowen Castle in Clifden for three nights. I was really looking forward to staying there because as a child it was the best place to be. This was where the rich and famous stayed, and you would often see the helicopters landing in the front of the hotel followed by a flurry of activity.

At the same time, you never knew who was staying there until after they had left, and occasionally you would see a photograph in the paper of some film star. At school, we would be bamboozled as to why anyone would come to the sleepy town of Clifden, a place where nothing ever happened.

The highlight of the week would be that a missing sheep had been found or some mare had birthed a foal.

Before we knew it, we were leaving the hustle and bustle of the City life behind us as we left Galway and travelled West on the N59. We passed the quaint villages of Moycullen and Oughterard, where we stopped to top up with petrol and then went to the local hotel for coffee.

This would be our last stop before Clifden. The next landmarks would be Maam Cross and Recess before finally arriving at our destination.

"Mum, how are you feeling?" echoed the girls.

"Funnily enough, I am feeling very relaxed. Much more relaxed than I ever would have thought."

"That's great, Mum. You know we are here for you. We will be with you all of the way."

"Thank you, guys."

After we left there, the scenery totally changed. I told everyone they were 'in for a treat.' The next local hotspot was Maam Cross. I explained, "It was here they used to have 'Fair Days' once a week, where traders and farmers alike would meet to sell their wares.

"I am not sure if they still do it today. My grandmother used to say it was a great place to hear the local gossip and to meet your future husband or wife, or so rumour had it.

"It's also around here that the Quiet Man was filmed."

Neither Stuart or the girls had ever heard of it. I told them, "Shame on you guys. We will have to put it on our list of movies to watch."

"Are there any other movies made around here?"

"Yes, there was one made in Roundstone called 'The Matchmaker,' and one in Clifden called 'Three Wishes for Jamie,' and one in Leenane called 'The Field,' there may be others but they are the ones I have watched."

The tension was rising with each passing mile. Thankfully, the scenery was truly breath taking. It had us all mesmerised, and the Twelve Bens were amazing.

Every time you looked out you could see something different. It was every bit as beautiful as I had remembered and so much more. The light bouncing on the lakes, and the little Castle in the middle of the lake was still there, although a little smaller than I remembered. It was as if time had stood still, nothing had changed. There were no words I can use to describe the views, or how I was feeling. There is no place like this in the world. You could hear a pin drop in the car, the silence was deafening.

We were all lost in our worlds, the place was so enchanting, and it was putting a spell on us all. I was now excited that I had come home. All my fear had gone, temporarily at least.

Arriving in Clifden was the strangest experience ever. It was like I was back in a parallel universe. At first, the Galway road looked different. There were now shops where once there were open fields.

The place looked the same and yet so different, gone was the wool factory, the old train station, and the Convent. There was a new hotel, new houses, new shops and apartments everywhere.

I thought, Oh Jesus, how the times have changed, and there was even a new one-way system in town. When I was growing up you could never imagine that there would ever be a need for a one-way system due to the traffic jams in the town, you'd more likely to get stuck behind an ass and cart, but now traffic was at a standstill.

I guess the new curse of all small towns is the volume of cars on the road of all small towns, catches up with it in the end. It's the price of moving into the modern world.

Suddenly I thought, what in the name of all that is holy is that? I couldn't believe my eyes. On the Square was a huge cheese grater in place of where the Old Jack's used to be and the marketplace where they used to sell cattle and fresh food straight from the farms was gone. They used to have stalls here once a month. Hence the name Market Square.

I was not sure if it was meant to be a cheese grater but it was a wonderful piece of art. I couldn't help but wonder what John D'Arcy would have said if he was alive today. I was laughing like a lunatic, the others began looking at me as if I had lost my mind.

I just couldn't catch my breath to speak. I was hyperventilating and there were tears running down my face. I thought that I must look like a mad woman. I was trying to explain who John D'Arcy was, but my words didn't make much sense due to my inability to breathe.

Amelia, said, "If this is the effect this place has on her I think we should leave now." Sara and Stuart started to laugh at Amelia. It looked like I had lost my marbles, as I tried to explain what was so funny. I gave hand signals to Stuart as a direction to the hotel.

Stuart said it looked more like I was having a fit than giving directions, but now, we were all uncontrollable in fits of laughter. As we approached the hotel, Stuart said we would be locked up if we tried to check-in in our current state, so we took a drive up the Sky Road.

I pointed out the monument to John D'Arcy but as we drove past we agreed we would take a walk up there to explore the area.

I said, "If you want the best view, there is nowhere better than this to take advantage of this picturesque town."

We continued driving until we came to where the road divided into two. I knew it was a loop so we decided to go down the low road and come back into town via the high road. As we drove down there was silence in the car as we were all stunned by the beauty of the place. There were spectacular views of Clifden Bay and the offshore Islands of Innis Turk and Turbot.

I had never heard Stuart swear or pray before in all our time together. In fact, I was surprised to hear him saying Our Lord's prayer, as I didn't realise he was religious.

He began having a nervous breakdown as the road was so narrow and there was no safety net. One false move and you would be over the cliff and into the sea. He would say rather loudly as he was praying, that he hoped we wouldn't meet another car, and began swearing at every pothole. We were all unsure whether to laugh or cry.

Stuart was very relieved when we finally arrived outside the hotel. He jumped out of the car in a flash. He unloaded the bags then waited for us to get out of the car.

As we went inside we were welcomed by a crackling open fire and you were instantly drawn into the place. You couldn't but be intrigued by the history of the building. It oozed character, romance, and luxury.

After quickly checking in and a hasty change of clothing, we all arranged to meet up again in the bar for some refreshments, and more importantly to agree on a plan for the next few days.

Sitting there in rather comfortable surroundings, I thought that I could easily forget why I there in the first place. Sadly, Amelia and Sara had not had a lapse in memory so as soon as we had ordered, they jumped right to the core issue.

"Mum, we were thinking when we were unpacked that it might be best for you to go out to the grave today, and not to have it hanging over you like a dark cloud."

To be honest I had to agree with them before I lost my nerve. We chatted casually over the food and the girls had put a list together of places they would like to visit.

I was not sure, however, if it would be possible to get all of it done in such a short space of time. After Sara paid the bill we headed straight for the car. The first spot was the flower shop in town as I wanted to get some for my grandmother and Mrs O'Brien's graves.

When Stuart pulled up outside the shop the girls jumped out and said they wanted to get a bunch as well. Once inside, I found myself ordering three bunches, and an extra one for my parents' grave.

I was at a loss to know why, but thought, here goes. Once back in the car I gave Stuart directions to Ballyconneely. Once again, the landscape had changed slightly. There were now more houses and the local secondary school that I had gone to for such a short time had gone and was now replaced by a huge modern building.

As we passed the old school, my nerves were beginning to take over. I was not sure what I would do if the girls had not been there to distract me. By the time we stopped outside the graveyard I was shaking like a leaf.

We were just about to get out of the car when I spoke for the first time in ages, and I found myself asking if they would wait here for a while as I needed to go by myself, as I wanted some time alone with my grandmother.

All three of them jumped out of the car and spoke in unison, "That's OK, but you are not alone. We are here for you and will wait as long as you need us to, we love you more than words."

By the time my hand touched the graveyard gate, my whole body was shaking. I was unsure if my legs would carry me as they were so wobbly, and more like jelly. I was trying to focus on my breathing just to keep myself going.

When I reached my grandparents' grave, I fell to my knees and began weeping like a baby. All the years that had passed simply vanished, and it was as if I had just lost her. I cried for all the years we had together and for all the years since she had gone.

Then from nowhere, I could hear a voice singing the Galway Shawl. It was slow and low, my body moving to the music. It was sometime before I recognised the voice as my own. I was surprised to discover that I still knew the words, or that my voice sounded so sweet and in control.

I found myself being soothed by the sounds of the sea. Sometime later, the girls approached me to ask if was OK if they could come up now. I stood there with pride and introduced them to my Grandmother, and told them I knew she would be so proud of them and would have loved them almost as much as I did.

Before leaving the grave, I placed the flowers on Mrs O'Brien's grave followed by my parents. It was strange, but suddenly I no longer felt any resentment towards them, and I felt free for the first time in my life.

As we returned to the car Stuart suggested we go to the local pub for a stiff one after everything that had happened, he thought we needed it to help celebrate just how far I had come in such a short space of time.

None of us needed much persuasion to go to the pub and I felt I now had a new sense of being in myself. As soon as we opened the door we were engulfed in the atmosphere, the place was rocking to the sounds of traditional Irish music. It was music to heal the soul.

It was reminiscent of the music of my childhood, the songs had a familiar ring to them, and nearly everyone in the bar got up to either sing or dance.

Stuart and the girls were fascinated by the whole experience and the fact everyone knew everyone. At times they were confused as they couldn't understand why they kept insulting each other, and would then the buy the other a drink.

The girls were trying Guinness under the direction of the barman who said that for anyone on their first trip to Ireland it was 'a must,' and as a first-time visitor to his fine establishment, it would be irresponsible of him if he let them leave without tasting it. He would be forever known as a failure of a barman.

I couldn't stop laughing when they told me. I never told them that most barmen in the country had the gift of the gab. I had a gin and tonic, as I could not stand the smell of Guinness, and the fact I was force-fed it as a child mixed with milk, as a cure for all illness.

Stuart ordered himself a brandy. We had planned to stay for one or two drinks, but the next thing we knew, it was nearly two in the morning and the musicians were packing away their equipment.

He had stopped drinking after his first brandy. I know he wished I had done the same as my head now was spinning. As we left the pub worse for wear we agreed that the next day we would return and visit the graves again and take a drive down past the old house.

By the time we got back to the hotel, I was exhausted in every sense of the word, mentally, physically and emotionally.

The following day we visited the Marconi site and the place where Alcock and Brown had crash-landed in a bog in their modified Vickers Vimy aeroplane. It was the first nonstop transatlantic flight from St John's Newfoundland to Clifden. Later, we went for a walk over to the monument, where we were rewarded for our efforts when we reached the summit with the 'Twelve Bens' as the town's backdrop. Its famous views were justified.

We later walked down the beach road and on to Clifden Castle, the home of John D'Arcy. We must have spent an hour or so exploring the grounds, but none of us were brave enough to go inside, as it was unsafe to do so.

Some of the stones looked precarious. The castle had taken a beating from the severe winters over the years. It was safe to say that John D'Arcy found the best part of the town to build his Castle.

We wondered at the reason why no one had ever bought the place and restored it to its former glory, as there are no words to fully describe the beauty of the magnificent views of Clifden Bay.

I thought it would make an amazing boutique hotel, great for weddings, and you would be rewarded with one of a kind wedding photos. They would be the envy of the rich and famous, near and far.

The next day after breakfast we went into town before heading out to Ballyconnelly. After leaving the graveyard we went down to the old Boreen to see my old family home.

Pulling up outside the gate with a new sense of strength, I climbed over the rusty gate and walked up the overgrown path. What a sight lay before us. Half the roof was now missing, windows were broken, and the front door was rotten.

I held my breath as I stepped inside. Although there were now weeds and moss growing out the walls, it was unmistakably a very strange feeling that came rushing back. I could still see my grandmother making treacle bread, and scones. The image felt so real that I could nearly smell them baking.

In my mind, I could see her sewing was neatly laid out in the corner and her soft voice humming away to herself as she worked. I was transported back to the happy days of my childhood.

I was unsure how long we just stood there watching what felt like a movie or if the others could actually see what I could see. It was the sound of the girls talking that eventually brought me back to reality.

After leaving the house we went for a walk around the land and up by the lake and I showed them the place where we used to pick winkles. After I explained to them what they were, I became a little sad as we climbed over the fence, got into the car and drove away.

I later took them over to the beach where I had spent much of my childhood in the days when life was so simple. We then drove out as far as Errismore and I relayed the fun we once had there at the races, then drove down to the fishing village of Roundstone before heading back out to Clifden.

When we returned to town we spent some time looking at the shops and buying souvenirs. We had the best cheesecake and eclairs we had ever eaten in a local café.

It was going to be our last night there so we decided we would visit the local pubs, as I heard that one of the bars had recently won an award for being one of the best pubs in Ireland. As we sat there enjoying the music, the girls and Stuart said that they had fallen for the charm of the place.

It was everything I had remembered and so much more. The one thing we all knew for sure was that this place was going to play a big part in all of our lives going forward. We planned to return during the summer and to spend some more time visiting other local places of interest.

I often heard Mrs O Brien talking about Innis Boffin and I told them all that I would love to take a trek out there for a few days.

It was safe to say the trip was a success and I had never felt so happy as I had at that moment. Once again it was a late night as I don't think they believe in closing the bar, unlike the UK where they are very strict.

We wobbled back to the hotel a little unsteady on our feet. We had Irish coffees before heading to bed. In the morning, we were up nice and early.

# Chapter 29

We were just about to check out of the hotel when the owner suddenly approached us looking very sheepish and rather unsure of himself. He said he had someone in his office who wanted to speak to me. I was shocked and told him that there was no way there could be anyone there for me as I didn't know anyone.

He said, "I am sorry but they insisted. They said that they can't leave till they talk with you."

"Do you know what they want? Do you know who they are?"

"Sorry, but they asked that I say nothing else except that it is very important. I am sure it's nothing. Perhaps they have mistaken you for someone else."

Stuart stepped forward and said, "Would you mind if we have a minute?"

"No, not at all, take as much time as you need."

I started to panic and kept saying, "Shit, shit, what do you think this is all about? It was alright when I was a stranger here but, now I am not sure. What if someone has recognised me?"

The twins replied, "Don't be ridiculous Mom, there is no way someone would have recognised you. You must have changed so much since you were thirteen."

"Amelia is right," said Sara. "I'm sure this nothing to be worried about. We can all go with you if that will make it any easier."

I was so nervous that my knees began knocking against each other as we walked up the stairs towards the manager's office. I was leaning on Stuart so much it was as if he was carrying me.

I was not able to speak let alone walk, then I suddenly thought, sweet Mother Divine. I was now regretting coming back. This was becoming my worst nightmare!

I considered, what if they arrest me? After all, I was still a runaway! I thought I must be on a missing persons list somewhere. My head was working overtime and it felt like it was going to explode.

I was not sure if my heart could take any more of it as it was racing so fast I could almost hear it. The walk up to the office was one of the longest walks of my life. Each step was like a needle being pierced into my feet. The closer we got the more effort it took.

By the time we got to the door, I was no longer able to speak. My mind just went blank. The lights were on but there was no one home. The manager opened the door and asked if we wanted tea or coffee. I just wanted to scream, 'are you off your head, tea or coffee will be of no use to me now, how about a bottle of poteen?'

Thankfully, Stuart took charge and responded with 'no thanks, I think we will be fine.' As we walked into the room a young lady, her hair scraped back to an inch of its life, jumped up and came racing towards us with her hand stretched out towards me.

She looked like she was just out of school, dressed in a grown-up pinstriped suit.

"My Name is Grainne Kennedy. I am a solicitor here in the town. Now I'm sure you are wondering why I am here."

"Yes," replied Stuart, as he seemed to be the only one of us that had not lost his voice. He remained calm, grounded and very much in control, unlike the three of us who must have looked like real idiots.

"Can you please tell us what all this is about?" asked Stuart.

"Of Course," said Grainne, "I'm sorry to intrude on your holiday but I was informed that you have been to visit the Lynch's farm out in Ballyconneely a few days ago. You see, it's a small community out there and everyone looks out for each other. One of the neighbours saw three ladies and a man walking around the house and down by the lakes. The same neighbour also saw you in town last night and followed you back to your hotel. So that's why I am here. I need to know if it was you that was seen."

"Why is it so important to you if we were?"

"Nobody has been out to the farm since Mr and Mrs Lynch died some years back. We have it on record that there was a daughter but it was way before my time. There are stories she ran away when she was around thirteen or so. I am sorry but I don't know the full story about the place.

"As with all small towns and villages across the country, there is always small talk. I just need to check to see if you had any connection to the family?"

Stuart very quickly said, "Yes, it was us."

He explained that we were just visiting the area, and we're looking at the property for a project as the place had some real charm.

Stuart asked, "Do you know if the place is for sale? We are sorry if we have caused anyone any distress by visiting the place as that was not our intention."

She replied, "Now that I can answer. No, the place is not for sale, as my firm has been tasked with finding the owner Ms Maeve Lynch!"

It was at this stage that I let out a strange howling sound and fainted. I fell to the floor like a sack of spuds. I'm not sure how long I passed out for but by the time I regained consciousness, I was lying on a couch with a strange face looking at me.

I tried to jump up but Stuart and the other man put a hand on my shoulders and told me that I needed to rest.

"You must have had quite a fright, Mrs Reid. Let me introduce myself. I am Doctor O'Halloran, and I must insist that you rest for a bit as you have fainted and banged your head on the floor, and there is a possibility you are a little concussed.

"I strongly recommend we call an ambulance to take you to the regional for an X-ray. They might want to keep you in for the night for observations."

I sat up and said, "I am sorry Doctor but there's no need for an ambulance, I am just fine."

"Well, in that case, you will need to stay here for at least another night and I will pop back this evening to check on you. If you have any concerns please call me right away. Here is a list of the symptoms to look out for. If you have any one of them you must call an ambulance straight away."

I was trying to form my words to say that we were going home that day when Amelia and Sara both spoke at the same time. "It's alright Mum. We have already booked to stay on here for another night or two."

After the doctor left, Stuart and the girls fussed around me like mother hens.

In fact, I had temporarily forgotten about Grainne Kennedy until Sara said that she was still waiting in the bar downstairs and that she had stayed and there was no rush, but she still needed to talk with me.

The manager could not have been more helpful as he quickly took our bags back to our rooms. Stuart carried me in his arms back to our room and as luck would have it, it was on the same floor.

Stuart laid me on the bed and kissed me gently and then said he would go down to speak to Grainne to ask her to come back later when I was feeling a bit better.

Stuart arrived back ten minutes later, to say Grainne would be back at 4.30pm.

I told him, "Thanks, Stuart. I don't think I could answer her questions right now. I am so grateful to have your guys with me. I don't think I could do any of this without your support."

"Nonsense, now that she has gone for a while we have time to think about what to do next. But first, you should get some rest, as you need to be in top form when she comes back."

I then sent the girls away and told them to go into town or to take a breather. I also sent Stuart down to the gym to release some steam.

I needed some time to think about what to do. I thought, 'Do I come clean or continue as I have done for a very long time?' As my family had left me to the silence of the room, I quickly made up my mind to make a full disclosure, regardless of the consequences.

Stuart and the girls were due back at 3.30pm so I had a few hours to kill. I rang reception to see if the hairdresser was available. I was in luck and was told to go down in fifteen minutes. I wanted to look my best to face my ghosts.

The gang arrived back to my room earlier that I had planned. They were amazed that I was now so calm, I told them it was time to finally tell the truth.

By the time Grainne returned, I was in a much better place. I apologised to her for all that had happened earlier, and for any inconvenience I may have caused.

I admitted, "I am Maeve Lynch, Ms Kennedy. The story you had been told about me running away when I was thirteen is true."

"Well, in that case, Ms Lynch, I am very pleased to meet you. My boss will be delighted you have finally been found. He will be very pleased indeed. Can you please call into the office tomorrow on Main Street any time after 9.30pm, I will make sure all the paperwork will be ready. Goodbye Ms Lynch."

"Goodbye Ms Kennedy, see you in the morning."

After she left we just sat there for a while in silence. It was all so surreal. I was unsure how I had got to this point, but thought that now I was here, it had not been as scary as I thought it might be.

Amelia was the first to suggest we went out for dinner to celebrate. To be honest, I would have preferred to have stayed in the hotel, but then Stuart reminded us that the Doctor would be calling back later, so best all round to have dinner there.

The Doctor came back at seven and gave me the all clear. We had a very pleasant meal washed down with a bottle of champagne. My toast was simple, 'onwards and upwards' from this day forth.

It was ten thirty the following morning when we parked outside the offices of O'Neill solicitors. Grainne Kennedy was there to greet us as soon as we opened the door.

"Your very welcome Ms Lynch, now if you would come with me into the meeting room, I will get the papers for you. I will also let Mr O'Shea know you're here. Would you like tea or coffee?"

We had just taken a seat as her colleague Mr O'Shea came into the room.

"Maeve is that really you?"

As I turned around, I was stunned to discover that it was Jack, my old school friend. I asked him, "Jack is that really you?"

He hadn't changed a bit. He still had the same dark curly hair that did its own thing. We hugged each other.

"Maeve my old friend," Jack confirmed.

"Jesus Maeve you look amazing. Still as beautiful as ever. I wouldn't have known you if I met you in the street. I would have walked straight past you."

"Well Jack, you look exactly the same, except, perhaps, for the waistline."

"Ha, ha!" he commented, "Still as funny as ever!"

He admitted, "Maeve it's safe to say you have caused quite a commotion around here. You had us all wondering if the queer fella had killed you and put you in the lake. He had said he would often enough.

"The only thing that saved his arse was Mrs O'Brien, who swore black and blue that you were alive and well, but she would never tell anyone where you were. So the firm here has always kept an open mind."

I replied, "I have to say, I am surprised my father didn't sell the place or lose everything gambling?"

"Well, it's not that he didn't try."

"I don't understand Jack, what would stop him?"

"When I took over the practice from Mr O'Neill, he told me that he believed your father had killed you because he lost it when he tried to sell the farm and was stopped because it was neither his nor your mothers to sell.

"You see your grandmother left everything to you. After you left he nearly got away with selling the place only for Mrs O'Brien to come to see O'Neill. She swore under oath that you were still alive and well and would come back home when you were ready.

"He drove him and your mother around the twist. He had a nasty temper that fella. There is not a person around the place that had a good word to say about him. He destroyed nearly everything he touched including your mother. She was the finest lady in town before he got his claws into her. Sure, you don't need me to tell you that your grandparents were the best you could find anywhere.

"Your grandmother made sure your mother always had a roof over her head and food in her belly long after she had gone. I don't remember your grandfather myself, but I do remember your grandmother. What a lady she was. She would be very proud of you if she could see you now."

We had both forgotten that the girls and Stuart were also in the room until Grainne came back with teas and coffees.

I then said, "I am so sorry. You must think I am awfully rude. I would like to introduce my daughters Amelia and Sara, and my partner Stuart."

"Well Ladies, you are the image of your mother. Stuart, you are one lucky guy. I hope you are looking after our Maeve, or you would have plenty of trouble around these parts."

We all started to laugh. I gave Jack a brief update on my situation in the strictest of confidence. I never told him the full truth, just that I changed my name when I ran off to England some years before.

After we signed all the paperwork, we returned to Ballyconneely and went up to the house with a different view. I couldn't believe the place was now mine.

Without even thinking about it, I knew I would have to renovate the place to bring new life back, and for it to be a place of happiness joy and laughter just like it once was.

We said we would be using this place a lot just to get away from the hustle and bustle of busy London life. It would become our sanctuary. Afterwards, we went over to call on the O'Brien boys, as I had not seen them since their mum was in the hospital all those years ago.

Driving past the O'Brien farm, I could see the two lads leaning against their shovels debating something or other. When the boys turned around, I thought they were going to have a heart attack, and it took them a good few minutes before they could talk or move. They nearly crushed the life out of me, but eventually, they let me out of their grip. I introduced them to my girls and Stuart.

We followed them up to the farmhouse.

I said, "Oh my, this place looks a lot different from what I remember."

They both laughed so hard, "Ah Jesus, our little Maeve, you are not the only one to have upgraded. How we never got pneumonia from the place was a miracle. The place was so draughty and damp. Sure you couldn't keep any heat in the place.'

I said, "I remember our house was exactly the same. You had to get undressed under the bed covers in winter to keep warm."

Just then, the wife of one of the boys came in, she was carrying one of their grandchildren. He could not have been more than six months old.

We spent several hours in the O'Brien's house catching up. They were shocked and over the moon when I told them that my grandmother had left the house to me and that we were going to do a complete renovation of the place.

"So, I guess we are going to be neighbours again", I confirmed, which resulted in loud cheers all around.

"Time to celebrate," the boys roared, and several glasses of wine later we eventually left slightly light-headed.

The Girls were giggling like teenagers, "Mum, I think we are going to have to go into detox when we go home."

"I agree, as I don't think I have ever drunk as much as I have in the last few days."

We were armed with names and telephones for an architect, builders, plumbers, an electrician, and every other trade you could possibly think of.  The boys and their wives were going to join us later in the hotel for dinner. I told everyone that it would be great to have a catch-up.

That night over more late night drinks, we agreed that Stuart and I would stay for another week so that we could talk to the architect about drawing up some plans and planning permissions. The girls would head back to the UK as they both had work commitments.

# Chapter 30

Over the next twelve months, it became as chaotic as ever. We were all so busy, Stuart was scarcely ever home. He was spending more and more time away in Europe and at times wouldn't be back home for months.

Sara was still in the States working on both a new play and a pilot for a movie. The movie was due to hit the screens in the next month or two, but unfortunately one of the actors let slip some details on the movie before it was due to become public knowledge, and as a result the media attention was relentless, which now meant they were under extra pressure to finish filming before anything else was leaked.

Some of the media stories and speculation was off the wall. You would wonder where they got all their ideas from. Sara found it funny most of the time. She said that maybe the leak had done them a favour as they were now getting so much publicity that it would reduce the amount of advertising required.

Amelia was flat out in the hospital as usual. There was a shortage of staff - surprise, surprise. Meanwhile, the office was crazy. I couldn't believe that it could get any busier. We had taken on some new staff over six months ago but we were already recruiting again.

Sometimes it took all my willpower to stay calm. It would be wrong for me to say it was easy. Whatever Poppy was doing, it was working. We were all having a problem in keeping up with her. Hiring her was a great decision. Even if we had to run to keep pace with her. I said it was better to have her on my team rather than a competitor.

To top it all off, the building team in Ballyconneely were also on top of their game. I found it very hard to concentrate on work. My mind kept wandering over to the building site. I was lucky, the builder Mike would send an email most days with an update on the progress, and even some photos.

I had to admit though, a lot of the technical details went over my head. I tried to get over at least once a month for a quick visit. On these visits, I could really see the progress in all its beauty. I have to confess that I looked forward to going back.

If you had told me about this, all those years ago, I would have said you were insane. Most of the time though, I had to go by myself as my co-pilots were always busy. I found that when I was there, however, I was always surrounded by peace and calmness. It allowed me valuable time to think.

When the girls would come over, they would always find it hard going back. I was amazed when Amelia offered to go over by herself just to check things were going to plan.

The builder said they would be finished by 30th October. I was surprised, but I was taken back, even more, when the builder called on the 30th September and asked if I could meet him at the house as soon as possible as he needed to run the last few changes past me.

He promised this would be my last site visit before he handed over the keys. He swore black and blue they would be finished on schedule and there would be no delays.

As luck would have it, Stuart was home and had to be in Dublin for a meeting later on the following week, so he was more than happy to have a few quiet days in Clifden after all the madness of recent months.

We both enjoyed the long walks along the beach where we could walk for miles and not see another soul, followed by a pint in the local. We arrived in Ballyconneely on 5<sup>th</sup> October, driving up to the place it looked spectacular, but I was struck by how quiet it was.

I said, "There must be a problem, otherwise the place would be crawling with workmen. I have never been here with the place so empty."

As we arrived at the back door, Mike popped up out of nowhere with a devilish grin on his face. "Good to see you guys. Glad you could make it. Let's go inside and I'll show you where we have a problem."

Inside and sitting on the table was a bottle of champagne and a set of keys. We looked at each other bemused.

He said, "Elizabeth, I am sorry I got you here under false pretences. I hope you can forgive me but I just couldn't wait any longer to share this with you. Many congratulations, your home is finished. Here are your keys."

I was speechless and quite unsure of what to say. I simply couldn't believe it. I was totally flabbergasted.

"I was not expecting this," I explained somewhat bemused.

Everything was in place, and amazingly all the furniture had arrived ahead of schedule – which never usually happens in Ireland!

Mike just touched his nose and smiled, saying, "I called in a few favours from the suppliers, and had to threaten some of them that I would never buy from them again if they didn't deliver everything by yesterday. I was lucky a couple of the lads went into Galway this morning and picked up the last few bits."

"Thank you, Mike, I just can't believe it. The place is amazing. It's so beautiful that it's hard to have the right words."

"No, thank you, Elizabeth, for allowing me to work on your home. It has been a great pleasure. I just wished that all my clients were as easy to work with as you were. I hope you have many years of happiness here."

With that, Mike went out of the door, and shouted back, "I will call you later after you have had a chance to take it all in."

It was later in the evening when I realised that it was exactly thirty-four years ago to the day, 5th October, that I left for Dublin, and where my life changed beyond anything thing I could ever have imagined.

I was sure it was no coincidence that the dates collided. I now know for sure that my grandmother was still beside me, guiding me to this point and to bring me home. I spoke to her out loud for the first time in a long time, I said, "I hope you like what we have done with the old place, thank you, Gran, for bringing me back home."

Before we opened the champagne, Stuart went back to the village to pick up a takeaway, and a few basic supplies and some new bed linen.

I was alone in the house for the first time in many years. It was a very surreal feeling. There were so many mixed emotions running through me. But the greatest feeling of all was a sense of completion, a oneness with myself.

It was good to be back. I just knew deep down that this was one of my best moves yet, I knew we would be very happy there. I could feel the presence of my grandmother all over the place. I could feel her sense of pride in a job well done. I thought, now this home can once again return to be the safe haven it once was. A place of joy, love, and laughter, a place where you are completely welcomed day or night.

I just knew this place will be somewhere where all of us could receive the soul healing we require. I knew that I would now be able to fully focus on the future and would no longer be haunted by the past.

I couldn't wait for the girls to come and see the place. I could barely believe it was true. It still felt like a dream, I had never imagined coming back again. Now I was actually there, I retained this overwhelming sense of peace and a oneness with myself.

I was startled when Stuart opened the door and was suddenly transported back to reality as he dropped the bags in the kitchen. The smell of the takeaway suddenly meant I was starving. He placed the food on the plates and I lit the fire in the hearth for the first time in well over thirty years.

After we had eaten, we called the girls to let them know the place was now finished and asked them how soon could they get there. Both girls were so excited and agreed to come over at the weekend.

I also spoke with Isabelle and agreed that I would stay there for another week or so. Stuart was only able to stay for two days, as he needed to be in Dublin for a meeting. If I was honest, I was delighted to have had the opportunity to be there by myself with just my sketchpad for company.

Lucky for me the weather was exceptionally good for that time of the year and I was able to spend a lot of time up at the lake, sketching like a mad woman. Sometimes I would forget to stop for food as I was so engrossed in a design.

As I finished one design and would be about to put the pencil down my mind would suddenly go into overdrive. At times, my hand would be aching to keep up. All thoughts of the busy streets of London were very far from my mind.

The girls were flying into Dublin on the Friday afternoon and Stuart agreed to pick them up before heading West. It was late in the evening when he finally arrived with the girls. To say they were amazed at the sight before them was an understatement.

We had the most fantastic weekend possible and all of us were sad at the thought of leaving on Sunday night but agreed we would be back often. As we were driving out of Clifden, Sara suggested we should have a housewarming party, but before I had a chance to say anything, Amelia jumped on the bandwagon as well.

There was no way to talk them out of it once they had that look on their faces. Before I knew it, the decision to spend Christmas in Ballyconneely was agreed upon and the party had grown legs, the best time to have the party would be New Year's Eve. The girls said they would do all the organising, so I agreed to let them off.

The rest of October and November disappeared in a flash as we were all so busy, and we forgot about our promise to make it back to Galway at least once a month, if only for a weekend.

Stuart and I took the ferry from Holyhead to Dublin on 20th December. It would be another first for me, and in the past twelve months there seemed to be no end of firsts, but this one would be the last from the past. This time, however, I had no fears or concerns about going back.

We stopped in Galway to pick up a Christmas tree, some decorations, and other bits and bobs. When the girls arrived on the 23rd we would come back and picked up the food and the booze for the party.

After my initial reservations, I was really looking forward to hosting the party.

Isabelle, Poppy and their families, and a few other close friends from work would also becoming and staying in the local hotel. Sara and her boyfriend Alex would also be staying for the holidays.

Amelia said she was going to feel like a spare part with all this coupling that she too would need to find herself a man in the New Year. She was nursing a wounded heart as she had broken up with her boyfriend of three years just a few months before. She insisted that she was fine but I knew she still felt a bit sore.

Well, what can I say about Christmas in Ballyconneely except that it was idyllic. It was as if it was something out of a movie. The fire burning and the smell of turf brought back all sorts of memories. We had a feast that started as soon as we got up and it lasted all day.

By late afternoon, we were nodding asleep, so it was decided that we should all go for a walk along the beach where we were nearly swept away by the Atlantic. By the time we returned to the house we looked like drowned rats, and as if we had been dragged through the hedge backwards.

We were laughing like lunatics and there were definitely saner people in the madhouse in Ballinasloe. Once inside, we changed into dry clothes and huddled up by the fire with cups of steaming hot chocolate wrapped around our fingers. We were as happy as we had ever been.

The sense of contentment that the house filled us with left no adequate words to describe it. Time moved at a different pace there. We lost track of time and days. In what felt like a flash of an eye it was the morning of the party. The girls and I were busy in the kitchen getting the food ready and the boys were setting up the drinks. The neighbours were in and out through the day dropping in flowers, extra tables and chairs.

I had forgotten how people just called in without a moment's notice. There was an air of excitement felt by everyone. The guests were due at 8.00pm with the exception of the gang from the UK. They were coming over as soon as they checked into their hotel.

By 6.45pm the doorbell started to ring. I shouted out, "Shit! Shit!"

People were beginning to arrive early. I was still in the shower but had to get dressed really quickly. I had no idea how my makeup went on and prayed that I looked alright as I had not even had a chance to look in the mirror.

"Oh Hell," I thought the Irish are not like the English. They don't believe in looking at their watches or sticking to the times given. By 8.00pm the place was packed to the rafters. Thankfully, everyone began helping themselves to food and drink.

I was slowly trying to make my way to say hello to everyone. The compliments about the house were overwhelming. The building team were beaming from ear to ear. I was taken aback by the generosity of guests and with the amount of gifts. My favourite was from the O'Briens. They gave me the most precious of them all. It was a horseshoe that Mrs O'Brien received from my grandfather many years ago when first married.

He had a very simple engraving on it, 'May this home be filled with laughter, good health, plenty of food and a warm fire to warm your bones and good friends to share the load.'

It was close to 3.00am when the last person finally staggered out of the door. I was completely knackered and as high as a kite. It was a night for spontaneous 'ceol agus craic,' most of the songs I had not heard since my grandmother died.

It was like taking a trip to another world. Stuart and the girls were in awe at how the Irish party. It was their first time to experience how food and drinks turned into a ceili. There was no need to ever hire entertainment. They were astounded at how happy the whole community were that I was now back, and 'back where I belonged' they said.

The girls were also at home. The older generation regaled stories of their great grandparents, and of what your mum was like as a youngster. They never once mentioned my parents or the terrible events that took place.

With everyone now gone, it looked like a bomb had hit the place, but I didn't care. The girls and Alex went to bed. Stuart and I had a nightcap re-living the success of the evening. I was trying to work out if we had spoken to everyone. Neither of us was sure we had, but one thing for sure we had not had enough time to catch up with everyone.

There were many faces I recognised and many more who had to tell me who they were. I guess you could say there was a lot of catching up to do with everyone over the next few months.

Stuart stood up to top-up our drinks but after he handed me my drink, he fell to the floor, and before I had a chance to move or say a word he just blurted out, "Marry me Elizabeth. Make me a very happy man."

"Jesus, get up you big ape," I told him, "What are you trying to do, give me a coronary? For the love of God, I thought you were actually having a heart attack. What has gotten into you? You must have had one too many."

"I am serious, marry me, make an honest man out of me."

"Please say yes, so I can get up?"

With that Stuart grabbed my hand and stared into my eyes. "Elizabeth, I have never been so serious about anything in my life before," and with that, he pulled a beautiful diamond ring out of his pocket.

I was speechless, it was something I have never experienced before. I couldn't find the words. All I could do was nod and as he placed the ring on my finger.

The rest of the night was a blur, so much so that later I thought I had dreamt it but after I woke up in the morning. I was in the kitchen making coffee when Amelia suddenly let out a roar, "Sara, come here quick!"

"Sara, do you notice anything different about Mum this morning?" She looks bemused and replied, "No?"

"Look closer," she said, and with that, she leaned over and whispered into her ear, "Look at her finger."

The whole time I just stood there wondering what on earth was she was talking about, until she jumped up and pulled my hand, "Mum, when did this happen? Why have you not told us? Spill the beans now. That is an order!"

Just then, Stuart rolled into the kitchen with his eyes still full of sleep. He was never fully awake until he had at least a couple of cups of coffee.

"Hey ladies", he said, as he wrapped his arms around me.

He was the first to speak and smiled at the girls, saying, "Well, what do you think of our news? Do you think I will ever be good enough for your Mum? I promise you that I will make her very happy."

"Wait," I said. "You mean to say I was not dreaming last night. We did get engaged?"

With that, he gave me a most serious look. "Please Elizabeth, marry me!"

This time I had no problem answering. "Yes Stuart, I would love to be your wife."

The twins were dancing around the kitchen looking for a bottle of champagne. After we poured the drinks, the twins jumped up and said we should get dressed and make our way up to the hotel to tell Isabelle and the gang.

The rest of our time soon vanished and once again, we were soon heading back to the UK. When back in London though, my heart remained in Ballyconneely.

We promised we would go back as soon as we could. Amelia had some holidays owed to her from the hospital so she decided to go back to Galway for a rest and to think about what she wanted to do with her life.

I envied her, as I too would have loved to have gone back for a few weeks. She said she needed some peace and quiet. I was delighted that the house would be used by the girls. It was just what I was hoping for when I had it renovated.

# Chapter 31

Stuart and I set the date for our wedding for 26<sup>th</sup> August. We planned a small ceremony by the lake at the back of the house with a small gathering of family and friends. We would hire a marquee for the afterwards, and a local band would take care of the music.

This was not going to be a traditional Irish wedding as such. I wasn't sure how the locals would react as they had never been to a wedding that was not in the local church. We had a Shaman from Cork coming over to officiate the union.

We were having a non-religious wedding as I had dropped my Catholic beliefs and Stuart was non-religious. Everything was booked so all I had to do was design the invites and make my dress. The Twins were busy working on their dresses with the ladies in the office, and I was not allowed to know anything about them until the big day.

Over the next few months, Amelia spent more and more time in Galway. She was taken by the place, however, I was flabbergasted when she announced she was giving up her job in the hospital and was moving to Clifden to take up a job in the local surgery.

She was planning to set up a more inclusive service for expectant mothers, and to reduce the number of trips to Galway.

Her idea was to provide a better link between the hospital and a GP. She was planning to finish at the hospital in June and to move to Clifden in July.

She was going to stay in the house for a while until she made up her mind, on whether she needed to be closer to town. I was a very suspicious person and believed there was more to this tale than she was willing to tell.

My over-active imagination believed there must a man in the mix somewhere, but there was no point in quizzing her until she was ready to explain and not a minute before.

When our Wedding Day finally arrived, I could hardly believe it was the day I would finally say my vows and become Stuart's wife. As I sat in the hairdresser's getting my hair guided into place, I found it hard to imagine how my life had been.

I counted my blessings every day for the magnificent life I had had. I could never have dreamed that my life would ever have turned out that way. In fact, if anyone would have told the 13-year old me that this would be my life I would have laughed at them and told them they were completely mad.

We were lucky with the weather that week and it looked like it would be yet another great day. Even though I was not sure it had much to do with luck but more to do with half the village putting out their statue of Prague, which every Irish person knows is the only way to guarantee good weather.

My dress, just like the wedding was anything but the norm. I thought that maybe I should have stuck to something more traditional.

My dress had a Bateau neckline that followed the curve of my collarbone to the very tip of the shoulders, and closely followed the contours of my body.

It was in a lightweight semi-lustrous soft satin-like to touch with the slight hint of baby blue and a layer of Chantilly lace with a very delicate lace and a sheer look with very small hand stitched flowers and ribbons.

I could not wear white, and blue was traditionally worn by Irish brides for centuries, right up until Queen Victoria made white a popular choice in 1840.

I hoped everyone would like the dress as I'd mixed a few different ideas together. I was very nervous about the reaction and after applying my makeup, I had a few rare minutes to myself where my thoughts turned to Edward.

I sent up a silent prayer to tell him I still loved him and to thank him for all the great years we'd had together and finally, to ask for his blessing, even though I knew I already had it.

In the next room, I could hear the twins chatting to Stuart if you could call it that. It was more like, "Time you weren't here. Sorry to say this, but get out! See you up at the lake in twenty minutes."

Just as he was leaving, I could hear them calling after him, "Does this mean we have to call you Dad now?"

He replied with the deepest chuckle I have ever heard from him, "I am honoured ladies, but Stuart will do."

"OK then, out now."

They knocked on my door a few minutes later, asking, "Are you ready for us Mum?"

"I am always ready for you two... Wow! Wow! You both look amazing!"

Their dresses looked superb, a very simple chiffon fit and flare with a strapless sweetheart neckline, with a cream sash wrapped around their tiny waists.

The colour was a slightly darker blue than my own dress. It was uncanny how close in colour they were. The dresses were all the more special because they had cut the material and sewn the dress themselves under the careful supervision of Marion.

It was then time to remove my dressing gown and show them my dress. I stood there like a bag of nerves as I slowly slipped off my gown to reveal my beautiful dress.

"Mum, the dress is incredible, you're a genius. It's simple but stunning. Wait until Stuart sees you. He might just pass out before he has a chance to say 'I Do.'"

"Stop it, girls, you're wicked!"

"Are you sure it looks OK? What do you think of the colour?"

"It's perfect in every way. Now stop worrying and finish your drink, we have plenty of time. Alex will come and let us know when everyone is seated and ready for us. So let's raise our glasses. "A toast to our wonderful mother."

"Mum, just wait and see what Stuart and the guys have done up at the lake. It looks like something from a magazine, you will love it."

It seemed like an eternity waiting for Alex to come, so much so that we nearly jumped out of our skin when he finally knocked on the door. We were so giddy at that stage that we had to take time to steady ourselves. We were worse than a group of kids.

Sara handed me a bunch of wildflowers that had been collected from the garden and lovingly crafted into an amazing bouquet. They would have paid a small fortune for something like that in London.

The girls were right, the place was unrecognisable. Stuart had transformed it into a fairytale scene. All the guests were seated on bales of hay with a white cloth to protect their best clothes. The O'Brien's supplied the bales. I saw my groom standing under a rose covered gazebo overlooking the lake. He was looking so nervous it was funny. The music started to play and the girls walked down the makeshift aisle before me.

I slowly made my way to Stuart. When he took my hand and looked into my eyes, I noticed that his were misty. He helped me into my spot in the middle of a most beautiful arrangement of flowers from the garden that were spread on the ground in the shape of a horseshoe. Later he told me this was to honour my grandfather.

He whispered into my ear, "You are the most stunning bride I have ever laid eyes on", but before I had a chance to respond, the ceremony began.

The official gave everyone a brief rundown on how the ceremony was going to proceed, and he slowly started to tell us about hand fasting, which was an Ancient Pagan Celtic Custom that had died out years ago but was slowly coming back into vogue.

In the olden days, a couple would have their hand fastening ceremony a year before the wedding. It was believed that if a couple were still blissfully in love at the end of 365-days, they would remain that way, so were given the tribes blessing in their union. If not, it was then recommended that they should part ways with no hard feelings.

He said, "Now let's begin the final part of today's ritual. Stuart, and Elizabeth, you have chosen to stand here in front of your family and friends to seal your commitment to each other by the Ancient

Celtic Ritual of handfasting.

"In doing so you are not only honouring each other but also your ancestors. You are sending out a clear message to one and all that you are entering into this marriage by your own free will. Your paths have crossed in this life, but you have also formed an eternal bond to each other.

"Now, Stuart and Elizabeth, if you could hold hands, right hand to right hand, left hand to left hand… As I wrap this cord around your hands as a symbol of your union, you are bound together and are now entering into the union of trust and love. Your marriage is not formed by these cords, but by the vows you declare to each other. You and you alone hold the fate of this union in your hands. As Above, so Below… Above you are the stars, Below you is the Earth.

"Like the stars that light up the night skies, even on the darkest of night. You too are promising to light up each other's lives. Even when life challenges you, and forces you out of your comfort zone.

"Just as the Earth holds the roots of the tallest of trees, through days filled with sun rain and winds, it holds them tightly in place.

"You also agree to help steady and ground each other to hold each other firmly through any storms that may come your way. Stuart, and Elizabeth, it's time for you to exchange the vows you have prepared for each other.

"I seal this marriage with a traditional Irish Blessing that has been used for many years. May your hands be forever clasped in Friendship and your Hearts joined Forever in Love. May Joy and Peace surround you, Contentment Latch your door, and Happiness be with you now and Bless you forevermore.

"Ladies and Gentlemen, Please give the new Mr and Mrs

Richardson a round of applause."

As we walked down the aisle, we were showered with lavender branches, and as we moved over towards the marquee where the drinks were being served, the inside now resembled a wondrous cave.

The day and the evening were filled with laughter, song and plenty of dancing. It was the early hours in the morning when the last of the guests left, 6.45am to be exact. We should have been tired out but instead, we were just happy to get the most out of the day.

I was totally blindsided when I noticed Amelia and Dermot O'Brien, Oliver O'Brien's oldest son, looking very cosy on the dance floor. Unless my imagination was running away with me, it looked like they were madly in love. I was thinking, you couldn't make it up if you tried!

The following day Amelia told us she had been going out with Dermot O'Brien for the last few months, and this formed a key part in the reason why she had suddenly relocated from London.

He had just come home from working in Canada where he had been living for the last few years. Seeing my twins so loved-up was the best gift of all. I don't think it will be too long before there will be another wedding or two... and hopefully the sound of the patter of little feet running around the place.

I might have to look more seriously at opening that Shop in Galway after all. That no doubt would make Izzy a very happy lady, it would be like she gets her wish after all.

**The End**

Mary Hughes

Printed in Poland
by Amazon Fulfillment
Poland Sp. z o.o., Wrocław